Hold Me Forever

Enjoy the Ride

What Reviewers Say About D. Jackson Leigh's Work

"…a thrilling and enthralling novel of love, lies, intrigue and Southern charm."—*Bibliophilic Book Blog*

"D. Jackson Leigh understands the value of branding and delivers more of the familiar and welcome story elements that set her novels apart from other authors in the romance genre."—*The Rainbow Reader*

"D. Jackson Leigh has created very likeable characters in the throes of making very realistic life decisions. She's also written an enjoyable novel full of humor and great love scenes."—*Just About Write*

"Her prose is clean, lean, and mean—elegantly descriptive…"—*Out in Print*

By the Author

The Cherokee Falls series:

Bareback

Longshot

Every Second Counts

Southern Secrets series:

Call Me Softly

Touch Me Gently

Hold Me Forever

Hold Me Forever

by

D. Jackson Leigh

BOLD STROKES BOOKS

2013

HOLD ME FOREVER

ISBN 10: 1-60282-944-6
ISBN 13: 978-1-60282-944-2

This Trade Paperback Original Is Published By
Bold Strokes Books, Inc.
P.O. Box 249
Valley Falls, NY 12185

First Edition: September 2013

Credits
Editor: Shelley Thrasher
Production Design: Susan Ramundo
Cover Design By Sheri (graphicartist2020@hotmail.com)

Acknowledgments

Two years ago, my close friend, Phoebe, gifted me with a calendar that had a different Southern saying for each day of the year. Many of them were familiar; most made me chuckle. So when I set out to write the third of what I call my Southern Secrets romances, I knew I had to incorporate that in the texture of the tale. Thanks, Phoebe.

The story stayed on simmer, however, while I wrote *Every Second Counts* because there was an ingredient still missing. Whit Casey was clear in my mind, but the woman who would complete the dance of romance with her remained elusive until I was dragged to a reunion of former co-workers in my home state, Georgia. There, my second character, Mae St. John, came into sharp focus.

I've always been fascinated by that class of true "steel magnolias" who exude a sense of style and grace, a wicked sense of humor, and the will to not only survive, but conquer anything life throws at them. That reunion gave me the chance to see how several of my co-workers from twenty-two years ago had matured into incredible women. My thanks to three really entertaining steel magnolias I've had the pleasure to know: Cas Shearin, Martha Anne Tudor, and Mary Miller.

The story, however, is never done until your beta readers find the holes and raise the important questions. My humble thanks to Jenny Harmon, Joanie Bassler, Ellen Greenblatt, Carol Poynor, and Gail Holley. I really depend on you guys.

Finally, as always, my thanks to my amazing editor, Shelley Thrasher, and to Len Barot for establishing the Bold Strokes Books family. Becoming a BSB author has changed my life into a wonderful adventure of stories, travel, and awesome friends both near and far away.

Dedication

In memory of Mae Eugenia Jackson, 1934-2012.

CHAPTER ONE

"Every day can't be Sunday."

Mae St. John huffed impatiently. With one hand she held tight to the wide, floppy brim of her hat in a tug-of-war with the sporadic wind. Between gusts, she vigorously waved away the pesky gnats with a paddle-style fan imprinted with the funeral home's logo.

Her black Milan hat was a welcome shelter from the sweltering August sun, but whoever in the fashion world had decided to revive this seventies-style millinery hadn't considered that car seats now had headrests. She'd had to lean forward halfway between the seat and the steering wheel the entire thirty-minute drive out to the country cemetery. She didn't dare take the hat off and lay it on the seat because the car's mirrors were too small to ensure it wouldn't be seated cattywampus on her head when she put it on again.

The intermittent breeze did little to temper the sultry humidity, and nothing to dispel the swarm of gnats that emerged from the surrounding woods every time the wind died down. Mae could swear they were the same insects that plagued the family reunions held outside the small church located down the hill and across the road.

She had loved those reunions when she was a child, but the advent of air-conditioning had lowered Southerners' tolerance for outdoor meetings, and modern warnings about mayonnaise exposed to the heat frightened the younger, coddled generations. So, the annual event had been moved into the new fellowship hall. It had refrigerators, air-conditioning, and freedom from insects. But gathering in the plain, concrete-block building stole the charm of an old-fashioned dinner-on-the-ground under the shade of giant oaks, and people stopped coming.

Times were changing.

Mae let the funeral director guide her to a seat among metal folding chairs grouped under the dark-blue canopy. She was front and center one last time before the grandmother who had reared her with a firm but loving hand.

She stared at the pearl-blue casket with ornate silver handles. The open grave waiting to receive Big Mae St. John for the rest of eternity was the biggest change Mae had encountered in her twenty-eight years. She had no idea what she would do without the dynamic and stabilizing presence of her grandmother.

"For everything there is a season, and a time for every matter under heaven. A time to be born and a time to die…" The words of the deep-voiced Episcopal priest were meant to soothe, but Mae's anxiety rose as each verse took her closer to being totally alone in this world.

"…a time to kill, and a time to heal…"

How would she live in the big, old house without Big Mae?

"…a time to cast stones, and a time to gather stones together…"

She had considered suing the Palmer Country Club for serving Big Mae, who was actually a small, thin woman, that fifth whiskey sour, then letting her get behind the wheel of her Mercedes. But she knew how well her grandmother could disguise her inebriation and how intimidating she could be to a young valet who might have hesitated before handing over Big Mae's car keys.

"…a time to keep silent, and a time to speak…"

If she had pressed the matter, the local media surely would have been alerted to the illegal level of alcohol in Big Mae's bloodstream when her car slipped off the edge of the roadway and overcorrected to shoot onto the fifteenth fairway and into an irrigation holding pond, scattering ducks and sinking quickly beneath the lily pads.

One young groundskeeper had valiantly tried to rescue Big Mae, but he was unable to open a door or break a window. John Hatley, chairman of the board that governed the club and Big Mae's attorney, told her privately that the boy had said Big Mae hadn't been wearing her seat belt and appeared mercifully unconscious as the car filled with water. Her cause of death was ruled as drowning.

"...a time for war, and a time for peace..."

No, she couldn't sue. Big Mae would have been appalled at the public scrutiny of her final hours.

Mae sighed. Why couldn't Big Mae have died of some lingering illness, so she'd have had time to ask her grandmother what she should do now? It was regrettable, but Big Mae's advice would have been the same as always—marry well and the rest will fall into place.

The priest's litany pulled her back to the present. "And now we commit this body to the ground: earth to earth, ashes to ashes, dust to dust. The Lord bless our sister, Evelyn Mae St. John, and keep her for all of eternity."

As amens chorused around her, Mae stood and placed a single white lily atop her grandmother's casket. She straightened her shoulders and hobbled to the limousine with as much dignity as possible, considering her four-inch heels sank into the damp cemetery dirt with every step.

If she could weather the next couple of hours in that dreary fellowship hall accepting sad condolences and answering whispered questions about who did Big Mae's hair and makeup for the funeral, she could finally go home and fall apart.

❖

"I can hardly believe she's gone." John Hatley's hands were sweaty as he clasped Mae's. "Your grandmother may have been a small woman, but, by God, she filled up a room when she walked in."

Mae followed him into his richly appointed office and sat in an elegant wingback chair as he moved behind his mahogany desk. She listened politely as he continued to ramble, even though she wanted to scream for him to just read the damn will.

The past week had been filled with so much nervous expectation that she'd nearly resorted to taking one of Big Mae's nerve pills. If the will had been written and signed years ago, why in the world did it take a week before he could read it to her? Big Mae had told her nothing about their finances, and she needed to schedule the paying of bills and other things. She hated to be disorganized.

Hatley finally left off his reminiscing and began to shuffle the papers on his desk. Mae shifted forward in her seat. Had Big Mae left a personal letter for her, like in the movies? She longed to hear her grandmother's final advice. Big Mae had given it constantly and freely throughout Mae's life, whether she sought it or not. Why would she be silent now?

Hatley cleared his throat. "I'm not sure how much your grandmother shared about her finances with you."

Mae frowned. "Unfortunately, she considered it unseemly for women to discuss money."

"Then what I'm about to tell you may come as a bit of a shock."

"Nothing about my grandmother could shock me." Mae didn't care about the money. She really didn't. What words of wisdom, what message had she left?

"Your grandfather left Big Mae financially comfortable, but the stock-market plunge a few years back drained her funds."

Mae hesitated to let his words sink in. "How badly drained?" Okay. Maybe she did care about money.

"I'm afraid I'd have to recommend that you let her house go into foreclosure. It's already mortgaged for more than it's worth, and she quit paying the mortgage life-insurance policy on it when the market went bad."

Mae didn't want to give up the house. She had grown up there. It had been in the family for generations. "Surely she had other assets I could sell. How did she pay her dues at the country club or have cash for clothes and groceries? She never once mentioned a need to conserve."

"You've been living off the loan she took out against the house and its contents. She's actually a year behind in her dues at the club, but, as chairman, I convinced the board that to kick out a member with such high social standing would be indecorous."

"But she never said a word. She paid my college tuition and sorority dues every year without complaint." Surely Big Mae would have given some indication they needed to be prudent with their spending.

"I believe she hoped you would marry well and your future husband would remedy the family money problem."

How archaic was that? Mae straightened in her chair and glared at the man. "Mr. Hatley, my grandmother would never barter me in marriage like a cow."

He raised a hand to ward off her anger. "Precisely why she refused to do more than gently press you in that direction, and, most likely, why she never advised you of the money situation. She wouldn't force you."

His concession did little to damper Mae's indignation. "If we needed money that badly, why didn't she remarry? At least a dozen men would have jumped at the chance."

"I asked her the same thing. She said she'd done her duty to the male population. She might die poor, but she'd die on her own terms."

Mae stared at him for a long moment. "So, there's nothing?"

He shook his head. "I didn't say that." He pushed a contract across the table for her to read. "She left a very small trust that is protected from her creditors. It will pay you fifteen thousand a year as long as you produce annual veterinarian statements that her poodle is in the best possible health for his age and all his vaccinations are up to date." He laid a check before her. "The first fifteen thousand is yours when you sign the contract, agreeing to the terms."

Rhett? Big Mae provided for Rhett and not her? She grabbed the offered pen and scribbled her name where he indicated. Big Mae didn't raise her to be a fool. "Apparently, I don't have a lot of options." She folded the check and slipped it into her purse.

Hatley took the signed contract, glancing to confirm her signature. "I have to warn you that should he die, the rest of the trust will immediately go to the local SPCA. So, I'd be careful about letting him off leash."

The large office had grown claustrophobic, pressing in around her. This was a nightmare. Mae closed her eyes and put her hand to her forehead. Maybe she had a fever and was delirious. When the fever broke, she would realize this was all a bad dream.

"There's more," Hatley said.

"Of course there is," she muttered.

When she opened her eyes, he handed over a sealed envelope. At last. This must be the missive she had hoped for when she first sat in this chair of doom.

"It's a personal note, I believe. I can leave you alone to read it if you like."

Mae stood. Probably half his office had already discussed her financial plight around the copy machine, and her misfortune will surely be the buzz of the country club soon enough. She would not read this letter here and suffer an emotional breakdown that would add fuel to the gossip.

"Thank you, but I think I'll read it at home."

She started for the door, then turned back to Hatley. "How long before the bank takes the house?"

Hatley didn't meet her eyes and adjusted his tie nervously. "The mortgage is already two months behind. I'll notify them that you intend to let it go into foreclosure, and you should have another month to make arrangements to relocate."

Mae nodded. She had a lot to do in a month and no idea where to begin.

❖

Mae was so numb that the next time she became aware of her surroundings, she was sitting in the house that would soon belong to the bank, stroking Rhett's black curls while he licked her hands. She didn't remember driving home or coming inside. She didn't know how long she'd been sitting there. But she did still have the letter in her hand and carefully slit it open with her fingernail, something she'd watched Big Mae do a thousand times. The letter began without preamble.

I know you may be angry now, but you will eventually thank me.

It's true I'm not bequeathing you a fortune, but I've passed on something much more important. You are a strong Southern woman bred from a long line of strong women. We all have survived by our own wits and resources. You will do the same.

Don't hold Rhett's trust fund against him. I know you love him as much as I do. He is much more agreeable than any husband.

Rhett's trust, along with a paltry ten thousand dollars secreted in my library and what I'm about to reveal, should give you a good start.

Your father was not killed in a car crash. Michael Dupree is a wealthy lawyer, alive and well in Opelousas, Louisiana. He was an attorney being groomed for a career as a political insider when he met your mother. She was a student at Emory and they worked together on a local campaign. But he was already married to a woman his family endorsed, and, when they discovered Maggie was pregnant, Michael's father paid your mother to have an abortion and never go near his son again. Obviously, she didn't go through with it or you wouldn't be reading this letter. Whether you reveal yourself to him is your decision to make.

Good luck, my granddaughter. I have every confidence in you. Since that day your mother took her own life, you have been such a joy and source of pride for me.

All my love,
Big Mae

P.S. Almost forgot your traveling money. Look to another strong Southern woman, but take more than the bills you'll find tucked between her pages. Take the life lessons that she learned in her struggle to prosper.

Mae blinked. She had a father? All these years and nobody had told her? A tentative ray penetrated her gloom. She wasn't alone. She had a father.

She sprang from the sofa so quickly that Rhett tumbled to the floor. She grabbed him up and held him against her chest. "Are you okay?" God, she had to be more careful. This dog was currently her only meal ticket. She kissed the top of his head. Big Mae was right. She did love him. She would have cared for him even without a trust fund. But since there *was* one…"I suppose that, despite my best efforts, I do find myself relying on a man to support me. So, don't even think about running under a speeding car, Mister."

She placed him gently on the floor and he followed her to the library. The walls were filled with shelves, and the shelves overflowed with books. She supposed she'd have to take down each one and thumb through it for the money. But what else did she have to do?

She was halfway through the top shelves when a dust-instigated sneezing fit forced her to scramble down to get a tissue from the faux-gold dispenser on the desk. She blew her nose and looked at Rhett.

"When's the last time anyone dusted these nasty books?"

Rhett sneezed in sympathy and wagged his stumpy tail. She smiled at him and turned back to the books. A strong Southern woman. She scanned the titles. It was right before her face. *Gone with the Wind* by Margaret Mitchell. Scarlett O'Hara had always been Big Mae's favorite flawed heroine.

She pulled the book from the middle shelf and shook it over the desk. Hundred-dollar bills, tucked between every other page, fluttered down. After careful inspection, she extracted one hundred of the bills, ten thousand dollars total, as Big Mae had promised.

Several pages had been torn out to allow for the extra bulk of the money, which made Mae laugh for the first time since she learned of her grandmother's fatal accident. The missing pages contained the scene where Scarlett drove a poor mule until he died of exhaustion as they escaped from the burning of Atlanta. A true animal lover, Big Mae had detested that part of the story.

Mae picked up the book and the money and beckoned Rhett to follow. She kicked off her shoes and, together, they curled up on Big Mae's bed. It smelled faintly of powder and jasmine, and the familiar scent comforted her. Rhett settled next to her hip as she opened the book and began to read.

Tonight, she would relive Scarlett's journey. Tomorrow, she'd start finding out everything she could about Michael Dupree to begin a journey of her own.

CHAPTER TWO

"She's got more in her cheek than she can chew."

Whit Casey looked up from her stopwatch as the pounding of hooves against the sparse turf grew louder. The slim jockey stretched forward over the neck of the sleek, dark bay colt as they thundered toward her. She stared at the finish post and clicked the watch the instant Raising the Bar's nose broke in front of it.

She grinned at her father. "Twenty-two-oh-two. Can't wait to see what he does on a real track."

Clinton Casey nodded and tongued his toothpick to the other side of his mouth. "Greased lightning, that's for sure. Best ace I ever played."

Whit shook her head. "I can't believe you won a colt like that in a card game, Pop."

"Well, the feller that had him was a few cards short of a full deck or he'd have never put that pedigree on the table. He's got Lena's Bar and Beduino appendix blood, you know," he said.

"Yeah. You told me that." Actually, Pop had mentioned it several times. "You think you'll get him on a track soon?"

"I reckon we should train at Carencro for a couple weeks before the season starts at Evangeline Downs."

"I need to find what you did with his registration papers." Raising the Bar couldn't be entered in any race unless the paperwork was in order.

He frowned. "You don't have his papers?"

"Pop, we talked about this last night."

"Could be in some mail I ain't opened."

"I went through everything that was in the house."

"Might be some more in the barn."

"Why didn't you tell me that before?"

"Must'a slipped my mind." Pop's hand trembled as he lifted his dirty John Deere cap and resettled it on his head. Whit recognized what she had recently figured out was a sign that he was tired and needed a nap. Fatigue made him less coherent.

"You know, I think I might have left Ellie shut up in the house. Why don't you go check on her for me? I'll take care of the colt."

He'd stubbornly refuse if she told him to go take a rest, but he'd collapse in his recliner and sleep for two hours if she gave him an excuse to go indoors.

"You and that damned dog." He spit a stream of tobacco juice on the ground. "She's into everything. Can't even breed her. She and Jack'd made fine puppies if you hadn't had her fixed. Just 'cause you don't want nothing to do with a man doesn't mean she doesn't."

Ellie, Whit's Jack Russell terrier, was only two years old, but there was no point in reminding Pop that his male terrier had been dead for years.

"Thanks. Just don't feed her any more treats. She's getting fat."

He feigned a scowl. "I believe those chickens roost at your barn. She ain't been here long enough for me to make her fat." He grumbled to himself as he headed for the farmhouse. "You sure got bossy living down there in the city."

The colt rounded the corner again, this time at a walk, and Whit strode out to meet them.

"Let's walk him around again, Tyree. I'll walk with you."

"Yes, ma'am."

"How'd he feel?"

Tyree Boudreaux's face lit up like the sun. "He's fit, Miss Whitley. When he hits his stride, he's smooth as the glider on my mama's front porch."

Whit smiled up at the teen. When Pop's client list dwindled, he didn't have enough work to keep a regular exercise jockey busy, so he hired the boy to both ride and help around the barn. Tyree was only sixteen, but she valued his opinion. His father was a professional jockey who floated in and out of Tyree's life. When he was around, he taught the boy everything he knew about perching on the back of a racehorse.

"How'd he handle the distance?" She'd clocked him on the standard four-forty but was interested to see if he could go the distance, which was twice that far.

"He was still picking up speed. You thinking of running him long?"

"Maybe, but if he had that much left in him, then we need to up his speed on the front end. I don't want to really turn him loose, though, until we're on a real track."

The track at her father's quarter-horse training farm outside Opelousas was nothing more than a path worn in the grass along the outside of an oval, four-foot-tall, wood rail. Even though there was no outside rail, it had once been a decent track, with a wide strip that could easily run three horses abreast. The footing had been several inches of rich dirt raked daily with a tractor to keep it soft. But it was one of the things Pop had neglected, and the pasture grass had quickly encroached.

"I'd like to see him run straighter along the rail. He tends to drift to the outside."

"He don't like the rail, Miss Whitley. He slows down when I hold him close to it."

She pursed her lips. This colt needed to be trained on a good track where he could run with other horses. That would cost her.

❖

Whit stared at the pile of unopened mail. Apparently, Pop often came straight from the mailbox to the barn and had absently laid the mail down in odd places. She discovered a stack on the dusty desk in the barn office and also handfuls in several places in the tack room, the feed room, and on the shelves in the wash stall.

"I found some he'd left on the ledge in Dream Girl's stall," Tyree said softly. He stood in the doorway, looking worried. "I picked up what I could, but Dream had already found it and ripped up most of it. I put what was left on the desk. After that, I tried to keep an eye on Mr. Clinton when he came in with mail in his hands, but sometimes I was out riding one of the horses and didn't see where he put it."

"Thank you, Tyree." She studied the teen. His father was Puerto Rican, but he had his African-American mother's rich brown skin, and, although he was slender like his father, he would soon be too tall to be a professional jockey. "I appreciate you hanging in with Pop when everybody else left."

"I like Mr. Clinton. My daddy says he's one of the best trainers in Louisiana. He's just been forgetful lately. My granny was that way when she got real old."

A loud clap of thunder shook the barn and they both jumped, then chuckled at their reaction.

"I reckon I'll go ahead and bring the horses in for the night, if that's all right," Tyree said. "It's a couple hours early, but this storm might scare the foals."

"Do you need some help?" Whit stood to go with him.

"No, ma'am. When I holler for them, they'll think it's feeding time already and come on up." He glanced at the littered desk as he turned to leave. "Looks like you've got enough to do right here."

Whit ran her hand through her brown curls in frustration. The shoulder-length hair was hot and bothersome now that she was working outdoors again. She planned to get it cut short like she used to wear it, but she'd had a million other things to do, and the past month already had been a hectic blur.

After a confusing call from Pop about some legal papers he'd gotten in the mail, she'd made a rare trip home. Since her mother had died three years ago, she'd promised herself she would visit more often. But Pop had seemed okay with his horses to keep him busy, and her own business had begun to flourish, so it'd been a while since her last visit. What she found when she arrived had shocked her.

The housekeeping service she'd arranged had quit coming, probably because of their unpaid billing statements she found in the stack of delinquent bills that littered the house, along with other unopened mail, dirty dishes, and soiled laundry. The once-lush pastures of the farm were going to seed because they hadn't been mowed or fertilized, and broken rails on the wood fences hadn't been mended.

Only the horses were still well tended. Five of Pop's six breeding mares had foals at their sides. But the stable of horses he was training had dwindled to this new two-year-old colt, three yearlings, and the two racers owned by his only remaining client. Pop had much more money going out than he had coming in.

Whit had contacted a few of his former clients, and they all told the same story. They had moved their horses to another training farm after Pop had confused dates and missed races where the clients had already paid entry fees.

Her weekend trip had turned into a weeklong visit. Whit cleaned the house, used her own savings to catch up his bills, and, after an extended argument, drove him to his doctor for a complete physical. Pop seemed much older than his sixty-eight years, and it wasn't just because of his long years of hard outdoor work.

She was back in Baton Rouge when his doctor called her with the results. He had a good bit of arthritis from age, but his heart and cholesterol were excellent. However, his mental deterioration alarmed her. The doctor was still waiting for more test results to confirm it, but Pop's symptoms all pointed to Alzheimer's.

She considered taking him to live with her in the city, but it felt unusually cruel to remove him from his beloved farm and horses that had kept him going after her mom died. Moving back home seemed to be the only solution.

It'd been nearly twenty-five years ago that she'd left to attend Louisiana State University. After graduation, she'd settled in Baton Rouge because the city had something rural Louisiana lacked—a thriving lesbian community.

She started out working as a journalist with the Baton Rouge newspaper and freelanced articles to racing publications. When the newspaper industry began to crash with the economy and she was laid off, she took business-management and web-design classes while she collected unemployment. Then she launched *Quarter Track*, her own racing dot-com and an every-other-month glossy magazine.

It was a financial struggle for a while, but the Casey name got her the best interviews and a step ahead of the other media in ferreting out news tips. It paid off. She started out doing it all—writing, photography, layout, even selling ads. But as her advertising base grew, she hired a friend's company to handle advertising and marketing and used several freelancers to help with the editorial content. She still did key interviews, but mainly worked from her condo as editor and layout artist for the magazine and producer for the website.

So, it was no problem to move her business to Opelousas. In fact, it was helpful to be closer to the Evangeline Racetrack and Casino. Straightening out Pop's financial mess and balancing her workload with his horse-training duties was her biggest problem. And then, there was Avery.

Whit was thirty when she met the up-and-coming young assistant district attorney at a chamber-of-commerce function. Avery was beautiful, bold in the courtroom, a natural at handling the media, and deeply closeted. Their first two years were hot and sexy. Whit couldn't get enough of the auburn-haired, blue-eyed prosecutor.

Then Whit's life began to change, and it had taken ten years for her to admit the changes were all for Avery's benefit. Avery had chided her for looking like a lesbian stereotype and persuaded Whit to let her short curls grow long and upgrade her comfortable clothes and boots to designer jeans and trendy shoes.

"Soon," Avery would say when Whit pressed for them to move in together. But when her father rose in politics from a district judgeship to the state legislature, Avery explained that she couldn't risk the media uncovering that he had a lesbian daughter when he toed the Republican Party's line against gay rights.

Those first years of special weekends and hot sex became a distant memory. The time they did spend together was frequently interrupted by "social responsibilities." Avery began to attend her father's political fund-raisers on the arm of another closet case, a young gay prosecutor who also had political ambitions.

They still socialized with lesbian friends and vacationed at the beach together, but their kisses were passionless, and lovemaking became so one-sided, Whit no longer broached the subject. She'd rather take care of her urges herself than endure Avery's mechanical reciprocation.

Over the years, Avery's criticisms became more frequent and less veiled. Whit needed to exercise because her hard body had grown soft sitting at a computer all day. Whit snored in her sleep. Whit should wear a little makeup. Whit should color the gray hair beginning to show at her temples. Whit was being overly sensitive when Avery was just making a small suggestion.

So, in a way, the decision to move back to the farm to rescue Pop really rescued her from a relationship that was chipping away at her self-esteem. Still, Whit's heart mourned those early years of passion and romance, emotions Avery said couples always outgrew.

She sighed. Maybe she had been too sensitive to Avery's comments. Maybe forty-two *was* too old for romance.

She began separating the mail into piles. It was mostly junk, but she also uncovered several letters from attorneys notifying Pop that the races he missed were a breach of contract. Another letter, from the racing commission, advised him that missing more events without properly scratching his entry could get him suspended from Louisiana racing. It was too late to answer the attorneys' letters. Those clients had already moved on to another trainer. But she should write a letter to the racing board to explain her father's lapse.

Thunder rolled over the barn in a long rumble, and Whit decided to make a dash for the house before the sky let loose. She gathered up the mail, noting as she walked through the barn that all but the yearlings were in their stalls. Tyree had worked fast while she was woolgathering at the desk.

Huge drops began to pelt down just as she was stepping onto the porch, and Whit took a moment to rest her back against the side of the house to breathe in the fresh smell of rain. She closed her eyes and smiled. How in the world had she survived surrounded by city pavement for the past twenty-five years?

She was about to go inside when she heard shouting. Tyree was running across the pasture, waving his arms.

"Miss Whitley! You gotta come quick. Pan has barbed wire wrapped all around his legs. I couldn't get him loose."

Whit opened the door and threw her armful of mail onto the table just inside. Pop was snoring in his recliner, as expected, but Ellie rocketed out the door to follow as Whit ran to the barn to find some wire cutters.

Tyree's eyes were wide, and he shifted from foot to foot as Whit rummaged through the toolbox in the tack room. "It looks bad, Miss Whitley. Pan's legs are all cut up."

Whit's heart sank. Pandemonium was Pop's most promising yearling. She desperately needed to sell him for a good price at the upcoming yearling auction to fund Raising the Bar's training. She found the heavy wire cutters and grabbed a rain slicker from a hanger on the wall before ducking into the barn office to load a syringe with a dose of tranquilizer. Then she pulled her cell phone from her pocket as they hurried to the pasture. Best call now to get the veterinarian to start heading this way.

By the time they reached the yearling, her phone was ringing with the vet's callback. She pulled the hood of her poncho up to shield the phone as she held it to her ear. "Hey, Stacy."

"Heard you were back. I know Clinton must be happy."

"Yeah, I guess. You on your way?"

"I'm at least thirty minutes out. The answering service said you have a horse with barbed wire wrapped around his legs."

"One of the yearlings. It's Pan." She waited while Tyree slipped a halter over Pan's head and talked softly to soothe the frightened colt. He held tight to the halter as Whit turned up Pan's lip to check his gums. "He doesn't seem too shocky and the cuts don't look real deep, but he's named Pandemonium for a reason. I probably need to sedate him so he won't struggle while I cut him free."

"What do you have on hand?"

"Pop had some Dormosedan. I loaded a syringe and put it in my pocket in case you gave me the okay."

"Don't give him too much. Start with four-tenths of a cc. If I'm not there in twenty minutes and he's still struggling, give him three-tenths more. But be careful. You don't want him keeling over on you."

"A permanently lame racehorse might as well be dead," she said grimly. "If we're not at the barn when you get here, we'll be all the way on the other side of the big pasture. Close the gate when you drive in because the other two yearlings are out here, too.

"Be there in a few."

Whit tucked the phone back into her pocket and pushed the bulky hood back, ignoring the rain. She quickly injected the tranquilizer into a vein in the colt's neck and studied the wire while the drug did its work. When he visibly relaxed, she squatted to snip away at the barbed strands and carefully remove them.

Two hours later, the yearling had a crisscross of stitches on both front legs and was groggily munching his nightly grain.

"You were lucky," Stacy said, gathering her instruments into a stainless-steel bucket.

Dr. Stacy James had followed her father's footsteps into equine medicine and was the long-time veterinarian for the Casey farm. Eight years older than Whit, she had married a geeky software designer who worked from home and managed their four children while Stacy treated horses across three parishes.

"Not lucky enough. I was about to list him at the yearling auction."

"It looks a lot worse than it is. He'll race fine if he doesn't get an infection. The cuts were superficial."

"Nobody's going to pay top dollar for a racing prospect with his legs full of stitches."

"This colt has a great pedigree. I figured Clinton would keep him."

"Pop needs the money to campaign Raising the Bar. Now, I'll probably have to keep Pan and train him myself."

Stacy picked up her bucket, and Whit followed her outside. The storm had been furious but brief, and the late-afternoon sun was already drying the grass. They were quiet until Stacy put her equipment away and closed the back of her truck.

"He's getting bad, isn't he?"

"Doctor says it's Alzheimer's."

"Makes sense. I noticed things going downhill around here. Last time I came out to breed mares, Clinton called the very next morning and didn't remember we'd just inseminated the day before."

Whit rubbed her temple, trying to ward off the headache that was building. "Damn it. I should have come to visit more often. I would have seen that things weren't right, and maybe I could have helped before he'd dug himself into such a deep hole. I suppose he owes you money, too?"

"Yeah. He should have the bills tucked away here somewhere."

"They're probably in the mail I just found today. I was about to open it all when Tyree found Pan." Whit ran her fingers through her hair. "How much does he owe? I'll go get my checkbook."

Stacy waved her off. "I'll send you a new bill, including the charges for today. Zach landed a big software contract, so we're not hurting. You can pay some on Clinton's bill after you get things straightened out here." She stared at the ground and scratched her tanned cheek.

"Is there more I should know?"

Stacy climbed into her truck and closed the door, but lowered the window and leaned out. "As long as I've known Clinton Casey, he's never had a single strand of barbed wire on his farm."

Whit frowned. "He never let his bills go unpaid or missed a race where he had a horse entered either."

"Word is he's borrowed money from somebody he shouldn't. You need to ask him about that. I'd tell you to go look at the road that runs behind your pasture, but the storm probably washed away any tire tracks."

She stared at Stacy. "You think somebody hurt Pan deliberately? Who would do that?"

Stacy shook her head. "I don't know. Don't know who Clinton's been doing business with. Just telling you I've heard rumors."

"That wire's probably been in the ground for years and just worked its way up. You know that can happen."

Stacy started the truck. "Could be. All the same, I'd be keeping a sharp eye on things if I were you. Talk to your father." She waved as the truck rolled down the drive and turned onto the highway.

Whit kicked the toe of her boot against a clump of weeds that had taken root among the pasture grass. Could things get any worse?

CHAPTER THREE

"If all you've got is grease, then it's time to make gravy."

Mae smoothed the flared skirt of her conservative sundress and took a deep breath to calm her nerves. She'd lingered in the house where she grew up as long as the bank would allow, but she'd only been putting off the inevitable.

She'd spent her last month there reading everything she could find on the Internet about Michael Dupree, even paying the fee to an agency that did criminal-background checks and making arrangements to head west. Everything she couldn't pack in her suitcase or that the bank didn't claim as collateral was stored in a unit that rented by the month. She transferred her meager $25,000 into a bank that had branches in Louisiana, had her car serviced, visited her hairdresser and manicurist, and took Rhett to his favorite groomer for the last time.

When her time had run out, she turned her twelve-year-old Lexus onto Interstate 20 for the eight-hour drive to Jackson, Mississippi, where she and Rhett spent the night before she drove on to Opelousas, Louisiana.

She had called and made an appointment through Dupree's secretary, saying simply that she was new to the area and had gotten his name from one of his former colleagues.

Now Mae perched nervously on the edge of a chair in the lobby of Dupree's law office. She hoped he wasn't allergic to animals. The Louisiana heat made it impossible to leave Rhett in the car, and she hadn't checked into a hotel yet to leave him there. Her throat tightened. Actually, Rhett was the only remnant of her life in Georgia, and she didn't think she could bear to be apart from him, even for an hour. The poodle was being unusually well behaved, sitting quietly at her feet, and she hoped that would continue. He tended to lick his privates when he got nervous, which was totally inappropriate in public.

"Mr. Dupree will see you now, Ms. St. John." The secretary had emerged from Dupree's office and was gesturing toward the open door. The woman smiled warmly at Rhett and Mae relaxed a little. After all, this was still the South, and Southerners do love their dogs.

A heavyset gentleman with a full head of gray hair stood and came around the desk. He was short for a man, only about an inch taller than Mae's five feet, six inches, and had eyes the same shade of brown as hers. His suit was expensive and he smelled faintly of a fine cigar. He extended his hand. "I'm Michael Dupree. I'm pleased to meet you, Ms. St. John."

She clasped his hand briefly. It was soft and well manicured. She hated men who were poorly groomed. "Thank you." She wanted to prompt him to use her given name. After all, he was her father. But he didn't know that, and it wouldn't be appropriate until she revealed their family tie.

"Please, have a seat. What can I help you with?"

She stared at him, at a loss for where to begin. The words she had rehearsed over and over had flown from her brain. Her mouth was suddenly so dry she could barely speak. "I'm here because—" Her first words were choked and ended in a raspy cough.

Michael sprang to his feet. "I'm so sorry. It's been a busy day and I've forgotten my manners." He walked over to an oak credenza that served as a liquor cabinet and pulled a bottle of chilled water from a small refrigerator hidden within. He poured the water into a glass and she accepted it gratefully.

After a few swallows, her throat relaxed and she took a deep breath. "I'm not sure where to begin," she said, relieved to have regained her voice.

Michael abandoned his desk and sat in the chair across from her. He seemed to really see her for the first time, and his evaluating gaze wasn't entirely fatherly. Rhett stood and growled softly until

Mae silenced him with the same glare her grandmother had often used on her.

Michael didn't seem to notice the dog. "My secretary said I was recommended to you by a past colleague of mine."

Mae licked her lips. "Yes. My mother. Margaret St. John." Rhett began to lick his privates, and she nudged him with her toe.

"Maggie?" He sat back in his chair and rubbed the fine sandpaper stubble on his chin. "Maggie St. John? I haven't heard that name in years." He studied Mae again, this time with a different, more appropriate gaze. "You look like her. How is she?"

"My mother died, committed suicide shortly after I was born. They blamed it on post-partum depression."

He stared at her, his mouth open as though he was searching for something to say but the words wouldn't come. Finally, he cleared his throat. "I'm sorry. I've read that can be a very serious illness."

His disorientation steadied her. "My grandmother raised me. She's actually the one who gave me your name."

He straightened in his chair and his expression turned wary. Mae supposed he was beginning to guess this was more than a referral for legal assistance.

"I'm surprised Big Mae remembered my name," he said cautiously. "It's been what? More than twenty years?"

"Twenty-eight, to be precise. That's how old I am. Big Mae said *you* are my father."

His hand dropped discreetly to cover his lap, and Rhett resumed licking himself. Two men betrayed by their manhood.

As she held Michael's gaze, Mae could see his legal mind evaluating her motive and the possible consequences. Part of her wanted to scream, "Why didn't you want to be my father?" Another part reasoned that he had been young and married and bullied by his powerful father.

She supposed she should make her intentions known, rather than let him flap in the wind. Folding her hands in her lap, she stared down at them. "I don't want to make trouble for you. It's just that, well, Big Mae died recently and I don't have any other family. I was hoping, maybe, that we could get to know each other." Michael didn't answer and, after a long moment, she looked up.

His smile was wistful. "My father was friends with a Georgia congressman and sent me to work on his re-election campaign to get experience. That's where I met Maggie. I was in my early thirties, my prime. She was young and beautiful, inside and out, and I was defenseless against her charm. We were careless." He stood and went to the credenza and poured himself two fingers of whiskey. "When Father found out Maggie was pregnant, he ordered me back to Louisiana. What could I do? I was married. When I got back to Opelousas, my wife announced that *she* was pregnant. Later, my father told me Maggie had an abortion and her family had forbidden her to ever see me again."

"I didn't come here to judge you."

"I appreciate that." He blinked at her, then wrinkled his brow. "So, how long do you plan to visit?"

"Although I wasn't completely forthcoming when I made the appointment to see you, it is true that I hope to relocate here."

"I'm sorry. I know nothing about you. Do you have a career opportunity here?" He stopped and threw his head back in a laugh. "You probably don't have to work. Maggie said your family was old Georgia money."

She shook her head. "That was once true, but the family investments apparently didn't survive the recent economic crisis. I have a small nest egg that's enough to arrange housing and tide me over until I'm able to find suitable work."

"What would you like to do?"

That was the question she was still asking herself. Rhett left off his licking and began a brisk scratch behind his ears.

"I have degrees in art history, sociology, and English literature, with a minor in criminal justice."

His eyes widened. "That's quite an assortment."

"I had difficulty choosing. I loved college and my sorority sisters. Big Mae never complained about paying my expenses, so I lingered until this past spring."

He nodded. "You could have earned a medical or law degree by now."

"Unfortunately, I faint at the sight of blood. That's why I only completed a minor in criminal justice."

"You wanted to be a cop or maybe an FBI agent?" He eyed her delicate features and sundress. "I thought most of those women were lesbians, and you don't look anything like a lesbian."

His stereotyping didn't sit well with her, but she decided to let it pass this time, given the more pressing issues at the moment. "I had hoped to try my hand at writing crime novels, but I'm afraid my circumstances demand I find more immediate employment."

"Hmm. You aspire to be a writer, then."

"One of my professors encouraged me in that direction. I also was the official scribe for my sorority, and I've kept a journal for years."

He tapped the glass in his hand as though ticking off his thoughts. Then he downed the remaining whiskey. He'd clearly made some kind of decision.

"I'm still married to the same woman. We have three ungrateful sons. Helen never knew about Maggie, and I've never been unfaithful to her since." He bent forward and touched her knee in a tentative, fatherly gesture. "I would like very much to get to know this beautiful young woman sitting before me." He stood and paced back to the credenza to pour more whiskey. "But, being raised by Big Mae, you'll surely understand my need for discretion."

"As I said before, I didn't come here to cause trouble for you, Mr. Dupree."

He regarded her. "That seems a little formal, considering our family relationship. Please, call me Michael."

Mae smiled at him and nodded. "Michael."

He drummed his fingers against his leg and then brightened. "I have a friend whose daughter owns a trade publication that could probably use a promising young writer. Do you know anything about horse racing?"

Thoroughly cleaned and scratched, Rhett straightened and tilted his head as if considering the question.

"Not a lot, but I've always followed the Triple Crown each year." That wasn't entirely true. She'd paid more attention to the Derby fashions than the horses.

"This publication concerns quarter-horse racing. They're the sprinters of the horse-racing world. We have several tracks in Louisiana, including a rather busy one here in Opelousas."

She had closed a lot of doors when she left Georgia, and this was the first that had opened in her uncertain future. "I'm a quick study, and it sounds very interesting." She tried not to sound too anxious.

Michael went to his desk and scribbled down an address. "I'll call tonight and arrange an interview for you tomorrow. Will that be too soon?"

"No. I'll have to check into a hotel until I can find a suitable place to live, but I'm sure being employed would improve my application to any rental agencies."

Michael's smile broadened and he wrote down another address. "I can help with that, too. I own several apartment properties in the historic district. One's just become available. It's a beautiful part of downtown that has been reclaimed and gentrified."

"It sounds wonderful, but with limited funds, I'd have to consider the cost."

"How about the first month free to see if you like it? We can talk about a lease later. Oh, and utilities are part of the lease, so you won't need to transfer anything into your name."

Mae stood. "That's very generous of you," she said, taking the addresses he held out to her. She wasn't really in the position to refuse.

He smiled. "It's not every day I learn I have a daughter." He pulled a business card from his desk and scribbled a phone number on the back. "This is my cell phone." He handed it to her, along with a notepad and pen. "If you'll write down your number, I'll give you a call to let you know what time you should go for that interview tomorrow."

"Of course." She wrote quickly and gave it back to him. "I…I'm at a loss. I only wanted to meet you and perhaps have lunch occasionally to get to know you. I never expected you to welcome me so generously."

He came around the desk and wrapped a fatherly arm around her shoulders as they walked out of the office. "It's the least I can do." He released her as they stepped onto the sidewalk. "I cared very much for your mother." He sucked in a deep breath and sighed as he shook his head. "If only things could have been different. She's been my one real regret in life." He smiled at her. "Now that I've met you, maybe it's not so regrettable, after all."

Mae was overwhelmed by their meeting and his warmth.

"Well, I'm sure you want to get settled after your long trip." He pointed down Bellevue Street, better known as Lawyer's Row. "Go several blocks and you'll see Liberty Street. Turn right and it's on the left—huge old house that's been converted into four individual apartments."

Mae stepped away from him, giving in to Rhett's tug toward the huge oak in front of Michael's office. She struggled for words as Rhett lifted his leg and watered the gnarled roots that invaded and cracked the old sidewalk. "I don't know how to thank you."

Michael waved a dismissive hand. "Go on. Get settled. I'll call you later."

❖

"I can't believe how much they're charging for track fees now." Whit went over the figures for the third time.

Although they lived minutes from Evangeline Downs, it wasn't practical to haul a horse back and forth each day. Every trailer ride increased the risk for injury, so she had no choice but to pay to board in the backstretch stables.

"You can't get lard unless you boil the whole hog."

She stared at Pop. "In case you hadn't noticed, we have a shortage of hogs around here to boil. I'd hoped selling Pandemonium at the auction next week would cover Raising the Bar's track fees, but I can't sell Pan with stitches all over his legs. The other two yearlings won't bring as much, but maybe if I sell both, we can raise enough to campaign Bar."

"Can't sell any of 'em." He dug a plug of tobacco from his Red Man foil pouch and stuffed it deep in his cheek.

"Pop, I'm trying to scrape up the money to campaign one horse. We don't have the money to absorb the expense of training three more that still have a year to go before they can enter a money race."

"Can't run with the big dogs unless you get off the porch, Whit."

She dropped her chin to her chest and dug her fingers into her curls. A few more minutes of trying to reason with him and she wouldn't need a haircut, because she was going to pull out every last strand.

Whit pushed back her chair and went to sit on the ottoman next to his recliner, where he was watching old television reruns. "We have to sell some of the stock. It's either the yearlings or a couple of the brood mares."

He avoided her gaze. "It's not that I won't sell them. We can't sell them," he said, gruffly.

"What do you mean?"

"I needed feed and hay and a lot of other stuff around here, so I had to get money the best way I could until the colt starts running for us."

Whit frowned. "What did you do?"

"I got a loan and put the farm and stock up as collateral."

Getting information out of Pop these days was like pulling teeth. "You took out a second mortgage on the farm?"

"Tried to, but the bank turned me down."

Whit's gut clenched. "Tell me you didn't go to one of those loan sharks at the track."

"I ain't no fool." Pop spit into the old-fashioned spittoon beside his chair, and Whit jerked out of the way. In his younger days, he never missed. But now the carpet around the brass bucket was stained with errant tobacco juice. "Michael hooked me up with a group of fellows who want to see the colt run."

"You sold shares in Raising the Bar?"

"Nope. If I'd done that, the money could only be used for his training. That's why I had to put the farm up as collateral."

Whit frowned. Pop had befriended Michael Dupree when they were just kids, but Whit didn't like him. As far as she was concerned, he was a poor little rich boy who always wanted what Pop had—friends and respect. He'd also wanted Whit's mother.

She was twelve when she'd walked in on Michael, who stood behind her mother where she was washing dishes. He pressed against her back, pinning her against the sink.

"Don't make me hurt you, Michael."

"Just a kiss, Celeste. A hundred bucks for a kiss. Clinton doesn't have to know."

"No amount of money would make me be untrue to my husband."

"Five hundred. Whitley could use some school clothes. The girl's jeans are two inches too short. You know what it's like to be in the seventh grade and dressed like a hobo?"

When he rubbed his hips against her and put his mouth on her neck, she elbowed him hard enough to nearly knock him down.

"Shit." He wheezed and held his ribs. "You didn't have to do that."

"You're lucky it was just your ribs." Celeste dried her soapy hands. "Next time it'll be something more vital."

"Mama?"

The adults whirled toward her.

"Whit, honey, I didn't see you there. Do you need something?"

"What were y'all doing?"

"I was just looking for Clinton," Michael said.

"Pop's at the barn." She turned to her mother. "He wanted me to get us a couple of Cokes."

"There's some in the fridge, honey. Get one for Mr. Dupree, too, and show him where to find your father."

She stuck her head in the refrigerator to dig out the icy bottles of Coca-Cola, but she could still hear their fierce whispers.

"You gonna tell Clinton?"

"No. But only because you aren't worth going to jail over, and he'd certainly kill you."

"I'm sorry."

"You're going to be more than sorry, Michael Dupree, if you ever try that again."

He must have taken that to heart, because Pop never found out and Michael was still alive and hanging around. Best to let sleeping dogs lie, but that didn't mean Whit had to trust him.

"Exactly who are the men who made you the loan?"

"Don't know and don't care. Michael said it was a group of fellows who made investments but didn't want everybody in their business, so who's in the group is kept secret."

"A blind consortium."

"He didn't say anything about them being blind."

"I don't mean literally blind. I meant…never mind." It wasn't worth explaining. Whit didn't like it. Besides being a lawyer, Michael was a successful businessman, but there had always been a lot of innuendo around town concerning his lack of ethics and shark-like deals. "Do you have a copy of the loan papers? I'd like to take a look at them."

"Michael has them at his office. I know you don't like him, but he's been a good friend. Never charges me for legal work. I was about to lose everything to the bank when he came up with this loan for me."

"What's the interest rate?"

Pop scratched his head, but then the phone rang and he abandoned his memory search to answer it.

Whit left him to his phone call and went back to her calculations. Any money Pop had gotten from that blind consortium was gone or hidden in an account she hadn't found yet. He had only a couple hundred dollars left in the farm account.

Pop hung up the phone and looked over at her. "That was Michael. Says he'll fax you a copy of the loan agreement."

"Thanks."

"He also said he's sending a girl out here tomorrow to talk to you about a writing job for your magazine."

"Pop, I'm not hiring anybody."

"You've been complaining since you got here that you ain't got enough time to train horses and run your business. You need some help, so I told him you'd talk to her."

"Pop!"

He stood up slowly, and she bit back the impulse to rush over and steady him until he gained his balance. It still surprised her to see how much he'd aged since her mother died.

"He's asking as a favor, Whit. He's done me plenty, so I'd appreciate it if you'd give her a chance."

Whit sighed. Everybody around town knew about the "girls" he recommended for jobs. Not that they weren't competent workers on occasion, but she wondered if his wife knew how those women got his endorsement. She wasn't sure she'd be able to look this person in the face when she showed up, but she did need some help. "Okay, Pop. I'm not promising anything, but I'll talk to her."

Satisfied, he nodded and limped down the hall toward the bathroom.

Whit thumped her pencil against the legal pad she'd filled with figures. The income from her business was paying the bills now and buying their groceries. But she'd have to use the last of her savings to campaign Raising the Bar. He was fast enough that she was sure he'd make money. How much was always a gamble. Even a mild injury or getting boxed in by other horses could steal a big race from the fastest horse.

Pop had summed it up. She had no choice but to get off the porch and find out if she could run with the big dogs.

CHAPTER FOUR

"Don't name the turkey you plan to eat."

Whit slapped Raising the Bar on the rump and grinned. "Great run today."

"That's for sure, Miss Whitley. He felt good. I could hardly hold him back."

"Tyree, if we're going to work together every day, I'd rather you call me Whit and stop saying ma'am to me."

"Yes, ma'am...I mean, okay, Whit."

Whit slipped the bridle from the colt's head and replaced it with a halter, then clipped him into the cross ties of the wash stall. "Damn, it's hot," she said. She turned on the hose and bent to run the cool water over the back of her neck. It soaked the front of her shirt, but she didn't care as she stood and pulled off her ball cap to shake her hair loose, gather it with her fingers, and rethread it though the back of the cap to keep it off her neck. "I've been working in air-conditioning too long and lost my tolerance for these Louisiana summers."

"Mama don't turn on the air-conditioning at home unless it gets over a hundred, and I work outside all the time, but that don't make it any less hot to me." Tyree shed his shirt and took his turn with the hose. Then he grabbed the sweaty saddle and bridle and settled on an upturned bucket in the wide center aisle of the barn to clean sweat from the tack while Whit washed down the colt.

"You should be riding at the track, Tyree, not doing barn chores for me. You're a good jock." She glanced at the boy as she ran the soapy sponge over the colt's glistening flank.

"I'm right where I want to be, Miss Whitley. I mean, Whit." He soaped the leather carefully. "Riding at the track might earn me more money now, but I'm gonna be too big in another year or so. What I'm learning from you and Mr. Clinton is my ticket. I want to be a trainer, too."

Whit smiled at him. "Then we'll have to make sure you learn what you need. I don't know anybody better than Clinton Casey to teach you." She just hoped Tyree could learn enough before Pop's memory disappeared altogether. Hell, she hoped that after her long absence from the farm, she could remember enough of what Pop had taught her to successfully run Raising the Bar. She needed him to win, not just for the money, but to build her reputation as a trainer so maybe she could bring some clients back to the farm and get it operating in the black again.

"Hello?"

When Tyree stood and quickly pulled on his T-shirt, Whit ducked around the colt to check out the source of the melodic feminine voice that floated through the barn. She raised an eyebrow at their attractive visitor—or rather visitors.

The woman was slender, dressed in a beige business suit. The scoop-necked coral silk shell under her jacket was almost a perfect match to the orange dust that settled on her beige, three-inch heels as she approached down the hard-packed clay floor of the barn. A medium-sized black poodle pranced at her side. A potential client?

Whit turned off the hose and stepped out of the wash stall. "Can I help you?"

The woman tucked an errant strand of dark, silky hair behind her ear and shifted the dog's leash in her hands. "I'm looking for Whitley Casey. We have an appointment?"

The woman's genteel accent was definitely Southern, but not Louisianan. Whit dried her hands on a clean towel. "I'm Whit Casey."

Her perfectly manicured hand was soft in Whit's, but the handshake firm.

"How do you do? I'm Mae St. John. Mr. Dupree called yesterday about me?"

"You're the writer."

"Yes. Well, I've done some writing. Not for magazines, specifically."

The colt bobbed his head, impatiently rattling the cross ties, and Mae flinched, taking a step back. She eyed the horse, her nervousness obvious.

"Spend much time around horses, Ms. St. John?"

"Not really. But I like animals." She glanced down at the poodle as if to confirm him as evidence.

It took some effort for Whit to keep her expression neutral. This brush-off was going to be easier than she thought, but she needed to at least give the appearance of an interview to satisfy Pop and Michael.

"How about if we continue this some place that's cooler? Tyree, can you finish up here?"

"Sure can."

Whit gestured toward the farmhouse. "This way, Ms. St. John."

They were halfway to the house when Whit's Jack Russell terrier came barreling around the barn, fresh from a hunt for field mice. She spied the poodle and put her head down to run faster. Before Whit could yell, the poodle had evaluated the situation and leapt into Mae's arms. Ellie circled and growled while the poodle shook.

"Ellie. Mind your manners. Sit." The terrier obeyed but continued to growl, her hackles raised along her spine.

Mae frowned. "Why, Rhett, I never knew you for a coward." She thrust the poodle at Whit. "Do you mind holding him for a minute?"

It wasn't a question because she'd already pressed the dog into Whit's hands and squatted to hold hers out to Ellie. "What a beautiful little girl you are. And so brave."

Ellie's ears pricked forward at the sight of the intruder pressed against her mistress's chest, and, as any jealous terrier would, she turned her back on Whit. She instead gave her attention to the woman handing out soft compliments and wagged her stubby tail.

"How rude of me to bring him into your yard without a proper introduction," Mae said, stroking Ellie's head and earning a tongue swipe across her wrist. "He's really not such a coward. You just startled him. He's quite handsome if you would stop growling long enough to notice."

Whit watched in fascination as Mae held Ellie's rapt attention, stroking down the terrier's neck and scratching behind her ears. Ellie wagged her tail again. "Okay, put him down on my other side," she said to Whit.

Ellie started to growl. "Sit." Mae's command held such authority that Whit almost dropped to the ground herself. She was surprised that the terrier complied, since it was only a fluke that she had obeyed Whit before.

The poodle sat, too, peeking around Mae at Ellie. He was twice her size but clearly didn't have Ellie's alpha instincts.

"Ellie, this is Rhett." Mae brushed her hand over the poodle and held his scent out for Ellie to smell. "Rhett, this lovely little lady is Ellie." She repeated the gesture, letting Rhett smell Ellie's scent on her other hand. He wagged his tail. "Now y'all get to know each other, and no growling."

Mae stood and Whit tensed to grab Ellie if she lunged for Rhett's neck. Rhett sat very still, except for his tail frantically wagging, as Ellie sniffed him up and down. Satisfied, she went to the nearest bush and wet it down in a display of dominance. Mae unclipped his leash and Rhett followed to add his contribution, then continued after Ellie to the next marking spot.

"I'm so sorry," Mae said, turning to Whit. "I know it's unprofessional to take my dog along on a job interview, but we just arrived in town yesterday, and when I started to leave him in our new apartment, he howled like somebody was killing him. I was afraid my new neighbors would throw us out before we've even gotten settled."

"It's okay. They seem fine now," Whit said gruffly. She turned toward the house in long strides and left Mae to follow.

They stepped onto the porch where Pop sat in his second-favorite spot, a straight-backed chair tilted to rest against the house.

"That was an impressive feat of dog whispering, young lady."

Mae smiled sweetly. "Thank you, sir." She extended her hand. "Mae St. John."

Pop stood and took her hand in both of his. "Pleased to meet you, Miss St. John. I'm Clinton Casey, sire to this one here with the disposition of a porcupine."

"Pop," Whit growled.

But Pop waved off her warning. "Y'all go on inside and chat. I'll keep an eye on the dogs."

Mae glanced back at the pups but seemed satisfied that Rhett was happy enough following Ellie around the yard. "That's very kind of you," she said, giving Pop a blazing smile.

"It's no trouble, young lady," he said, smiling back at her. "Sometimes I prefer the company of dogs over some people I know." He glanced in Whit's direction to make his point.

Whit stared at him. Just yesterday, he'd been complaining about Ellie's hair in his recliner and her water dish that he constantly stumbled over.

He held the screen door open for Mae to enter. Whit caught his eye and shook her head in disgust, and he retaliated by letting it go when she walked through so that it bumped her in the back. She answered by closing the heavy oak door with a firm thump.

Whit ducked her head sheepishly when Mae jumped at the loud slam. "Uh, wind must have caught it."

Mae nodded and stood uncertainly in the area between the kitchen and living room, fidgeting with Rhett's leash.

"I just moved *Quarter Track* here from Baton Rouge so I haven't had time to really get an office set up."

She led Mae into the dining room. Nobody had eaten there since her mom died, so Whit decided she would convert it into an office for her magazine. Several file cabinets were crammed haphazardly against the wall, and stacks of back issues and other reference material covered the dining table. In the midst of the chaos was Whit's desktop computer. A massive sideboard still filled with dishes dominated the far wall. Once she bought a desk, she'd hire someone to help move the old furniture into storage.

"Ninety percent is done by me from home. I pay a marketing agency to sell the ads, and I use freelancers to write for the magazine. Maintaining the website mostly involves collecting daily stats and bits of news from other sources and posting them on my site. I normally do that, but right now I'm paying a friend in Baton Rouge to handle it until I get some things cleared up here at the farm."

She turned to Mae. "I'm afraid Mr. Dupree had the mistaken impression that I was looking to hire someone, but you can see that I'm nowhere near that point. I don't even have a desk for myself, much less somebody else."

Mae was about to speak when Pop clumped in with the two dogs. Ellie went straight to her water bowl with Rhett on her heels as Pop glared at Whit.

"I'd swear your mother taught you better manners, even if you did live in the barn more than the house growing up." He took off his cap and pointed it at Whit. She sighed and pulled hers from her head, letting her hair fall to her shoulders. He nodded his approval. "Now, would you like something to drink, Miss St. John?"

Whit interrupted. "Ms. St. John was on her way out. I explained to her that I'm not in a position to hire anyone right now."

"Thank you, Mr. Casey. I'd love a glass of water." She turned to Whit. "Can we sit down a moment?"

Whit scowled but nodded, and they both sat down at the table. Mae pulled a folded paper from her purse and handed it to Whit. "This is a sample of my writing."

It was titled *The Imagery of Christ in William Faulkner's* Unvanquished. Her only example of her work was a paper she wrote for a college class? It was all she could do not to roll her eyes. "Ms. St. John—"

"Please, call me Mae."

Whit drummed her fingers on the table. She didn't want to like this woman with whiskey eyes, a melodic accent, and shining dark hair. She didn't want to call her by her first name. Pop taught her early not to name the turkey they planned to butcher for Thanksgiving, and Whit planned to make this woman disappear before supper time ever got here. "Ms. St. John, it is customary to present clips of news articles you have written when applying for a job with a magazine or newspaper."

"I'm afraid I don't have such examples."

"What do you have?"

Mae drew another paper from her purse. It was a typed resume.

"As you can see, I have three degrees from Emory University."

Whit nodded, scanning the list of academic and social accomplishments. "That's an impressive education, but your resume shows absolutely no job experience." She scanned the single page. "I see you've listed positions as secretary, treasurer, and, finally, events coordinator of your college sorority."

"Events coordinator was a huge responsibility."

"I'm sure, but as I explained, I don't have a job opening, and I don't anticipate having one for an events coordinator."

Mae swept her hand toward the jumble of papers that covered the table. "Yet, you obviously need help with your workload."

Whit's frown deepened. "I thought you wanted to write."

"I do. But I can do other things as well. I'm a *very* organized person."

"I hear they're hiring at the Evangeline Downs casino."

"Big Mae would roll over in her grave if I worked at a casino."

"Big Mae?"

"My grandmother. My mother died young, and Big Mae raised me."

"I'm sorry about your mother, but I don't have a job for you here."

"All I'm asking for is a chance."

Maybe if she approached this differently, the woman would see how ill suited she was for Whit's business. "When I asked if you had experience with horses and you said, 'Not really,' what exactly did you mean?"

Mae squirmed in her chair and looked down at her hands. "I went to pony camp when I was ten."

Oh, this was rich. Whit could picture herself sharing a beer with her friends in Baton Rouge and telling them about the woman who came looking for a job with pony camp and her sorority on her resume. They'd laugh their butts off.

As though reading her thoughts, Mae lifted her chin and looked Whit directly in the eye. "I'll make you a deal," she said.

"A deal?"

"Yes. I'll work exactly one month for free. I have the resources to do that. At the end of that month, if you're not satisfied that I've been beneficial to your business, I'll leave."

"Can't beat that," Pop yelled from his recliner in the living room. The old coot was eavesdropping.

Whit sighed. She had so much on her plate, the last thing she needed was to spend time breaking in a new employee she didn't even want.

"Please. I know I can do this."

Whit stared at her boots. It felt so wrong. This woman was inexperienced, obviously pampered, straight—not that Whit had anything against straight women—and had some connection to Michael Dupree. When she looked up four sets of eyes were watching her—Pop, Ellie, Rhett, and Mae—but it was Mae's hopeful whiskey-brown ones that were her doom.

"Okay."

Mae's smile lit up the room.

"But I don't even have a computer for you." She pointed to the desktop Dell. "That one's mine."

"I can bring my laptop to work on as long as you have wireless here."

Whit nodded. "I do."

"Then I'll see you first thing in the morning."

"Since tomorrow is Friday, why don't you start Monday around nine? That will give me time to figure out what I need for you to do."

"Monday, then." Mae stood and shook Whit's hand again. "I promise you won't regret this."

Whit shook her head. "I'm going to hold you to that." She followed Mae as she collected Rhett and walked to her car. "By the way, dress is casual. I wear jeans or shorts if I'm going to be outdoors in the heat. And you can bring the dog with you. Since Ellie didn't chew him up, she must like him. Maybe hanging out with him will keep her from pestering the barn cats."

Mae smiled broadly, got in the car, and waved as she drove away with Rhett sitting proudly in the passenger seat.

Pop was standing so close that Whit bumped into him when she turned to go inside. "Dang, Pop."

"Mark my words. That little lady is a Thoroughbred in a herd of donkeys." He watched the Lexus crunch carefully down the gravel drive. "If I was forty years younger, I'd be saddling up to go after that one."

"Calm down, old man. Don't make me get out the shock paddles because you've gone and had a coronary over a woman a third of your age."

"Just sayin'. A loose horse ought to be looking for new pasture, and since the only thing you brought with you from the city is that bossy little dog, I reckon you're pulling single traces."

"I've got two businesses to run, Pop. I don't have time for anything else." She stomped into the house with him right behind her. "Besides, women are nothing but trouble."

"I might be forgetting a few things, but I haven't turned stupid. I know you're working harder than a borrowed mule. I'm just saying your load would be lighter if you'd hitch up to double traces and share that burden."

Chapter Five

"That dog's barking up the wrong tree."

Mae twisted her hands together and scanned the restaurant. She had good reason for being nervous at their first meeting, but it didn't make sense that she was this anxious about having lunch with Michael today. He'd been nothing but welcoming.

When two men stood up at a table in the far corner she recognized her lunch date. Thank God he'd brought someone else so it wouldn't just be the two of them trying to make conversation. Not that she was ever at a loss for words, but it could happen. One day. And she didn't want it to be today.

Michael waved her over. "Mae, I'm so glad you could join us. This is Jean Paul Broussard, a colleague in the local legal community. I hope you don't mind if he joins us."

"I don't mind at all." Mae eyed the handsome stranger. His dark hair and eyes reminded her of Al Pacino, except he was taller. She held out her hand. "Pleased to make your acquaintance, Mr. Broussard."

"Please, it's Jean Paul. I'm honored to meet you." His accent was a smooth blend of cultured French and Southern drawl. He gently clasped her outstretched hand in a respectfully brief greeting and pulled out a chair to seat her between him and Michael.

"How'd your interview go with the Casey girl?" Michael asked.

"I start on Monday." She unfolded her napkin and placed it in her lap. "Thank you for recommending me."

"Did she offer you a decent salary?"

Mae hesitated. It was incredibly improper for him to ask, even if he was her biological father. "It is entirely commensurate with my experience." It wasn't a real answer, but something told her not to confide her deal with Whit Casey. Michael frowned and Mae gave him a sweet smile meant to disarm, and then changed the subject. "What do you recommend on the menu?"

"The crawfish have gone out of season, but even though they've been frozen, the bisque is excellent," Jean Paul said. "You may want to request it without their trademark crawfish head floating in it. It can be an appetite killer if you aren't accustomed to the quirks of bayou cuisine."

Mae smiled at him. "Not at all. Big Mae's cook liked to simmer a combination of fish and crawfish heads to make a good stock for her catfish stew. She swore the crawfish were the key to a good flavor."

The men shared looks of approval, and Mae knew she had scored. Men were easy to manipulate. Her grandmother had been a consummate instructor in the art, and Mae was an apt student. It was one of her many skills. She also found most men eager to impart their superior knowledge to seemingly clueless women.

"I've been reading up on quarter-horse racing, because I don't want to seem like a complete idiot at my first day of work on Monday. However, I'd like to see it up close. I was thinking of going to Evangeline Downs tomorrow. Can anyone wander around the barns where they keep the horses? I don't want to get arrested for being in the wrong place."

"What you need is a tour guide, but I'm afraid I have to go out of town on business this weekend." Michael looked up from his menu. "Jean Paul knows his way around Evangeline Downs. He'll be glad to show you around."

"I don't want to be a bother."

"Escorting a beautiful woman to the track is no hardship," Jean Paul said smoothly.

She regarded him, judging him to be in his mid-thirties. His good looks and silky accent came across as a bit slick, and she was irritated that Michael automatically assumed she would be comfortable spending the day with this man she'd just met. Still, she tucked her concerns away, because Michael had left her no room to decline without offending. “That would be lovely,” she said.

“Excellent.” Michael waved their waitress over to place their orders.

“Quarter-horse racing doesn’t start at Evangeline for another month, but my family owns shares in several Thoroughbreds that are racing now, so I have passes that will get us in areas of the track usually off limits to the general public,” Jean Paul explained. “It means getting up very early though.”

“How early?”

“Five thirty in the morning. They start exercising the horses before the sun is barely up.”

“Good thing I’m an early riser. Are you sure you don’t have other plans?”

“Nothing that can’t be rescheduled,” Jean Paul said. “Besides, I want to check out the new colt that some people are saying is a clone of Funny Cide.”

Michael snorted. “You can’t be serious. There’s no way anyone could get a clone registered to race. Not a Thoroughbred or a quarter horse.”

“There is always a way,” Jean Paul said matter-of-factly.

“Cloned? I read about them cloning sheep, but I didn’t know they were cloning horses.”

“They did it first at Texas A&M,” Michael said. “A few idiots have cloned performance horses for dressage or eventing, but it’s hardly worth the expense. Both Thoroughbred and quarter-horse racing have banned it.”

“If it costs so much, why would anyone want to do it?”

Jean Paul paused while the waitress delivered their food. “It costs thousands of dollars for the cloning procedure, but a top racer is worth millions. The Thoroughbred, Funny Cide, was gelded, so they couldn’t breed him. John Henry, twice Horse of the Year, was a gelding.”

Mae could see now that she needed to do a lot more reading before Monday.

Michael stabbed a fried oyster with his fork and waved it at them. “I still say it’s hogwash.”

Jean Paul raised an eyebrow at Michael's dismissal. "Two lawsuits were filed just last week to get the Quarter Horse Registry to withdraw its ban on cloning. Thoroughbred racing is next. It's just a matter of time."

Mae looked up from her very tasty seafood gumbo. "If that's true, then why would someone risk doing it now? Wouldn't that get them in a lot of legal trouble?"

"More than you know," Michael said. "Forging the registry paperwork alone would get you permanently thrown out of racing." He stared down at his plate and frowned. "You'd have to be really desperate to risk it," he said absently, as if his thoughts had gone elsewhere.

Mae turned his remark over in her mind. Suppose the rumors were true. This could be the big story that would make Whit Casey hire her for sure. "This sounds really interesting. I wouldn't mind learning more about it."

Michael seemed lost in his thoughts, but Jean Paul had more to say on the subject. "People shrug about it now, but cloning is going to be the next big legal battle. Just think. If they can successfully clone animal athletes, what's to stop them from eventually cloning human athletes?"

Michael shook his head. "Never happen, unless it's in some backward third-world country. No God-fearing nation would ever let it happen."

Mae had to agree that it was unlikely, at least in their lifetimes. "I admit it is a bit of a leap, but I think Jean Paul could be on to something where horses are concerned."

Michael stared at her for a few seconds, then nodded. "You could be right. Maybe you should look into that." He glanced at his watch and stood. "Hate to eat and run, but the case I've been trying this week didn't wrap up as quickly as I thought. I have to be back in court in ten minutes." He waved the waitress over and handed her three twenty-dollar bills. "There you go, hon. That should take care of our bill and a nice tip."

The young waitress tucked the cash in her pocket, her smile implying a bit more than appreciation. "Thanks, Mr. Dupree. You come back when you're not in such a hurry, and I'll make sure you get everything you need."

He winked at her, then turned back to Mae and Jean Paul. "Y'all take your time and get to know each other." With that parting remark, he left them alone.

Mae folded her napkin and placed it on the table. "Actually, I really should go, too. I've left Rhett alone for the first time, and I want to make sure he isn't howling up a storm and disturbing my neighbors."

Jean Paul also stood. "Rhett?"

"My grandmother's poodle I inherited, along with his trust fund."

"The dog has a trust fund? Your grandmother must have had a great sense of humor."

Mae realized it was the first time he had really smiled, and she was surprised at how much it warmed his dark features. "Big Mae had a wit sharper than a general's saber. I hope you're not allergic to dogs, because Rhett goes just about everywhere with me. He's very well-behaved."

"Except for howling when left alone?"

"Well, except for that and licking himself in inappropriate places."

Jean Paul threw his head back and laughed, his straight teeth a flash of white, then held out his hand. "It was a pleasure to meet you. I'll pick you—and Rhett—up early tomorrow. Wear comfortable shoes because we'll do a lot of walking."

"I will. Thank you," Mae replied, giving his hand a squeeze. She was rethinking her first impression of Jean Paul. Once he relaxed, she found him to be pleasant-enough company.

❖

Whit drummed her fingers on the table while she waited for her most recent website update to load. She really needed to upgrade something, but she wasn't a techno-type person and was at a loss to figure out what.

There had been a time when she was content sitting long hours at her computer, updating things on the *Quarter Track* website and trolling other similar websites for ideas. Lately, she could hardly tolerate an hour of computer work before she was itching to get outdoors. The fresh air and scent of horses and hay called to her. How she'd endured those years in the city, even thought she was happy, was now a mystery to her.

But she knew what had kept her in the city—women. Discovering bars and coffeehouses where lesbians gathered was like a kid walking into her first candy shop. Before college, she'd known only one other lesbian.

Katerina was a young exercise jockey, but experienced enough to recognize Whit's teen crush on her. The year before Whit left for Baton Rouge, they'd explored each of Whit's sexual fantasies and a few she'd never imagined. Then Kat announced she was moving to a track where she had a better chance to get her jockey's license. Whit left for Baton Rouge and her freshman year at LSU the day after Kat boarded a bus for California.

She absently wondered if Avery had moved on, too, like Kat and all Whit's girlfriends eventually did. She'd been back at the farm for nearly a month without hearing from her. Not that she expected to. Whit had made it clear that she wouldn't be returning to live in Baton Rouge again.

She didn't really miss her former haunts, but she sure missed female company. She had Pop and a handful of straight friends in Opelousas. But, even as accepting as they were, she still felt like a zebra in a herd of horses. She needed some herd time with other zebras.

The website finally flowed onto her screen, and she clicked through several pages to check the work she had done. Satisfied all was in order, she turned to her email inbox. At least thirty messages appeared when it opened, and she scanned them quickly. Nothing was urgent, so she decided to escape to the barn and handle her email after it was too dark to be outside.

She picked up her cell phone to pocket it, then juggled it awkwardly when its loud ringing startled her. She checked the caller ID. Huh. It was as if her thoughts had summoned the devil herself.

"Hello, Avery."

"Whit, honey. It's so good to hear your voice. Tell me that you're coming back to the city soon."

"As a matter of fact, I'm probably going to be in Baton Rouge sometime in the next couple of weeks. My real-estate agent called to say she has a contract on my condo. If it all works out, I'll have to drive over to sign the closing papers."

"Don't you think you're moving a little fast? I know you're upset about your father, but that's precisely why you shouldn't be making life-changing decisions right now."

Those very thoughts had nagged at Whit over the past weeks. Was she making decisions at the wrong time because she was in emergency mode? Her silence spoke those doubts clearly enough.

"Everybody misses you." Avery's voice softened. "I miss you. You're only a little over an hour away. Drive down and have dinner with me this weekend."

Whit missed some things about Avery, too. She missed Avery's soft skin and blue eyes. She missed kissing her. But the Avery she missed was the woman she had known early in their relationship. Not the workaholic, critical woman she'd turned out to be. It had taken years of indecision for her to make the break and save herself, her self-esteem. She was still angry with Avery. No, she was angry with herself for letting it happen. She knew it took two people to ruin a relationship, but she couldn't, shouldn't open that door again.

"I've got a lot going on here. I don't think I can get away right now."

Avery, her voice husky, continued as though Whit hadn't spoken. "A little candlelight, soft music, and good conversation. Who knows what it might lead to?"

"Avery—"

Avery's voice dropped another octave. "I won a big case this week and I need you to celebrate with me. You know what winning does to me."

Whit shivered and closed her eyes. She did remember. Winning made Avery assertive and insatiable in bed.

The first time had caught Whit by surprise. Sex between them had always been satisfying, but fairly vanilla until the day Avery came home with a guilty verdict in a big murder case and a swagger the size of Texas. Whit had been pleasantly sore for days.

But it had been several years since they'd shared that kind of passion. Was Avery sincere? Had Whit's absence made Avery realize that she'd taken Whit for granted?

"Even better, Tara and Joanie are having a few people over at their cabin on Lake Maurepas on Saturday. They've invited us for the entire weekend. Wouldn't that be fun, relaxing at the lake, having drinks with friends and cooking out?"

Ah. Now they were getting to the real reason for the call.

Tara Savoy was a behind-the-scene kingmaker in Baton Rouge politics. The alliance between her family and Avery's had spanned decades. Tara's family provided the money and influence, while Avery's family provided the politicians.

But Tara was approaching sixty, and her partner, Joanie, was twenty-five years younger. A drunken, one-night stand with Joanie many years before got Avery banned from Tara's gatherings until she and Whit became a couple. Only then did Tara trust Avery around Joanie, and Whit now suspected that Avery wasn't welcome at the cabin this weekend unless she had Whit by her side.

"I can't do that, Avery. Dinner is one thing, but I have Pop to care for and two businesses to run. I can't take the whole weekend off."

The silence lasted for a long moment.

"So, you don't have time for us anymore?" She gave a short, hard laugh. "Here I thought you were just pouting because *I* was tied up with work. I'd never have guessed you'd leave without discussing it with me."

Whit took a deep breath. This was it. They'd never officially broken up. Avery had been deep into preparation for a big trial during the weeks that Whit had discovered and struggled with what to do about Pop's situation. She had tried to talk to Avery, but she was too busy to meet for even a meal to talk out Whit's concerns or the reasons she was leaving Baton Rouge. Avery acted as if the situation would magically go away if she put Whit off long enough. So, in the end, she just packed up and left her condo with a real-estate agency to sell or rent. Her good-bye had been a message left on Avery's cell phone.

"We hadn't even had lunch together for more than a month," Whit said. "Normal couples find time for each other, no matter what life throws at them." The anger she had kept bottled up began to pour out, hot and bitter. "Normal couples make a life together. They live in the same house and make love. It's been more than a year, Avery, since we've been intimate, and longer than that since you made me feel like you were doing more than pacifying my needs."

Avery ignored the comment about living together. "Christ. I should have known this was about sex. It always comes back to that, doesn't it?"

Whit seethed. "You see, that's the real problem. It's just sex to you. It's much more than that to me. It's sharing intimacy with the person you love. You never did understand that."

"Real life isn't like one of your lesbian romance novels, Whitley."

"Avery, just let it go. We want different things."

"You need to grow up. You can't play with ponies and read those stupid lesbian romance stories all your life. You're not a twenty-year-old college student anymore."

The disconnect would have been more dramatic if they hadn't been on cell phones. Not even a dial tone filled the silence and the empty hole in Whit's chest.

CHAPTER SIX

"That dog still hunts."

Whit glanced between her stopwatch and the colt running the long oval track. Raising the Bar was getting faster every day. But she needed to move him to a real track and get him used to running with other horses.

"Good morning."

Preoccupied with the colt, she hadn't seen Mae approach. She didn't mean to stare, but, damn, the woman looked good. Better than good.

Not wearing a business suit today, Mae was a picture of casual elegance. The broad collar of her fuchsia-colored blouse lay open to reveal a sculpted collarbone and only a hint of modest cleavage. The toes of new, lace-up paddock boots peeked out from her boot-cut, hip-hugging jeans.

Mae frowned and glanced down at her outfit. "Is this okay for work? If it's not, I can wear something different tomorrow."

Whit coughed and her face warmed at being caught ogling like a teenager. "Uh, yeah. I mean, no, you look fine. The paddock boots are a good choice."

Mae looked relieved. "Well, I noticed that was what you were wearing last week. They're really quite comfortable and the store had a good selection."

The colt whizzed past and Whit absently clicked her stopwatch, having no idea if she'd done it at the right second.

Mae chattered on. "I bought four pairs in different colors. I just love shoes. I went to the track on Saturday and tried to get a feel for what might fit in before I went shopping, but I saw everything from shorts to dresses."

Whit looked down at the khaki cargo shorts, dirty leather sneakers, and T-shirt she wore. "I had jeans on last week because I'd been riding," she said, as if that explained her current sloppy attire. "It's still too hot in September to wear them all the time."

"Well, I figured I'd be in the office most of today, getting organized, so I should be fine. Still, Big Mae taught me to always be prepared. I have several other outfits in the car in case I need a wardrobe change."

Whit mentally sighed. She hoped Mae could forget her wardrobe selection long enough to be at least a little help. But if she couldn't, then, hell, it wasn't like she was actually paying her. "I'm just saying, there's no dress code for this job. I just wear what's comfortable."

"I'll bet all those pockets come in handy when you're out here doing horse things." Mae shook her head. "I can't wear those types of shorts myself. They make my butt and thighs look like the broad side of a barn. They're fine on you because you're so tall."

Whit doubted anything could make Mae's shapely hips look big, but clamped her lips together before the thought could become words and the compliment possibly misinterpreted. She did *not* hit on employees, much less straight women.

Mae, however, didn't seem to require that Whit contribute much to the conversation.

"Anyway, the woman in the store was very helpful. I must have tried on outfits for hours. She even had some doggie treats for Rhett. Of course, I find people usually are helpful when you're spending money with them." She tilted her head as though she was examining the woman's motives. "Still, she was very nice, and even directed me to a few other stores to find what I needed."

"Did you leave him at home?" Whit broke in when Mae finally took a breath.

"Rhett? Heavens, no. He's at the house with Mr. Casey and Ellie. I think she's decided he's not too much of a bother. You don't think a horse will step on him or anything, do you? I couldn't bear it if something happened to him. He has a trust fund. Did I tell you that? Isn't that funny? A dog with a trust fund? I think it was Big Mae's final joke. She had quite a sense of humor."

Whit realized she'd completely missed timing the colt on his next whirl around the track, and Tyree was already slowing him to a trot. She decided she should jump in before Mae launched into more stories about this Big Mae character.

"You're early. It's only seven thirty."

"I know you said nine, but Jean Paul said horse people always start work really early before the day gets too hot."

"Jean Paul?"

"Jean Paul Broussard. Do you know him?"

"No."

"He's a lawyer friend of Michael's, uh, Mr. Dupree's. His family owns shares in several racehorses. He gave me a thorough tour of Evangeline Downs on Saturday. It was very nice of him."

Whit doubted it was much of a hardship for the guy, unless Mae had talked him to death. At this point, she considered that to be a distinct possibility. Tyree reined the colt down to a prancing walk when she waved them over.

"Walk him out, Tyree. I'll see you back at the barn. Don't turn him out, though. I'm going to move him to the track next week, so I want to get him off grass and accustomed to being stall-bound most of the day."

"Yes, ma'am."

"What'd I tell you about saying ma'am to me?"

"Okay, Whit." He grinned at Mae. "I was being polite in front of the lady."

Mae shaded her eyes and smiled up at him. "Thank you, Tyree. That's very gentlemanly of you. But you can call me Mae. So you're a jockey?"

"Yes, ma'am. I mean, I'm only an exercise rider. I'm getting too big to be a jockey. I want to be a trainer. Mr. Clinton's teaching me."

"That's wonderful."

"Mae is going to be working on *Quarter Track* with me, so you'll see her around some," Whit said.

"I remember you. You were here last week. You had that dog with a funny haircut."

Mae put her fingers to her lips. "Don't say that in front of him. He's very sensitive about his haircut."

Tyree laughed. "I won't." He turned the colt homeward and they trailed after him.

When they reached the barn, Tyree unsaddled Bar, and Whit clipped him into the cross ties of the wash stall.

Mae edged closer. "He's beautiful. May I pet him?"

"If you want, but he's pretty sweaty." Whit squirted some soap into a bucket and reached for the hose.

Mae held out her hand and let the colt sniff her palm. "What's his name?"

"That's Raising the Bar," Tyree announced proudly. "He's gonna win Mr. Clinton a bundle of money."

"Bar's the two-year-old we're planning to race in another month when the quarter horses get their turn at Evangeline," Whit said.

"I learned something about that Saturday when I toured the track. I also read a lot about it on the Internet."

Whit had to give her credit for initiative. She turned on the hose. "You might want to stand back so you don't get wet."

Tyree ducked into the tack room and returned with a folding chair and small bucket filled with the things he needed to clean the sweaty saddle and bridle. He opened the chair next to an upturned five-gallon bucket. "You can sit here and watch, Miss Mae. I'm gonna sit on this bucket."

Mae settled in the chair and began to ask questions. "So, you and your father own all the horses here? Why do you have so many stalls? Are there more horses in a north-forty or something? That's what they call it in Western movies. I was never quite sure what a north-forty meant."

Whit chuckled at the barrage of questions. "This isn't a cattle ranch. It's a training farm. We don't have a 'north forty.' That refers to forty acres of pasture on the north part of a ranch. There are empty stalls because Pop's getting old. It's too much of a strain for him to train more than a few at a time now." It wasn't really a lie. "All of the horses here now are ours except for the racers in the last two stalls on the right."

Tyree gathered up the tack he'd finished cleaning. "Speaking of those two, I'm supposed to ride both of them this morning. You reckon Mr. Clinton will be out soon?"

Whit gestured toward the house. "Go see if he's ready yet. It takes him longer to get going these days, but he was up and eating breakfast when I left the house earlier." She eyed Mae as Tyree left. "I think I told you that I just moved back from Baton Rouge. Once I get a handle on what it's going to take to run my business and train horses, I'll probably pick up a few more clients for him."

"I didn't see a sign when I drove in. Does your farm have a name? I mean, everybody else seems to have a name, like Calumet Farms in Kentucky."

Whit smiled to herself. "Joie de Vivre Quarter Horses."

"If I remember my French lessons, it means something like 'love of life,' doesn't it?"

"Yeah. My mother named the farm. Pop's just an old Texas redneck, but Mama was Cajun." Whit finished sluicing the water from Bar's glistening hide and led him to his stall. She missed her mother even more fiercely now that she had to deal with Pop's illness. It was an ache she didn't want to prod by answering a lot of questions about the battle her mother had lost to cancer. "I've got to write down a few things from this morning's training session, and then we can go to the house and get started."

Mae followed her into the barn office. "So, have you sold shares in Raising the Bar? Some of the horses I saw Saturday were owned by groups of investors."

"No. You don't usually sell shares unless they've won several races and you need money to pay the fees for a really big race. Bar's barely two years old. He'll run his first race next month." Whit pulled a notebook from the desk drawer and checked her stopwatch before entering a few figures.

"You don't keep those records on computer? Why didn't you set up the *Quarter Track* office here?"

Geez. Was there no end to this woman's curiosity?

"The barn's too dusty to keep computers out here. I'd have to Sheetrock the walls and put in a ventilation system, or I'd be buying new equipment every six months." Actually, she spent most evenings working on *Quarter Track* business, and it was easier to keep an eye on Pop if she was in the house, not the barn.

❖

Halfway to the house, they encountered Clinton and Tyree. Clinton wore a neatly pressed cotton shirt buttoned to his neck and a leather jacket. Mae had to resist brushing away the bit of shaving cream that still clung to his earlobe. He touched his hair as if to ensure it was still neatly combed and smiled broadly at them. Tyree shifted nervously at his side.

"I see you finally got out of bed, Whitley. Getting ready to run that colt?"

The sadness that flashed in Whit's eyes made Mae's heart swell with empathy.

"I've been up for hours, Pop. We've already run Bar and put him back in the stall. What have you been doing all morning? Where are you going all dressed up?"

"I was thinking of taking your mother out to breakfast."

Whit's face flushed. She glanced at Tyree, who hung his head, then back at Clinton. "Pop—"

Mae touched Whit's shoulder to stop her. She'd had some experience with this, and she knew it was all new to Whit.

"Why, I just saw Mrs. Casey leave," she said, laying her hand on Clinton's arm. "She said she was going to town to get some groceries. She'll be really disappointed she missed a date with such a handsome fellow, but I'm afraid you're a few minutes too late."

Whit stared at her, eyebrow raised, but Clinton just shrugged. "Seems like I've been chasing that woman my entire life." He winked at Whit. "Who's this pretty lady? Somebody you're chasing?"

Whit's blush deepened. "This is Mae St. John. Michael recommended her to help me with *Quarter Track*, and you met her last week."

Clinton looked confused, so Mae gave his arm a reassuring squeeze. "I imagine you must meet so many women, it's hard to remember just one."

He straightened at her praise. "Celeste is the only girl for me, but I wouldn't forget meeting one as pretty as you."

"Oh, my. Handsome and charming. Mrs. Casey is a lucky woman." Mae actually meant every word of it. She tried to imagine the woman who had captured this Texan's heart. Was she tall with rich brown hair and swirling hazel eyes like Whit? She took Clinton's hand in hers. "We were just going inside so Whit can show me how to get started. It's my first day on the job, you know. I'm a little nervous."

Clinton smiled at Mae. "Then I'll let you gals get to it."

Tyree's shoulders relaxed and he tugged at Clinton's sleeve. "Mr. Clinton, we got two horses to run before it gets too warm. You told me it's not good to ride 'em when the sun gets too high."

"Why don't you let Whit take your jacket for you." Mae nodded for Tyree to help him pull it off. "It looks much too nice for the barn."

"Okay, but I don't have much time. We've got to run those ponies," Clinton said, handing his jacket to Whit. He patted his pockets. "Now where's my stopwatch?"

Whit handed over hers. "Here you go."

He looked at the watch. "This ain't mine."

"It's mine. You must have left yours in the house. Mae and I'll look for it when we get inside."

"It'll do, I reckon." Clinton looked at Mae. "It was nice to meet you, young lady. We'll have to have you over for dinner when Celeste comes home." He slapped Whit on the back. "Neither one of us can cook worth a damn." He turned toward the barn. "Come on, boy. We're burning daylight."

Tyree hung back a moment. "Thank you, Miss Mae," he said softly. "He gets confused sometimes, but he'll be okay."

Whit watched her father stride to the barn with new purpose. "You sure you don't need me to go with you?"

"Naw." Tyree smiled and waved her off. "His mind doesn't remember a lot of things, but it all comes back to him when there's a watch in his hand and a horse flying around the track."

Whit nodded and turned toward the house without a word. Mae's heart ached as she followed her inside. She watched as Whit aimlessly shifted some stacks of papers around, then stopped to stare down at the table.

"My father has Alzheimer's disease."

Mae wanted to give her a tight hug and tell her everything would be all right. Instead, she briefly squeezed Whit's hand. "I hope you don't mind, but Mr. Dupree told me a little about your parents."

"What exactly did Michael say?" Whit's gaze cut into hers like a laser so sharp, Mae wanted to step back. Instead, she stood her ground.

"Just enough to prepare me," she said softly. "He wasn't spreading gossip. He just didn't want me to say something awkward because I didn't know the situation."

Whit's shoulders dropped. "I'm sorry. Things have been a bit strained here lately."

"My sorority's community-service project was working with an Alzheimer's facility because one of our sisters had a grandfather there. The nurses taught us that it was better to just go with whatever part of the past the patient is living in at the moment. They deal with it better if you can redirect their focus rather than correct them." Mae smiled, hoping to put her at ease. "It must be a huge strain to have to shoulder this yourself. My sorority sister had a large family to help her. Hopefully, I can help you by taking some of the *Quarter Track* work off your must-do list. Let me run out to the car and get my laptop."

She rushed out to her car and, once there, took a few minutes to compose herself. She didn't want Whit to see the tears gathering in her eyes and mistake them for pity rather than compassion. God. What was wrong with her? She mentally checked the calendar to see if she could be PMSing. That was probably it. She hardly knew this woman, and she wasn't typically vulnerable to excessive empathy. Mae shook herself. A few deep breaths, a mental step back to clear her head, and she was ready to impress her new boss. She just hoped Whit would like her ideas.

When she returned to the house, they decided Mae's daily job would be to update certain calendars and statistics on the website. Whit showed her how to do that, and Mae was relieved that quartertrack used the same software as her sorority's website. Hopefully, that would help make up for her lack of racing knowledge. All the times and types of races were confusing, but Whit was a surprisingly patient teacher.

"I already have a few story ideas," Mae said, when they finished the updates. "I even wrote one up over the weekend." She was anxious to impress.

Whit looked skeptical. "You probably should have waited until I approved the idea. I don't want you to be too disappointed if you've wasted your time."

Mae made a quick decision. She'd pitch her story last. First, she had an idea she knew fit in with the serious racing theme of *Quarter Track*. "Well, how about this? When I was at the track Saturday, I overheard some men talking about a Canadian horse coming to race in Louisiana. They were wondering why its owners wanted to race in this state, rather than New Mexico or California. I thought I'd try to get in touch with the trainer and do an interview."

Whit nodded. "Not a bad idea. What about the one you said you already wrote?"

"I looked over several copies of the magazine, and frankly, it's all business and nothing fun."

Whit frowned. "It's for serious racing people, not a general audience."

"Why limit yourself?" Mae put up a hand before Whit could protest. "Just hear me out." She opened her photo software and angled her laptop so Whit could see it, too. "I'll click through these images while I explain."

The first photo showed a small black mutt following a groom under the eave of a row of stalls on the Evangeline backstretch.

"Did you take this?"

"I did. Yes."

Mae watched her examine the photo. She hadn't noticed before that Whit's serious hazel eyes turned almost blue when she was intent on something. She clicked to the next picture. The dog had stopped to sniff a hoof pick someone had dropped, and, in a third picture, he was trotting after the groom again and carrying the tool in his mouth. It was a cute sequence.

"Not bad," Whit murmured. "Not bad at all."

"I was the unofficial photographer of my sorority, so I took a couple of classes to improve my skills." It warmed Mae in an unfamiliar way that Whit liked her pictures. "I was thinking that maybe you could start a stand-alone photo feature of scenes around the track. I could take them, or we could invite your readers to submit photos for publication. It could broaden your audience."

Whit stared, her face unreadable. Mae fervently wished she could read minds, decipher what Whit was thinking. But she couldn't, so she forged ahead.

"Anyway, when I asked the dog's name, I found a cute story about how Blackie—that's his name—had just shown up there, half-starved and mangy. The grooms said he started bringing them dead rats he was killing around the barn. Apparently, the rats had become a problem since the barn cats would only catch mice."

The next picture showed Blackie, crooked teeth protruding from his over-long lower jaw, proudly sitting next to a dead rat and staring into the camera. The rat still made Mae shudder. She clicked quickly to the next picture where a horse had stretched his neck over the half door of his stall to touch noses with the little dog.

"How long were you at the track? It must have taken some patience to get these photos."

"Oh, I took the first three Saturday, but after I started writing Blackie's story Saturday night, I went back Sunday to get some more photos and talk to a few more people. He's a very busy little dog."

"Cute. But a lot of stables have mascots. You could probably sell this to the local newspaper, but my readers would shrug. Blackie doesn't seem any different from every other dog that hangs around barns."

"Oh, but he *is* special. The grooms swore that Blackie saved one horse's life because he alerted them that the horse was ill. The track veterinarian agreed that it was possible. He said some dogs can sniff diabetics and tell if their blood sugar is off, and Blackie must have been able to smell that the horse was ill."

Whit snorted. "It was probably a coincidence."

"Dr. Benjamin, the veterinarian, doesn't think so. He said Blackie has alerted them two other times. Those horses weren't ill, but had been doped for their race. You know, like Lance Armstrong and Barry Bonds."

Whit sat back, her expression so surprised it was almost comical. "I would have never guessed you to be a sports fan."

Mae raised a challenging eyebrow. "Isn't that just a little chauvinistic?"

"I guess it is. I apologize."

"No need." She waved her hand dismissively. "I'm actually not a sports fan, but I am a news junkie. I've been scanning the pages of *The New York Times* and the *Wall Street Journal* over breakfast with Big Mae since I was in elementary school."

"Really?" Whit sounded doubtful. "No offense, but I would have guessed…never mind."

She decided to ignore the near faux pas. She didn't want to know what Whit thought she read in her spare time. Grocery-store tabloids? Hmm. Perhaps she would keep her affection for romance novels to herself. "Back to my story. So, Dr. Benjamin says he's talking to a colleague, who does veterinary research at Texas A&M, about writing a grant application to study whether dogs can be used to sniff out doping in animal and human athletes."

Whit held her hands up for Mae to stop. "Okay, you've sold me. Print out the story and I'll take a look at it."

"I have a copy right here." Mae dug into her laptop case but held the pages to her chest rather than giving them to Whit. "This is only a first draft, but I'd like your suggestions before I do any more work on it."

A smile transformed Whit's face, and Mae decided her new boss was actually a very attractive woman. She handed over the pages and Whit leafed through them.

"Oh, and I meant to ask about social media. I couldn't seem to find *Quarter Track* on any of it."

Whit frowned. "That's because I don't waste my time on that stuff."

"But it's not a waste of time. Social media is the best marketing tool you can use."

"I have friends who spend all day piddling around with Facebook and have nothing to show for their time."

"The *Quarter Horse News* has a Facebook page with more than a hundred thousand followers. The page promotes articles in the magazine, so it sends the readers to their website to see the entire article. I'll bet they have even more Twitter fans."

Whit rubbed her forehead. "I just don't have time for all that."

"I can do it. I can set up the accounts and monitor them for you."

Whit seemed to think that over, then stood. "Okay. Have at it. I need to go check on Pop. I may be gone for a while, so help yourself to anything in the kitchen. There's drinks and stuff for sandwiches."

Mae squeezed Whit's hand. She'd show her how invaluable she could be. But it was more than that. Something drew her to Whit Casey. Maybe it was because they were both single women struggling to find their way. But as much as she wanted to prove herself, she felt compelled to reach out to this woman whose hazel eyes swirled with shards of soft blue and vibrant green, and shades of sadness. "I've got plenty to get me started. Take as long as you need."

Chapter Seven

"Can't keep trouble from coming to the door, but you don't have to invite it in."

I thought we were going to the racetrack."

Whit glanced at Mae's reflection in the rearview mirror. She was perched like a bird, head bobbing with the road bumps, next to Tyree on the wide backseat of the big crew cab Ford 350 dually.

"We're going to the old track that used to be Evangeline Downs before they built the casino and a new track next to it." They were hauling Raising the Bar and Pop's two client racers to Carencro for the nearly three weeks of training before racing season began at the Opelousas track. "The old place is a training facility now, and we need to train on a real track."

"Drop me off at the office so I can rent stalls and sign us up for track time," Pop said.

"I did that online already," Whit said, eyeing him.

He'd been animated and tireless over the past week, strutting around and spouting unnecessary instructions for Whit concerning the three racers they were training. She suspected it was to impress Mae, who encouraged him by asking question after question.

Whit glanced at Mae's reflection again. Her new employee had surprised them with a lunch of tomato soup and grilled-cheese sandwiches when they came in that first day from exercising the two client horses. She and Pop usually just wolfed down sandwiches with little conversation, but Mae drew Pop out of his shell with her million-and-one questions and intense focus on each answer.

She'd finally escaped the constant chatter when the farrier showed up. Even with fewer horses, it took all afternoon to trim hooves on the breeding mares and yearlings, then set new shoes on the three racers. It was after six when she returned to the house. Pop was snoring in his recliner, and the only trace of Mae was a note on the table that read: "Back at seven in the morning to show you the new social media pages I set up. Don't eat a big breakfast because I'm bringing donuts."

It had set a pattern for the rest of the week. Pop thrived under Mae's attention, but the anticipation of their change in schedule today had kept him wandering the house into the wee hours the night before, and he was still fatigued and grumpy today. She'd considered leaving him at home, but she realized he shouldn't be left alone. She made a mental note to call his doctor about his medicine dosage. A familiar wave of guilt washed over her, the same as every time she considered whether things would be different if she'd been around to recognize his symptoms earlier.

But, while Pop was quiet and grumpy, Mae was, as always, chatty and inquisitive. "Wow. How many barns do they have? Do they have horses here year round? Are some of them Thoroughbreds, or are they all quarter horses? I've been meaning to ask, how do you tell them apart? If some quarter horses race longer distances, why don't they just race against Thoroughbreds? Can Thoroughbreds enter quarter-horse races?"

Tyree bailed out as soon as the truck came to a stop, and Pop grunted with the effort to follow as quickly as he was able. "That girl's got more questions than a machine gun has bullets," he muttered.

Whit chuckled as she met Mae's puzzled gaze in the rearview mirror. She turned in the seat and Mae grinned.

"I guess I was asking too many questions, huh?"

"Well, I think Pop is worn out because he had a restless night, and you just plain scared Tyree. Men aren't generally much for talking unless it's about themselves."

The blush that crept up Mae's cheeks was an attractive accent to her dark hair and whiskey eyes. "Sorry. I just want to know so many things."

"There's nothing wrong with that, but how about this—I'll give you a tour of the place and explain things as we go. You can write down any questions that require more than a one- or two-word response, and I'll try to answer them at a leisurely pace when we're done."

"Okay. You've got a deal."

Whit was surprised to find she liked Mae's smile. In fact, Mae was full of surprises. Despite her lack of reporting experience, she was a very good writer. Her story about the little mutt at the Evangeline Downs backstretch was engaging, funny, and poignant. Whit wanted to go over a few points with her, but Mae was a natural storyteller.

They unloaded the horses and settled them in their new stalls, then parked and unhitched the gooseneck camper/horse trailer. Tyree would live in the camper, making use of the track's communal locker room for showers, during the weeks the horses trained there.

With Mae's encouragement, Pop retired to the trailer for a nap, and they left Ellie and Rhett in the camper with him. Tyree wandered off to mingle with the other exercise jockeys and collect track gossip, so Whit bought a bag of roasted peanuts and two drinks, then led Mae to the track bleachers to scope out the competition.

"Do they—"

Whit held up a hand. "Remember our agreement?"

"Oh. Sorry." Mae pulled a reporter's notepad from her purse and scribbled her question for later.

Whit set the open bag of peanuts between them to share and tried to anticipate some of Mae's questions.

"The difference between a quarter horse and a Thoroughbred is the ass."

Mae looked puzzled. "I don't understand. They breed them to donkeys?"

"Donkeys?" Whit chuckled. "Who said anything about donkeys? I'm talking about their butts, their hindquarters."

Mae blushed and smiled as she clasped Whit's forearm. "Duh. I just read something last week about breeding horses to donkeys."

Whit stared at her arm. Mae did that a lot—touch the people around her. Whit didn't usually like people to invade her personal space, but it didn't seem invasive when Mae did it. Her skin tingled under the light contact.

"But that produces a mule, right?"

Whit blinked. "Oh, uh, yeah." Christ, she was stuttering like a teenager. She cleared her throat and focused on the horses running around the track. "A quarter horse's back end is much heavier in comparison to a Thoroughbred's." She gestured to the track. "It's for quick bursts of speed because they were bred for sprinting after cattle. Thoroughbreds are longer legged, generally, and leaner in the haunches to build speed over a distance."

"Sort of like the difference between a skinny marathon runner and those sprinter guys with huge thighs?"

"Exactly. The breed gets its name from its speed over a quarter-mile distance, even though in the modern racing world, they compete over several different distances."

"This is so interesting." Mae stared at the horses. "But out there they still all look the same to me."

"Well, it takes a little time to always tell the difference. Most of the quarter-horse racers are appendix quarters, which means they have some Thoroughbred in their recent bloodline. The American Quarter Horse Registry allows it. Appendix quarter horses tend to be taller and less bulky than the quarter horses bred for other purposes. They're also the ones who will run the longer races. Raising the Bar is an appendix quarter horse. Let's go visit the barns and I'll show you what I'm talking about."

Whit easily hopped down from the end of the metal bleachers, but turned back when Mae didn't follow.

"I'm afraid my legs aren't as long as yours," she said, staring at the distance to the ground. "I'll have to go to the bottom."

People sat shoulder to shoulder on the bottom four rows, and Whit realized Mae would have to make her way through them or walk back to the other end to reach the ground. She huffed impatiently. "Come on, I'll help you down." Against her better judgment, she held up her arms. "Put your hands on my shoulders."

When Mae leaned over and did as she ordered, Whit grasped her waist and lifted her to the ground.

"Thank you," Mae said quietly. "I feel like I've been such a bother today."

They shifted uneasily at their close proximity and avoided each other's eyes. Whit released her and stepped back. "You're not a bother," she mumbled. But Mae—with her shining dark hair, impossibly thick lashes, and molasses accent—was bothering her. Fucking libido. She obviously needed to get laid, but she didn't have time for that. Maybe she'd unpack some of her erotica and go to bed early. She just needed a little alone time and, uh, tension release.

They strolled among the barns, and the uneasiness between them evaporated as Whit explained about quarter horses and how to train racers. Mae furiously scribbled questions on her notepad, until Whit gave in and told her just to go ahead and ask. It was like breaching a New Orleans levee. Her questions slowed only when people stopped them to welcome Whit back to the training track. A lot had changed in the twenty-odd years she'd been away, and she was amazed to still see so many familiar faces.

She was more surprised at how easily Mae warmed up to people. She had a way of making each person she met feel like they were truly interesting. Whit chuckled as another old groom fell under Mae's spell. She listened with rapt attention while he explained the merits of feeding bran mash. The woman could charm the ears off a donkey.

Whit's thoughts and her gaze drifted aimlessly as she waited for Mae to conclude her conversation. Hot walkers chatted as they led their sweaty equine charges to ensure overworked muscles didn't stiffen after a fast run. Grooms bathed and brushed coats, manes, and tails until they gleamed in the afternoon sun. A trainer was in deep conversation with his exercise jockey about a colt's performance. She relaxed into the feeling that she'd stepped back in time to when her biggest concern was begging Pop to let her stay overnight in the camper rather than going back to the farm at night with him. She hadn't realized how much she missed the track and the feeling of community in the backstretch stables.

Her eyes slid over two figures, then snapped back to the willowy blonde. Avery. What the hell was she doing here? Her good mood vanished. How did Avery know Michael Dupree?

Avery looked up and their eyes met. The stunned look on her face told Whit that she wasn't at the track to search for her. Avery spoke to Michael, pointed, and they headed toward her. Shit. Would Avery make a scene?

She glanced at Mae, who had also spotted them. "Michael, what a surprise. Checking up on me?" Mae's tone was teasing and her broad smile welcoming.

Michael beamed back. "Just making sure Whitley is treating you right."

Mae extended her hand to Avery. "I don't believe we've met. I'm Mae St. John."

"Avery Perrault." Avery's smile was forced, her fingers barely grasping Mae's in a limp greeting as she shot Whit a scathing glare. "You've been busy."

Michael glanced nervously between Avery and Whit. "Mae is the daughter of an old friend of mine from college. I recommended her to Whitley as a writer for her magazine." He stepped next to Mae and gave her a one-armed hug. "Did you enjoy Saturday at Evangeline with Jean Paul?"

Whit's hackles rose as his arm draped over Mae's shoulders. She didn't care that he was Pop's friend. She didn't like him. She really didn't like the way he failed to respect a woman's personal space. Still, she almost laughed at his clear message that Mae wasn't a threat to Avery. Apparently, he wanted to avoid a scene, too, but Mae seemed oblivious to the unspoken conversation. Whit figured she was clueless that she was standing between two lesbians, two former lovers.

"Jean Paul was an excellent guide," Mae said. "I found several stories to pitch for *Quarter Track*. Thank you for enlisting him to help me."

"I'm sure it was no hardship for him to spend the day with you." Michael gave her shoulders another squeeze and dropped his arm when she appropriately demurred at the compliment.

Mae smiled warmly at Avery. "Whit was educating me on quarter-horse racing. I'm afraid I'm new to the sport and have a lot to learn."

Avery looked Mae over with a touch of disdain. "I'm sure it's no hardship for Whit," she said, echoing Michael.

Burn. Whit searched for something, anything to say that would defuse Avery's snub.

But Mae only smiled and prattled on. "She's been very patient, but I'm afraid I don't know much about horse racing other than Derby fashion and pretty horses. Big Mae and I always watched the Derby and tried to pick which horse would win. I favor gray horses, if one is running. I think gray horses are so pretty, don't you?"

Avery's expression was predatory, like a fox stalking an oblivious chicken that was happily pecking away at scratch. Whit crossed her arms over her chest and stared across the backstretch, uncertain if she should rescue Mae from the condescending remark Avery was surely preparing to launch or just stay out of it. But Mae's embarrassing confession faded into the background when Whit spotted Pop standing between the long barns, both dogs at his feet.

"I'll be right back," she said.

Pop looked anxiously around the backstretch, but he appeared to relax when he spotted her coming toward him. His white hair stuck out in multiple directions, so Whit pulled off the ball cap she was wearing to keep her thick curls off her neck and settled it snugly on his head. "Where's your cap? You're going to get your bald spot sunburned."

"I don't have a bald spot, Celeste."

"Yes, you do, Pop."

He sighed. "I called you Celeste, didn't I?"

"It's okay."

"Every time I wake up, I imagine I can hear her in the kitchen, putting the coffee on." He rubbed his hand over his eyes. "When I woke up in that camper a few minutes ago, I couldn't remember where I was." He looked down. Ellie had wandered a short distance away to investigate the temperament of a fat orange barn cat, but Rhett remained at his side, watching him intently. "Then I saw this little fella and I remembered that pretty lady he belongs to."

"Mae."

He nodded. "That's right. He's pretty smart for a dog with a funny haircut. I said, 'where'd they go?' and he led me right out here."

"We're right over there." Whit gestured toward the others. "Michael's here. I know you'll want to say hello."

Pop and Rhett followed, and Ellie joined them after Whit whistled for her. Mae smiled warmly and Michael gave Pop a friendly clap on the back when they joined the group.

"Well, sir. It's been a long time," Pop said to Michael.

"Clinton, I just talked to you last week when I called to tell you about Mae."

Pop lifted his cap and resettled it on his head as if it would release the memory his brain had hidden inside. "Reckon I forgot." He grinned at Mae and held out his hand. She took it and he drew her to his side. "But I didn't forget this pretty lady. That dog of yours brought me right to you."

Mae squatted to ruffle Rhett's curls. "Good job, handsome." She stood and took Pop's hand again. "I'm afraid he had to learn to be a guide dog early. Big Mae could never remember where she parked at the country club, and Rhett would have to help her find the car."

"How charming."

Both men, obviously enamored with Mae, scowled at Avery's dry remark.

"Have we met?" Pop's tone was none too friendly.

"Several times, Mr. Casey. I'm Avery, a close friend of Whit's in Baton Rouge." She looked pointedly at Mae when she emphasized *close*.

"Huh. Can't say that I recall you." He turned to Michael, dismissing her. "What brings you down to the track today?"

"Miss Perrault's father is Senator Perrault. He's up for re-election this year, you know, and I'm putting my money on him to win another term in the state senate." Michael straightened his shoulders and looked like a rooster about to strut. "She's helping the senator with his campaign, and I've been talking with her today about legislation to provide some incentives for expanding Louisiana's racing industry. We could be as big as the Quarter Horse Triple Crown in New Mexico, if we get enough investors behind it."

Ah. That explained why Avery was with Michael and what she was doing at the training center. Avery had no interest in horse racing. She'd only gone once with her to Evangeline Downs, and she'd spent the entire time in the casino rather than watching Pop's racers with her.

"It could mean a lot of jobs if we turned the Carencro facility back into a racing track and built another casino here," Avery said.

Whit frowned. "That's crazy. Opelousas and Carencro are only eighteen miles apart. You'd just steal business from the track at Evangeline."

"Not if we do this right," Michael said. "We have a business consortium that's already talking with the folks at Dollywood about a similar theme park here and several of those showcase theaters like they have in Branson, Missouri. We can fill those eighteen miles with attractions and hotels. Just think of it."

Whit was thinking of it. She was thinking of all the farms along that eighteen-mile stretch of Interstate 49—including Joie de Vivre Quarter Horses. How many landowners would sell out when offered millions for their property? How many others would be forced out when the area was rezoned commercial and property taxes rose sky-high?

"Can't say I care much for the idea," Pop said. He spit on the ground, and Avery moved back as if he might soil her five-hundred-dollar boots. He glared at her. "You can remind your daddy for me that he represents everybody in Louisiana, not just the bankers and certainly not investors from outside this state."

Whit swelled with pride. Pop's growl was a glimpse of the former tough-as-nails Clinton Casey before his mental decline.

"The farmland between here and Opelousas has belonged to the same Louisiana families for generations," Pop said. "They've already given up enough land for that interstate highway. They're not likely to want to give up more."

"They won't have a choice if the legislature gets behind this," Michael said. "You can't stop progress, Clinton."

Avery eyed Pop cautiously. "We're talking about good-paying jobs for a lot of people, Mr. Casey. Not only that, it would certainly raise the purses of the races here with more people attending and betting. You wouldn't mind that, now would you?"

Ever the politician. Whit could easily see Avery running for the legislature one day, following in her father's footsteps. How could they have ever been lovers? They couldn't be more different. But then, they couldn't be more alike. Wasn't that what she was doing, too, following in her father's footsteps?

Mae, who had been busily typing into her phone, returned it to her shoulder bag and stepped between the two men. "I'm just about to wilt in this sun. Who would like to walk with me to the grandstand to get something cold to drink?" She linked arms with both men as she turned them toward the walkway that skirted around the track to the grandstand. "I understand you two have been friends since elementary school."

"We did go to the same school, but he's four years older than me," Michael said.

"He might be younger, but I'm prettier," Pop declared.

Mae laughed. "I'm still impressed. Things move so fast these days, people just don't make lifetime friendships anymore."

Whit stared after them until Mae glanced over her shoulder. "Y'all coming?"

"We'll be along," Avery called after them. Her hand on Whit's arm stopped her, too. "Can I talk to you in private…just for a minute?"

Avery didn't look like she was angry. She looked hot. The good kind of hot. The flowing blond locks, low-slung skinny jeans, and knee-high fashion boots kind of hot. She pulled her sunglasses off and Whit nearly groaned. Avery knew her blue eyes were gasoline to Whit's flame. They were electric in the bright sun, reflecting the hue of her sleeveless blouse. Whit took a deep breath and jammed her hands in her pockets in an attempt to appear unaffected. "What's up?"

"I want to apologize for hanging up on you the other day."

"I think we'd said all we needed to say."

"I didn't say what I really wanted to." Avery bit her lower lip. It was a nervous gesture Whit used to find endearing. Now she just wondered if it was another calculated move like priming her with those baby blues.

"I'm listening."

"I was wrong, okay. We both got so caught up in work, and when you realized we had drifted apart, I was still too busy to stop and do anything about it. You tried to tell me it wasn't working for you, but I always thought I'd have time to fix it later."

"Avery, I don't see any way to fix it now. Christ, you're working for your father's conservative Republican campaign. How is that going to help us?"

Avery put her hands up. "Please, I don't want to talk about our differences right now. I want to try to remember the good part of us. Have dinner with me, Whit. Give us a chance to rekindle what we had. We were good together once. We can tackle the other stuff later."

She stared at the ground and shook her head. "I don't know."

Avery stepped closer, her fingers lightly caressing Whit's arm. "Remember the first time we made love? We snuck down to the lake after everybody was asleep and went skinny-dipping. I'll never forget that. You were gorgeous in the moonlight."

Whit shifted to ease the pulsing between her legs. She remembered. She closed her eyes to escape Avery's intense blue gaze, only to fall victim to images flashing through her brain of Avery's slender body and firm breasts bathed in the moonlight.

"You don't have to come all the way to Baton Rouge. I'll meet you in Lafayette. Saturday night at seven? Pamplona Tapas?"

Whit didn't hold out much hope that they could recapture what they once had, but she was tired of serial relationships. One of her friends joked that a lesbian's one-night stand lasted about two years before the morning-after hit. That pretty much characterized Whit's relationships before she met Avery, which was why Whit had been determined not to give up on their relationship once their hormones calmed down. She blew out a breath. "I really don't think it will do any good, but okay."

"Ground rules."

"Such as?"

"No talking about my father's campaign or your father's financial mess. This is just about us."

It went against her better judgment, but damn, she could use a night without thinking about all the ticking bombs threatening to detonate and destroy her life.

"Deal."

CHAPTER EIGHT

"Where there's smoke, there's fire."

Michael and Avery didn't stay much longer, and Whit had work to do. She and Tyree hosed down their three horses to cool them and walked them a bit to be sure they'd made the trailer ride without any signs of lameness. Pop seemed happy with Mae's company until Whit was free to go over their training plan with him and match it up with the schedule for their access to the track.

When they were ready to leave, Whit looked in on Raising the Bar one last time. He turned to greet her when she entered the stall and searched her hands for a treat. This colt wasn't just fast; he was even-tempered. Hardly anything rattled him. That would be sorely tested as he acclimated to standing in the stall more than twenty hours of his day and they increased the corn in his diet to amp his energy level to explode on the track.

She ran her hands over his legs once more, searching for warmth that would indicate inflammation. Satisfied that he was sound, she stepped back and pain seared through her right foot.

"Son of a bitch." She hopped over to the wall and pulled her foot up. A farrier's nail was imbedded in the sole of her boot. She tried not to think about the other end buried in the ball of her foot.

Tyree poked his head over the half door. "Everything okay, Boss?"

"Get Bar out of this stall, quick."

Tyree didn't ask questions. He grabbed a halter and led the colt outside.

Whit hopped after them and sat on an upturned bucket to rest her injured foot on her other knee. She stared at the nail and gulped deep breaths to fight the nausea that washed over her. She could feel the blood pooling in her boot.

"Oh, my God, what happened?" Mae peered at Whit's foot.

Whit looked up at Pop. "Nail. In his stall," she said through gritted teeth.

"God damn it." Pop took the colt's lead from Tyree. "Go get the barn manager." He lifted each one of Bar's feet to inspect them as Tyree took off at a run. When he straightened from examining the last hoof, he looked relieved. "Well, we were lucky. He looks clean."

Mae whirled on him. "Lucky? Whit has a nail stuck in her foot and y'all are worried about the horse?"

"He doesn't have medical insurance. Whit does," Pop said gruffly. He looked at Whit. "You okay? You ain't gonna pass out or puke, are you?"

Mae put her hands on her hips. "Clinton Casey. That's your daughter."

"I know that. Because she is my daughter, I also know she pukes at the sight of her own blood. That is, if she don't faint first." He narrowed his eyes at Whit. "I'd rather you pass out when we take that boot off. Nothing to clean up."

Mae slapped at his arm. "Stop it." She knelt next to Whit. "You *aren't* going to throw up, are you?"

Tyree slid to a stop, breathing hard from his run. "He's coming, Mr. Clinton. I told him we found a nail in the stall and his eyes nearly bugged out."

"I'll just bet. I'd be suing their pants off if my colt got hurt." Pop studied the nail protruding from the bottom of Whit's boot. "Go get me the nail puller and first-aid kit out of the trailer, Tyree."

"What are you going to do?" Mae stared up at him, realization dawning on her face. "She is *not* a horse. We have to take her to the emergency room."

"Hell, no. I'm not going to sit in an emergency room for five hours when Pop can get this nail out in two minutes." Whit knew she sounded braver than she felt. "Long as it didn't hit an artery, I'll be fine."

"Pull those laces out of your boot and tie them around your leg," Pop said. "Might keep that thing from spurting all over the place if it did."

Whit nodded, but leaned back against the barn siding and closed her eyes.

Mae gently removed the laces from Whit's paddock boot to make a tourniquet. "You're white as a sheet," she said softly. "Have you had a tetanus shot?"

Whit nodded. Her outburst over the emergency room roiled her stomach, and she was afraid she'd heave her lunch if she spoke again.

A middle-aged man approached with two teenaged boys in tow. "I'm Will Terry, assistant track manager. What's the problem?"

Pop pointed to Whit's foot. "What kind of half-assed farriers are you hiring these days? We're lucky Whit's big foot found it before my colt ended up with it in his hoof."

Mae made an impatient sound and shook her head.

Mr. Terry turned to the boys. "Strip that stall down to the dirt, but be careful. You find any more nails, I want to see them. And I want to inspect that stall before y'all put fresh bedding down."

The boys jogged off to get manure shovels and wheelbarrows, just as Tyree returned.

"I brought some clean towels, too, Mr. Clinton." He handed a bottle of water to Whit. "I thought it might help to sip on this. It's real cold."

"Give that to me, please, Tyree. And hand me one of those hand towels." Mae wet the towel and draped it around Whit's neck.

The icy cloth did quell her nausea a bit, and Whit wiped one end across her face, holding it to her temple for a moment. She looked up at Mae and tried to muster a smile. "Thanks. That helps."

"Ready, kiddo?" Pop held the heavy, pliers-like farrier tool at his side and gave her a reassuring smile. "We've done this before, haven't we?"

That did make her smile. She marveled that he could pull things out of the past but couldn't remember somebody from two days ago. She was nine years old and had ignored his caution to be careful where they were tearing down some old run-in sheds to build new ones. He'd pulled a nail from her foot then, too.

Pop gently lifted her leg and straddled it with his back to her, just like he would to remove a horse's shoe. She clenched her jaw tight as he worked the tool's teeth around the nail head and closed her eyes for the inevitable yank of the metal spike from her flesh. Mae's hand slipped into hers and squeezed tightly, diverting her attention from her foot. Despite his age and arthritis, Pop was still a strong man, and he snatched the nail from her foot in one clean stroke. Tyree produced another upturned bucket to rest her foot on while Pop tugged her boot off.

"Looks okay, Whit. It's bleeding good, but you're not spurting, so I think you missed the artery."

She gulped down a new wave of nausea, and Mae, her brow furrowed with concern, released her hand to replace the wet towel around her neck with a fresh one.

The boys finished stripping the stall, and Mr. Terry swept a large magnet over the floor to detect any nails that weren't visible in the dim lighting before giving them the okay to bring in fresh wood shavings. He spoke briefly into a radio, then turned to Pop and held out his hand for the nail.

"It's a new one, not one that's fallen out of a shoe," Pop said.

The two men shared a long look. "I'll have the boys sift the bedding to see if there were others," Mr. Terry said. When another teen he summoned jogged to them and handed Pop a plastic baggie full of ice, he added, "You might want to keep that on the wound for a few hours and prop that foot up."

Pop nodded. "Good advice."

He shook Pop's hand. "I'll be looking into this further, and we'll knock a week off your stall rent for your trouble."

"Fair enough," Pop said.

❖

Mae insisted on driving home so Whit could prop her throbbing foot up on the dash with the ice pack taped to it. Pop stretched out on the backseat, the two dogs on the floor snoring along with him.

The silence between them was comfortable as Mae guided the truck onto the interstate highway. She seemed perfectly at ease with the large powerful vehicle.

"Don't tell me...you drove the dually that pulled the homecoming float for your sorority."

Mae chuckled. "No. We hired someone to do that."

"I'm shocked."

"But a group of us did rent one of those big bus-like RVs when we went out of town to football games. I was always elected to drive because I'm not much of a drinker."

"Ah. So there *is* another sorority story to explain why you're good at this, too."

Mae smiled, but they rode in silence for several more minutes before she spoke. "I never had any family except Big Mae. Mama died when I was just a baby. I loved the sorority because it gave me the extended family I always wanted. I think that's why I stayed in college so long. Well, that and I really like learning new stuff."

"I'm sorry. I know I sound judgmental about you being a sorority girl."

"It's okay. A lot of them are shallow and self-involved."

It wasn't okay. Whit didn't like people making groundless judgments about her sexual orientation. She was embarrassed that she'd only been thinking about how different they were. They had some things in common, like their love of dogs and—"My mother died, too. I'm sure Michael told you. It was three years ago. Cancer."

Whit had grown so accustomed to Mae's smile and animated personality, the frown that darkened her beautiful face now seemed out of place. "My mother committed suicide," she said.

Whit couldn't seem to open her mouth without saying something stupid around Mae. "Damn. That's awful."

Mae shrugged. "I don't even remember her, of course, but I have to admit I've always been a little angry I wasn't enough reason for her to continue to live." She glanced in the rearview mirror and changed the subject. "Clinton must have cut quite a figure before he got sick. I saw a little of that when he took charge this afternoon."

Whit nodded. "Yeah." She stared out the window until she could swallow the tears that threatened. She was tired and her foot hurt. And her heart hurt for Pop. "He seems most confused at night and when he first wakes up. Tyree found him sleeping on some hay in the barn one morning last week. I didn't even know he'd left the house." She had no idea what she would do when she could no longer care for him and run two businesses.

"He doesn't like her, you know."

"Pop? Doesn't like who?"

"The blond woman at the track today. He doesn't like her."

"Avery?"

"Yes. That's the woman you were seeing in Baton Rouge, isn't it? He said, and I quote, 'If she really loved Whit, she wouldn't keep her in the cellar.'"

What the hell? "Keep me in the cellar?"

"I interpreted it to mean 'keep you in the closet.' He said you're nobody's dirty little secret, and any woman worth her salt would be proud to be with you."

Holy shit. Pop outed her? She didn't know what to say. She glanced at Mae. "When did he tell you this?"

"We talked about it the other day while you were putting shoes on the horses. Clinton told me about Mrs. Casey and about Avery. He's very proud of you, you know, starting your own business. He's even happier that you're back here training horses with him, but he worries that you'll be alone when he passes on to be with your mama."

"You must have had a long conversation." Whit wondered why Pop never talked to her about those things.

"You were hiding in the barn all afternoon."

"I was working with the farrier."

Mae chuckled. "Clinton says you were hiding because you aren't much of a talker and I was talking you to death."

She stared out the window, not really seeing the dark landscape. Was that why Mae had drawn things out of Pop that he hadn't told his own daughter? Because she never just sat down and engaged him in conversation? She frowned. Had she done this with Avery, too?

"Are you still seeing her?"

Whit blinked. "Seeing who?"

"The blonde."

Whit wanted to laugh at Mae's tone. It was as if she was holding up dirty underwear with her fingertips and asking what she should do with it. "I don't know."

"Well, either you are or you aren't. Which is it?" Mae's words were gentle but to the point.

"Does my sexual orientation make you uncomfortable?"

"Not in the least. I have gay friends. Well, they're mostly guys, but we had several sorority sisters who were lesbians."

"I'm surprised they were voted in if everybody knew they were lesbians."

"They were legacies so they had to be admitted, but the majority of the sisters didn't mind anyway. Since *Sex in the City* became popular, everybody thinks it's cool to have a lesbian or two as friends."

"I guess it helps that they don't have to worry about the lesbians stealing their boyfriends."

"Yes, and they were real handy at fixing things around the sorority house." Mae's glare glinted with the sarcasm in her voice.

Whit smiled. "Ouch. I guess you have a few thorns under that magnolia personality."

Mae stared at the road, but her lips twitched in a slight smile. "You didn't answer my question."

"What question?"

"Are you still seeing her?"

"Why do you want to know?" Christ, did that sound like she was flirting?

"Well, what if she calls the office? Should I hand the phone to you or tell her you're unavailable? And if she leaves a message, should I save it for you or throw it away?" Mae, eyes twinkling now, glanced over at Whit. "If another lesbian calls to ask if you're available, should I say yes or no? Better yet, should I invite my lesbian sorority sisters for a visit? Several of them are rather attractive."

Whit held out her hands and laughed. "Okay, okay. Enough."

"So?"

"The answer is no. At least, I don't think so." Whit sighed. "I guess I don't really know."

Mae turned down the farm's driveway and parked in front of the house. They sat there, neither moving after she switched off the ignition. Her gaze was soft. "I'm a good listener. Tell me about her."

Whit's hand rested on the door, but she didn't open it. She hadn't actually talked about her recent decisions with anybody. She wasn't close to Avery's friends, and she couldn't trust her own friends to be objective. Maybe she should talk to someone who didn't have a dog in the fight. Pop and the pups were still sleeping, so there was no reason to hurry into the house. She gathered her thoughts.

"I met Avery at a mixer for the annual gay film festival in Baton Rouge. She was fresh out of law school and starting to work for her father's firm. I was just beginning to make a profit with *Quarter Track*." Whit removed the melted ice pack on her foot and turned to face Mae. "She was beautiful and intelligent and understood my work ethic. That's what killed my previous relationships. My usual girlfriends wanted to party and work just enough to pay the bills. Avery understood my need to build a business." She snorted. "That's ironic, because I ended up leaving her because all she did was work."

"Was that the real reason? Or was her obsession with work just a symptom of some deeper problem?"

Whit's first instinct was to make a smart crack about her being the sorority psychologist, too, but Mae's dark-honey eyes were serious, her expression concerned. "No. She always had some excuse for why she wasn't engaged in our relationship—her next big case, her concern over her complicated relationship with her father, or just being too tired. But they were only excuses. I left her because she didn't, doesn't love me like I need to be loved." She rubbed her hands over her face. That really was it, wasn't it?

"How would you describe true love?"

Whit stared into the darkness. She'd never actually tried to define it. "Well, it certainly isn't like a romance novel."

Mae's eyes widened, and she pressed her hand to her chest. "There's no white horse, no castle, and no happily-ever-after?"

Whit smiled and shook her head. She was both relieved for a break in the seriousness of their talk and strangely disappointed that she still had no answers about Avery. "What about you? Have you left a string of devastated men in your wake?"

Mae wrinkled her nose as if she smelled something bad. "The only ones I could tolerate more than a month ended up being gay."

Huh. Whit wasn't sure what to make of that.

Mae twirled a lock of her dark hair around her finger. "They were the fun dates. They liked to shop and dance and meet for coffee. Other men just wanted to talk about themselves and fuck."

Whit laughed quietly, careful not to wake Pop. "I can't believe you said that word."

Mae grinned at her, then shrugged. "If Prince Charming isn't out there, I guess I'll just be an old maid."

"That would be a shame." The words slipped from her lips before she could censor them, and they stared at each other.

"Big Mae said I should marry the first man who could provide well for me, and if I needed more than that, she said I could get a puppy to love."

Whit gestured to the backseat where Ellie slept. "I've got a puppy. But it wasn't enough to save my relationship with Avery." She dropped her chin to her chest. "Shit."

"What is it?" Mae asked gently.

"I told Avery I'd meet her for dinner Saturday night. What was I thinking?"

"Then you are still seeing her?"

"Yes. No. I guess my heart still misses what we had in the beginning, but my head knows there's no future for us. Hell, maybe I don't know what real love is. Maybe I expect too much."

Mae grasped Whit's hand. "Tell me. What *should* we expect when we find true love?"

Whit looked into Mae's eyes. "A soul mate would put my needs before anyone else's and know that I would put hers before my own." Pop began to stir in the backseat, and Whit lowered her voice to a whisper. "She should need me both physically and emotionally every day for the rest of our lives."

"Exactly." Mae's voice was firm as she held Whit's gaze. "I want somebody who will hold me forever. I won't settle for less."

"I always thought lying and cheating were the only deal-breakers for me. But I can't say Avery ever lied to me, and if she cheated, I didn't know about it. Still, what we had wasn't enough. When I thought about what kind of future we'd have together, I knew I'd be miserable. I deserve better. I'd rather be alone than live like that."

Mae smiled and released Whit's hand to entwine only their pinkie fingers. She lifted their joined hands. "Let's swear a pact to never settle. We'll stay single forever if our prince—or princess—never finds us."

Whit shook her head at the silly gesture but smiled and declared, "Swear."

Chapter Nine

"You can never tell which way the pickle's gonna squirt."

"Www.quartertrack.com not responding."

It was the third time Mae had attempted to upload the new statistics. What was going on? She flipped to another screen and tried to load the website, only to watch the little wheel spin and spin and spin.

She was working from her apartment this morning because Whit and Clinton had returned to the Carencro training track at daybreak to exercise their horses. She checked her Internet connection. Still strong. She drummed her fingers on her small kitchen table. In an unconscious echo of Whit's arrangement, the table had become her home office since she did most of her dining at home on the coffee table in front of the television.

Still spinning. She reached for her cell phone. She knew Whit was busy, but she'd had a nagging impulse all morning to call her. Whit had opened up a little last night, enough that Mae felt she'd found a new friend and Louisiana suddenly felt a little less lonely.

"Hold on." Whit's answer was clipped. Mae could hear her talking to Tyree over the pounding of hooves in the background. She pictured Whit, tall and lean, stretched over the track railing toward Tyree as he perched on Raising the Bar and nodded at her instructions. "Okay. Sorry. What the hell is going on with the website today?"

"That's what I was calling to ask you. I've got all the stats updated, but they won't load, and I can't get the website to come up either."

"Yeah, I got a call about an hour ago from the company that hosts the website. They said quartertrack.com got so many hits overnight that it crashed their server. The guy said they'd give me more server space temporarily, but they want to shift me to something called a cloud."

"That may not be a bad idea. Are you going to do it?"

"I don't know. I'd have to sign a new contract and pay a lot more. I'm not going to do that until I figure out what's going on with the website. This has never happened before. Maybe it's been hacked. The guy was insulted that I suggested their server wasn't secure, but I still want to talk to my geek friend in Baton Rouge to see what she thinks."

"Have you checked the website email? If they are honest hits, maybe that would give you a clue what they're looking for on the website."

"I've been up since dawn, training racers. I haven't had time to deal with this."

Mae could hear the strain in Whit's voice. She also could hear Pop talking in the background and Whit telling him to give her another minute.

"Do you mind giving me the password to the email account? I can check it for you."

"j-o-i-e-numerical two-v-i-v-r-e. "

"I'll let you know what I find out." Her screen began to fill with the *Quarter Track* website. "Oh, looks like they got us back online. I'll upload these racing stats and check the site's mail."

"Thanks. We won't be here but a few more hours. Then we're going over to Evangeline Downs. I need to take care of some things there to get us booked for the racing season."

"Don't worry about the website. I'll see what I can do to sort it out for you."

"Mae, thanks. I'm really drowning here. I can't possibly let you keep working for free. We need to talk about that again when we have time."

Whit's low alto made her flush with pleasure. It was the first time since she'd watched them lower Big Mae into her final resting place that she felt a real sense of purpose. "There's no rush. Go back to Clinton and Tyree. I've got your back."

For some reason, it pleased Mae beyond reason to say that.

❖

Mae was nearly bursting with her news when she finally found Whit and Clinton nursing beers in the Evangeline Downs clubhouse. Even though October was only a few days away, summer was making one last stand before Louisiana weather gave in to cooler temperatures, and the restaurant's air-conditioning was a welcomed respite. Clinton's sweat-soaked shirt was probably why they were here. Whit was worrying the label on her beer and watching Clinton closely. She looked relieved when Mae sat down and waved a waitress over.

"Two sweet teas, please," she told the woman. She frowned at Clinton. "You look about to drop. You shouldn't be drinking alcohol. It will only dehydrate you more."

Whit glared at her father. "I already told him that, but he's stubborn as a mule."

Clinton scowled back at her. "A man ought to be able to drink a beer when he wants."

The waitress set two tall glasses on the table and Mae shoved one toward Clinton. "Drink it for me? Please? The sugar will make you feel better, too."

"I've always found it hard to say no to pretty ladies." Clinton took a big gulp. "You can just bring us a pitcher for the table if you want," he said to the waitress.

Mae laughed when Whit looked at him like he'd grown a second head. "I think I've figured out why the website crashed."

"Really?" Whit downed the rest of her beer and discreetly confiscated Clinton's. "I'm afraid to ask."

"We-e-ell." Mae drew the word to prolong the buildup. She wanted to savor Whit's reaction, obviously because it proved her worth to *Quarter Track*. But it was more than that. She wasn't sure why, but she wanted Whit's respect. "You know we talked about me starting up some social-media accounts for *Quarter Track*. So I did. And I linked our Google page and our Facebook page to a Twitter account."

Whit stared at her. "You're telling me that social media is responsible for getting us so many hits that it crashed the host server?"

"Not just the accounts themselves, but it appears that something I tweeted got a lot of attention. People are going to the website to see if we've posted a story."

"What the hell is tweeted?" Clinton looked at Whit suspiciously. "You're not doing anything illegal, are you?"

"No, Pop. I'll explain social media later." Whit watched him drain his glass and refill it from the pitcher of tea. "Scratch that. I'll let Mae explain it to you since you listen to her better than you listen to me." She turned back to Mae. "What exactly did you tweet?"

"I said there was a deal going on behind the scenes that could bring a second racetrack and casino to the area and turn the highway between the two into a mini-Vegas." She sat back and waited for the effusive praise.

Whit paled. "Oh. My. God. Avery is going to kill me."

"I thought you'd be pleased." Mae hadn't expected a hug and girlish squeal of delight, but she hadn't anticipated Whit's panicked expression either. Whit should be thanking her, not worrying about Miss I'm-better-than-everybody Avery. "Your email was filled with requests from half of Louisiana and a dozen business interests outside the state wanting to know when we're going to post more information. More than twelve-hundred people have subscribed to the *Quarter Track* website in the past twenty-four hours."

Whit chewed her lower lip so long Mae was about to channel Big Mae and order her to stop. Finally, she spoke. "You know what? You're right. To hell with Avery. Looks like I need to talk to a man about a cloud."

The ball of nausea that was forming in Mae's stomach popped like a bubble. They grinned at each other until the loud slap of Michael's hands on their table made them both jump and look up. Mae was startled by his dark expression. This was a side of Michael she hadn't seen, and it frightened her a little.

He glared at Whit. "Who gave you permission to go blabbing about the deal I'm working with Senator Perrault?

Whit matched his stare. "I don't need your permission to publish anything, Michael. As I recall, nobody specified our conversation was off the record. You and Avery spoke openly in a public setting."

"You know damn well that was a private conversation among friends."

"I know nothing of the sort."

"Then maybe you need a lesson about how things are done around here."

Whit stood and mirrored Michael's pose, hands flat on the table as they confronted each other like mongrels claiming the same bone. "Maybe you need a lesson in First Amendment law."

"I ought to shut your little magazine down."

"You just try it. You may think this little corner of Louisiana belongs to you and your political cronies, but—"

"Whit didn't let the horse out of the barn. I did." Mae flinched as two angry glares turned her way. Mercy. She took a deep breath. She'd negotiated peace among some real bitches in her sorority, so she should be able to handle two normally reasonable adults. "Please, can we all sit down and talk about this?"

Whit and Michael just scowled at her.

"Sit." She tried her best to inject some authority into the order, but it didn't work on these two. Obviously, unlike Rhett, they hadn't graduated from obedience training. "Okay. Don't sit. You can continue to stand and yell at each other. But if one of you turns up dead in the near future, every person in this restaurant can point to the other of you as a prime suspect. I can hear it now. 'Yes, your honor, they were arguing so loudly I thought they'd come to blows any minute.'"

Whit dropped into her chair. Even Michael seemed to give it serious consideration as he sank slowly into the empty seat next to Mae.

"Dead? Who killed who?" Clinton was having trouble following the argument.

Mae patted his hand. "Nobody's dead yet. But Big Mae said you shouldn't say or do anything in public this week that would make you look guilty in court next week. She believed in always being prepared."

Michael made a snorting sound. "I've heard that lecture before."

Mae suspected the "be prepared" lecture Big Mae gave him had more to do with wearing a condom. Did he really want to bring this up in front of Whit and Clinton? Michael shifted uneasily under her gaze, as though he could read her thoughts. Evidently not.

"Apparently, you didn't listen." Whit was still on their original subject, oblivious to the look that passed between Mae and Michael. "When you blab things in public, you can't expect the press to ignore them."

Michael glared at Whit again. "You publish one more thing about this, girl, and I'll have you so tied up in court you'll be busier than a cat trying to cover shit on a marble floor."

Whit half rose in her seat, poking her finger at Michael. "Don't threaten me, Dupree. I'm not afraid of you or Avery's father."

Mae grabbed her threatening finger and pulled her back down in her chair. Whit was shaking with anger. Clinton reached for Whit at the same time and knocked over his tea, spilling it across the table. Mae could have kissed him as they all jumped up and grabbed napkins to mop up the mess. It gave her time to think.

They sat again and she held up her hands to silence further argument. "I think we need to focus on the positive here. This can be good for everybody." She laid a hand on both Whit's and Michael's forearms, as though she could be a physical link to bring them together. She squared her shoulders and met Michael's angry gaze. "I tweeted the news while I was standing right there with both of you yesterday."

"You did what?" Michael frowned.

"Posted it through social media. Hear me out." She glanced at Whit, who was still glaring at Michael. "Whit didn't know anything about it until today. She was angry with me, too, at first." She squeezed Whit's arm to stop her protest. "Sure, it's tripled the traffic to *Quarter Track*, but it can be good for you, too, Michael."

He frowned. "How's that?"

"Well, you were just a behind-the-political-scenes guy before. Now, everybody will know you're a man with ideas and the clout to make things happen. You're going to have high-powered clients beating down your door. Why, you could even run for political office in the future. That is, if you want to."

Michael drummed his fingers on the table. After a moment, he sat back, puffed out his chest, and nodded. "Smart, very smart. Just like your mama."

Whit couldn't believe it. He'd rolled over like a hound begging for a belly scratch. How did Mae do that?

"So, you're not angry with me then?" Mae practically batted her eyelashes at him, and Whit choked back a laugh. "I was hoping you could give me a real interview—an exclusive—to get what information you can give me so I can write a real article for *Quarter Track*."

Michael pursed his lips, then nodded. "I have to meet with the senator at two o'clock. I'll talk with him to see what we feel we can say about it right now. How about you meet me at my office at four thirty?"

Mae beamed at him. "That would be wonderful. Thank you so much."

"You're very welcome." He stood and sneered down at Whit. "You could learn a thing or two from this young lady, Whitley. It's obvious she didn't grow up in a barn like you did." He shot Clinton an apologetic look. "Sorry, Clinton, but she could use a little polish."

"Polish what?" Pop frowned as Michael headed for the door.

Whit could see that his energy was flagging. She needed to get him home. But she was concerned about the interview Mae had arranged. Sure, Mae had done a good job with the feature story on the little dog, but Whit feared Michael and Senator Perrault would manipulate her to their advantage. She had no experience interviewing powerful men who had an agenda. "Can you come back to the farm? We need to talk about your interview with Michael."

"Of course. I want to show you some things about the website, too." Mae gently touched Pop's arm. His eyes were sleepy and his hands trembled faintly against the table. "I can see that we've worn Clinton out."

The genuine concern and the way Mae's eyes softened when she looked at Pop warmed Whit. It helped to have someone else share her concern for him. She clasped his shoulder. "Ready to go home, Pop?"

"We've got to run the horses. Where's Tyree?"

"We've already done that, Pop. Tyree's probably waiting on us around the barns. He wanted a ride to the farm so he could get his truck and drive it back to Carencro."

"Okay. I am a little tired."

Whit and Mae helped him stand and guided him outside.

"Where are you parked?" Whit asked.

"In the general parking lot." It was on the other side of the track.

"I'm parked right by the stables. We probably need to get you a media sticker for your car so you can park closer to the backstretch here. You go ahead and we'll meet you at the farm."

"I left Rhett with Tyree and Ellie. That's how I knew where to find you. Can you just bring him with you?"

Whit feigned surprise. "You trust me with your little trust fund?"

Mae smiled. "I trust Clinton and Ellie to look after him."

"I'm wounded."

"Well, Rhett is an obedience-school graduate, and there's the issue of you needing a little polish."

"Don't forget it was Pop who raised me in the barn."

Mae laughed. "I'll see you at the farm."

Whit grinned as Mae walked away. She enjoyed their easy repartee. She felt lighter, happier than she had in months. Somebody finally had her back. She had a wingman, a cohort. And it felt very good.

CHAPTER TEN

"Something smells as rotten as last year's Easter eggs."

What if I forget to ask something critical?" Mae was nervous about the interview. How could she be objective about this story? Her sense of Southern heritage wanted to side with the property owners who would be forced to sell land that had been in their families for generations or be sandwiched between casinos and clubs that would stay open all night. But Michael was her father, her only living relative, and this project was important to him. She couldn't exactly explain her dilemma though, because Whit thought Michael was just a friend of Mae's deceased mother, a mother she'd never known.

"Are you kidding? Pop was right when he said you're like a machine gun when you're asking questions. Just throw in the hard ones between a bunch of easy ones, and he'll give up the information before he knows what hit him."

Mae wrung her hands. She wished she could just tell Whit that Michael was her father, but she'd promised. Then it came to her, as clear as Big Mae's crystal. "I have a better idea. What if we both go and play good cop, bad cop?"

Whit chuckled and shook her head. "You've been watching too much television."

"No, really. Just listen." Mae mentally lined up her argument. "When *The New York Times* breaks a news story, there are always more stories in the following week as they learn more. Am I right?"

"Yeah, they always have follow-ups."

"If I go into the interview with guns blazing, asking questions Michael isn't comfortable answering, he might decide not to talk to me about the subject anymore. If we both go, I can pretend to be sympathetic to his side. You can sit back and just jump in occasionally to ask the hard questions. It wouldn't be much of a stretch, because you two don't seem to like each other much anyway. This way, he'll probably still talk to me later when we have more questions."

Whit scratched her cheek and frowned. "I'm not sure that's totally ethical, but I can't put my finger on why."

"What if Woodward and Bernstein had refused to listen to Deep Tonsils? They'd have never brought Nixon down."

Whit stared for a second then burst out laughing. She laughed until her eyes filled with tears and she doubled over.

Mae frowned. "I don't see what's so funny."

"Ton…tonsils. Deep Tonsils." She straightened and wiped at her eyes, but burst into laughter again when she looked at Mae.

"Well, that's what they called their secret source, wasn't it?"

Whit gasped for breath and tried again to compose herself. "Throat. Deep Throat."

Mae huffed, then smiled. She liked Whit's deep, full laugh. She felt she'd just glimpsed what Whit must be like without the weight of the world on her shoulders. "Tonsils, throat. There's not much difference."

"Okay, okay. I'll be Bernstein to your Woodward, but only if Tyree hasn't gone back to the track yet. He was getting some things out of the barn. I'll need him to stay with Pop while I'm gone." Clinton was snoring in his recliner, undisturbed by their conversation or Whit's raucous laughter.

"Thank you. I'll go find Tyree." Mae dashed to the barn. She didn't want to think about how she'd just played Whit. She knew, of course, that it was Deep Throat. She'd seen the movie twice. But she needed to plant a seed of doubt in Whit's mind that she maybe couldn't handle the interview alone. It had worked like a charm. So why did she feel so guilty?

❖

Michael wasn't happy when Whit showed up at his office along with Mae. He sat behind his desk after they settled into the two chairs in front of it and handed them each a single-page news release. "This is all we're prepared to say at this time, and I need one of those back when you leave." He glared at Whit. "I was only expecting Mae, and one is my personal copy."

Whit ignored his stare. She knew he had a copy machine in the next room. He was just making it clear that he preferred to deal with Mae. Seems Mae had called this right.

"These are some impressive numbers," Mae said. "More than a thousand jobs and millions in tax dollars for the state. Is it possible to estimate that? How does that work?"

Whit thought Michael would explode if his self-importance expanded his ego any larger.

"Even though the project is very preliminary, we do have handshake agreements with several investors and other parties interested in building commercial establishments along the highway corridor."

"So, these figures are contingent on the landowners selling and the project fully developing?"

"Those figures are actually very conservative, based only on the interest we have so far. If the legislature complies and offers some initial tax incentives, those numbers could double or triple as the project progresses."

Whit frowned at the paper. "Do any of these handshake agreements come from landowners willing to sell?"

"As a matter of fact, they do."

"I don't believe you."

Michael gave her a smug look. "I don't care if you don't." He turned to Mae, cutting off Whit's next question. "We have several signed options on some of the land parcels and leads on securing some others. Jean Paul, who by the way really enjoyed your company at the track, is in charge of securing the land options. He's a genius at real-estate procurement."

Mae looked up from her notes. "I thought Jean Paul was a lawyer."

"He is. A real-estate lawyer. He deals in commercial properties. He works for his father, who's a financier, but his involvement in this project is separate from his father's business."

Whit didn't like the sound of this. She needed to find out more about this Jean Paul guy. "How many?"

"How many what?" Michael gave Whit an irritated glance.

"How many landowners have signed options?"

"Everything I can divulge is in the news release."

"I might remind you that Senator Perrault is a sitting senator in the legislature. I can file a Freedom of Information Act request and get copies of all his emails. That could tell me what I want to know and more."

Michael called Whit's bluff. "Go ahead. You know as well as I do that real-estate negotiations and personnel are exempt from that law."

"Couldn't you just give us an estimated percentage?" Mae asked earnestly.

"Perhaps Jean Paul would be willing to discuss that with you… over dinner. He asked me for your phone number, but I told him I would need to get your permission first." Michael pointed at Mae to emphasize his words. "You could do much worse, young lady."

Something inside of Whit balked at him pimping Mae out, but before she could form a plausible objection, Mae demurred.

"He seems very nice, but I'd like to think about it. I'm very busy right now, trying to settle in, and I just started my new job."

"Even working girls need a little relaxation in their lives."

Whit wasn't sure why, but she didn't want to think about Mae with some guy. "We're getting off track here," she said.

Mae shot Whit an apologetic glance, then turned back to Michael. "I was just thinking that if the percentage of property options is high enough, it would reassure our readers that this project could really happen. It would give hope to all those who need jobs."

Michael considered this. "Sixty percent."

Whit jumped to her feet. "You're lying."

Michael shook his head. "You always were a hothead, Whitley. If you don't believe me, then talk to your neighbors."

The knock at the door kept Whit from responding.

"Yes, Evelyn?"

"I've got Mr. Beaumont on line one, Mr. Dupree. He wants to speak to you about the Anderson case. He said it's urgent or I wouldn't have interrupted."

"I'll take the call." He turned to Whit and Mae. "Could you ladies excuse me for minute? I won't be long, but please don't leave. I need to talk to Whitley about another matter."

Whit dropped her news release on his desk as they filed out of Michael's office. She considered leaving despite his request that they stay. She didn't want to talk to Michael if he was going to pressure her to let him preview the article.

Evelyn gave them an apologetic look. "There's fresh coffee in the conference room and some donuts left over from this morning. I'll come get you as soon as he's off the phone."

"Thank you." Mae was warmly gracious, as always, while Whit only offered a stern nod in response. She didn't like getting friendly with the enemy, and, right now, Michael's office was feeling more and more like hostile territory.

Mae fixed them both a cup of coffee while Whit checked out the donuts. She'd skipped lunch and it was almost dinnertime.

"Can you really get the senator's emails?" Mae asked as she stirred creamer into their coffees.

"Emails and text messages, if he lists his phone as a government expense."

"If that's possible, why wouldn't he just pay for his own phone and use that to text anything he didn't want the press to get access to?"

Whit chewed the cruller she selected, then swallowed. "The culling of electronic correspondence is still a relatively new area of investigation. Most people are too enamored with the convenience of it. They don't stop and think about how public it can be."

"So, what's next? Are there questions we still need to ask? The news release says they aren't at liberty to reveal any of the interested business partners."

At that moment, Whit's phone rang and she glanced at the caller ID. "Avery," she muttered, and signaled Mae to hold her thoughts.

"Hey, what's up?"

Mae turned back to the counter to add more sugar. If this coffee was fresh, she'd hate to taste it when it'd been warming all day. She knew, though, that her frown wasn't about the coffee. She was bothered by the huskiness in Whit's voice as she spoke on the phone.

"I'm good. Yeah, the colt's running really well."

Turning her back was only a polite illusion of privacy. It would have been rude to stare at Whit while she spoke with Avery. But it was impossible not to overhear. The conference room wasn't that large.

"So, you didn't go to the lake? I'm sorry. I just couldn't get away."

Mae didn't like the way Whit's voice had just lowered another octave.

"I don't know, Avery. I can't talk about that right now."

Mae walked to the windows on the other side of the room and stared out.

"Okay. Saturday night. Can you make the reservations for six? Late-night dinners aren't conducive to getting up at four thirty in the morning to train horses. That's fine."

She might even describe Whit's low, rich voice as sexy. That is, if she were a lesbian…which she wasn't. She examined her unexpected flush of jealousy. She just didn't like the way Avery played with Whit. She was concerned about her boss, but it was more than that. Whit and Clinton were her friends.

"I know. We'll talk Saturday. I promise."

Maybe she needed to expand her circle of new friends. Maybe she should go on a date with Jean Paul. He *was* pleasant company.

"Yeah. We're at his office now, but he's not telling us much. I don't want to get you in trouble with your father."

Mae abandoned her thoughts and focused on Whit. She strolled back to the coffeemaker where she could hear better and made a show of warming what was left in her cup. She held up the carafe in question, but Whit shook her head.

"Okay. We can talk about it Saturday. Yeah. Me, too. I know. Bye."

Whit stuffed her phone back in her pocket. "That was Avery."

"I wasn't trying to eavesdrop, but I gather she knows we're here? Is she mad about *Quarter Track* breaking the story?"

Whit shrugged. "Apparently not. I got the impression she was at the meeting Michael had with her father earlier." She frowned down at the conference table. "That's the problem with Louisiana. Too many people are related to each other. It makes it hard to know who to trust because you don't know where their loyalties lie."

Mae froze. She should tell Whit that Michael was her biological father. Would Whit fire her? If she didn't tell her now, would the consequences be worse later? Mae had always been an honest person. She never should have told Michael that she'd keep their relationship secret. But if she hadn't, would he have recommended her to Whit and rented an apartment to her? She'd just have to explain the situation and ask Whit to keep her secret.

"Whit—"

The door swung open and Evelyn waved for them to follow her. "Mr. Dupree is finished with his call now," she said.

Mae followed them down the hall but hung back when they reached Evelyn's desk. "You go ahead," she said to Whit. She wasn't sure she could face Michael right now, knowing that she'd decided to share their secret with Whit. She was afraid she'd lose her resolve. "I think I've asked all the questions I had. I can wait in the car for you."

Mae turned to leave, then stopped at Evelyn's desk. "Oh, and would you let Mr. Dupree know that he has my permission to give my phone number to Mr. Broussard?"

Whit stared at her, her expression unreadable, then disappeared into Michael's office.

❖

"Where's Mae?"

"Waiting in the car. She may have more questions later, but we need to check out what you've already told us. And I need to get home. Tyree is keeping an eye on Pop while I'm gone."

"That's what I wanted to talk about, Whitley. The men who hold the loan on your father's farm are pressing me for payment."

Whit stared at the floor and rubbed her chin. "I need more time. The horses start running in about two weeks, and Pop will have money coming in then to start making payments."

"You're betting on that colt of yours to bail him out? I know Clinton has always gambled his next meal on the horses winning, but I thought you were more practical than that."

She limped back and forth in front of his desk. Her foot was beginning to swell and throb in her boot again. She had to make him listen. It was her only chance. "This colt is really good, Michael. Probably the best Pop's ever had."

"Be reasonable, girl. The quarter horses might take the track in a few weeks, but the racing season is three months long. I'm telling you that Clinton's creditors aren't going to wait until the end of December for payment."

"I only need until mid-November. They're offering a million-dollar purse in the Louisiana Quarter Horse Breeders Association Futurity this year, and Raising the Bar can win it. He's that good."

Michael's jaw muscle jumped as he considered her words. "I can't do it."

Whit slapped both hands on his desk and thrust her face inches from his. "You're supposed to be his friend. You got him into this mess. Why didn't you let me know what was going on? I could have come back sooner, before it got so bad."

Michael dropped into his chair. "He wouldn't let me. I tried to tell him that he needed to talk to you, but he was too proud."

Whit straightened and stepped back. He wasn't telling her anything she didn't already suspect.

"I can find a buyer for the farm. With this project coming together, you could get a good price for the land. You could pay off the loan and have some left over to take care of Clinton." He studied her. "He's only going to get worse, you know."

"Pop is my problem. Holding off those loan sharks you hooked him up with is your problem." She wasn't buying Michael's show of sincerity. She didn't trust him. "Tell them I'll have their money after the Breeders Futurity."

"I'm telling you, they won't go for it. Let me find a buyer now. Otherwise, they're going to take it right out from under you for the measly three hundred thousand dollars Clinton owes them. Then they'll sit on it and eventually resell it to some casino builder for ten times that much."

"Tell them I'll pay half next week and the rest after the race."

Michael shook his head. "Where are you going to get a hundred and fifty thousand dollars?"

"I'm selling my condo in Baton Rouge. It's closing next week."

"That's insane. If you give them that money now and can't come up with the rest by mid-November, you won't have the farm or your condo. You and Clinton will be homeless."

"You let me worry about that. You just make them the offer."

"I think you're digging a hole you can't crawl out of, but I'll see what I can do."

Chapter Eleven

"She's got too much gravy and not enough biscuits."

Mae could feel the waves of tension rolling off Whit. They had driven together before without talking, but it was a light, comfortable silence. This silence was stifling. She wanted to talk to Whit about Michael, but this apparently wasn't a good time to bring it up. Still, if she didn't say something, anything, pretty soon, the quiet was going to smother her.

"Whit?"

"Huh?" It was more of a grunt than an answer.

"Is everything okay?"

"Yeah." Whit's knuckles were white as she gripped the steering wheel. "No."

"Want to talk about it?"

"No."

"Did I—"

"It's got nothing to do with you. Okay?"

Mae drew as far back against the door as she could. "I'm sorry." It wasn't that she thought Whit would hurt her in any way, but her anger just seemed so big that it needed extra space. She stared down at her hands folded in her lap and felt Whit sneaking glances at her.

"I'm sorry, Mae." She blew out a long breath. "I shouldn't snap at you."

"Whatever Michael said seems to have upset you."

Whit curled and uncurled her long fingers repeatedly as she gripped the steering wheel. Finally, her anger seemed to deflate like a balloon with a slow leak. "He wanted to talk to me about Pop, about planning for the inevitable."

"I see." Mae slid over so that she could rest her hand on Whit's thigh. Her heart ached for Whit's dilemma. "I guess Michael had some ideas?"

"I really don't want…I mean, I guess I'm not ready to talk about it."

Mae could hear the lack of certainty in her voice, so she gave Whit's thigh a reassuring squeeze and waited.

"He thinks I should get Pop to sell the farm because I'll need the money when he gets bad and needs twenty-four-hour care."

"You've got plenty of time before that happens, Whit. Really. You can do a lot of things to make it easier to keep him at home as long as possible. I know some from my community work, but I'm sure there's a local expert that could come evaluate the house and make suggestions."

Whit nodded, her throat working. "That farm is home to him. His memories of Mama are there. I can't take him from that until he's so gone he's unaware of where he is."

Mae was afraid if she answered, the soothing words she wanted to say would catch in her throat. So, she just stroked Whit's thigh like she did Rhett's ears when he trembled through a thunderstorm. A subject change was in order before they were both bawling. She gave Whit's thigh a pat and withdrew her hand. "You have a date with Avery on Saturday?"

"She wants to talk about the project since it's out in the open now."

Mae snorted. "Right. I'm sure that's all she wants." The blush that crept up Whit's cheeks was enough of an answer.

"You're giving Jean Paul your phone number. Have you even Googled him? You shouldn't be giving your number to strangers, even if Michael does know him."

"He's not a stranger. I've had lunch with him and Michael, and he escorted me to the track the next day. He was a perfect gentleman."

"What does he look like? I don't recognize the name."

"So you know everybody in Opelousas?"

Whit's jaw muscle jerked. "No, I don't. But he sounds like he may be about my age."

"How old are you?"

Whit hesitated, glancing at Mae. "Forty-two."

"Then he's younger. I'm guessing mid-thirties."

She grunted and frowned as she stared at the road. Mae decided to tease her. "He's tall and dark, like one of those Italian Mafia guys." She nodded firmly. "Yeah. That's what he reminds me of."

"So you're going out with Louisiana Mafia?"

"I didn't say he was Mafia. I said he looked like Mafia. He's actually sort of handsome. Now that Michael's admitted that he's part of the story we're working, maybe I can get some information from him over dinner."

Whit pulled up to the farmhouse and killed the engine. "You know, it's sort of unethical to date your sources. It sheds doubt on your objectivity when you do."

"But that doesn't apply to your date with Avery?"

Whit grimaced. "Touché. However, I dated Avery long before she had information I wanted. Just be careful, okay?"

"I will if you will. Avery might be much more dangerous than Jean Paul. I'm sure he's not stupid enough to offer pillow talk in exchange for information." She made an air-quotes gesture to signal that pillow talk was a euphemism for sex. "I wouldn't put it past Ms. Fancypants, though, to get naked if she thought it could influence how you cover this issue."

"She wouldn't…I wouldn't—" Whit sputtered, then waved dismissively at Mae. "Ain't gonna happen," she growled, climbing out of the truck.

Mae hopped out, too, and waited for Whit to join her by the porch steps. "I brought the ingredients for spaghetti. I thought maybe I'd cook dinner for all of us, since you two seem to live off of sandwiches and pizza."

Whit shifted and tossed her keys from hand to hand. "That sounds great, but could we take a rain check? I've got a mound of financial paperwork to sift through so I can fill out my quarterly tax forms the next couple of nights because my days are filled training horses and figuring out what to do about the website. How about Saturday night?"

"You have a date with Avery on Saturday night."

"Oh. Yeah. How about Sunday, if you don't have plans? Or we can do it on Monday so you don't have to drive out here on your day off."

"Sunday would be wonderful. My calendar is free, but I'll have to check Rhett's." Mae was relieved that her tease finally drew a small smile from Whit.

Still, the weariness in Whit's eyes sliced into her heart. She wanted to wrap Whit in a tight hug and hold on. She had no idea how it would be received, but she'd taken a tentative step toward her when Tyree opened the front door and the dogs scampered out to greet their mistresses. Ellie leapt into Whit's arms and began to coat her throat with doggie kisses, and Mae absently wondered how Whit's skin tasted. This would have concerned her, but she often had random, nonsensical thoughts. They never meant anything.

"Oh. I guess we should get something up on the website tonight since a hundred other media agencies are chasing the same story," Whit said. If she'd noticed Mae staring at her throat, she apparently was ignoring it. "I'll write up something short and post it, and then we can talk Sunday about something more in depth."

"You've got all that paperwork to handle. I can write something when I get home and email it to you. You can read over it and post it if you think it's okay."

"Thank you. That would be very helpful."

"You're welcome." Mae smiled to hide her disappointment. She could have written the article while the spaghetti sauce simmered. It would have been like a family—Whit filling out paperwork while she typed the article and Clinton napping in his recliner while the rich aroma of garlic and tomatoes filled the house. All that waited at home was an empty apartment and a lonely dinner for one. But Whit's dismissal was clear. She turned toward her car and slapped her thigh for Rhett to follow. "See you tomorrow."

"Good night," Whit called after her.

❖

Whit went over the figures again. Buying more bandwidth, enough to support the traffic quartertrack.com was now experiencing, would triple her costs. Plus, she needed to pay her web guys to redesign the site a bit to build in teasers to the features Mae wanted to write for the magazine. She didn't even want to think about the extra printing costs of more pages so she could add content.

Whoever said "it takes money to make money" was right. She was confident now that the changes Mae had suggested would attract more readers, but she also knew how writers tended to job-hop. Mae was just starting her career. What if she decided to look for employment back in Georgia, closer to her sorority sisters, after she published enough stories to put together a real resume? Whit didn't have time to interview candidates to replace Mae, and she sure didn't have time to do the work herself.

She shuffled the papers to find her latest bank statement, then closed her eyes and sucked in a deep breath. It had taken her two decades to save up her nest egg. It was the money she should be drawing on to invest in her business until the advertising returns began pouring in. But, after putting out the hottest of Pop's financial fires, she barely had enough left to finance the training and racing in the upcoming three-month season. She also had counted on the sale of her condo to give her a little breathing room, but now she'd committed that money to hold off the collection of Pop's loan.

On top of everything, she needed to start paying Mae. But where the hell would she get the money? She'd already cut all the expenses she possibly could. She could only feed Pop so much macaroni and cheese. He was starting to grump about wanting a steak and complain when she kept the air-conditioning on eighty degrees. She thought again about selling off one of the brood mares, but that would be like a vineyard owner selling his mature vines.

She put her head down in resignation, her forehead hitting the stack of paper with a soft thump. She thumped it several more times because, well, maybe it would shake some idea loose that could get her out of this mess. She'd jumped in to rescue Pop with little thought, and now the financial quicksand was pulling her under, too. No matter how she looked at it, she had too much gravy—too many bills—and not enough biscuits to sop it up.

She straightened and turned off the lamp next to her, sitting in the dark for a moment. There was nothing to do but pay for the extra bandwidth from her savings and run Bar in a few more of the smaller races so the winnings could pay the track bills. Pop would fight her on it. Bar would risk injury every time he ran and could peak too early, before the Breeders Futurity, but what else could she do?

She dreaded another night of tossing and turning with her worries, so she grabbed a bottle of brandy and stepped out into the warm evening. Maybe the liquor and the rhythm of the porch swing would calm her enough to sleep.

❖

Mae stared into her refrigerator but found no inspiration. Whit's polite rebuff was a softball-sized lump in her stomach that effectively killed her appetite. She could picture it, growing larger and larger as it absorbed her gastric juices. Gross. She closed the refrigerator in disgust.

She filled her teapot and put it on the burner, then flopped on the sofa. Rhett jumped up beside her and stared down with mournful eyes. Mae shook her head when her stomach growled loudly. Maybe it wasn't a dumpling growing in her stomach. Maybe it was a matzo ball. She giggled despite her morose mood. One of her sorority sisters had been Jewish and liked to yell it like a curse word because the sorority sisters all tittered any time someone said "balls."

"Oh, matzo balls!" She laughed at Rhett's surprised expression and scratched his ears. "I know. My brain just chatters away with the most stupid thoughts when I'm upset."

Rhett cocked his head.

"Well, it's not that I'm really upset. I'm disappointed."

Rhett looked skeptical.

"Okay, maybe I'm not just disappointed." She searched for the right word. "I'm disquieted, and I have no idea why." She sighed and resumed scratching Rhett's ears. "All I know is that I'm thinking about matzo balls, for Christ's sake, and talking to a dog."

Rhett whined.

"Oh, I'm sorry. You're not just a dog." She sat up to pull him into her lap and rolled him over to rub his chest and belly. "I'm sorry I'm in such a mood. It's just, well, I was looking forward to eating dinner with someone who can carry on a conversation." She kissed his curly head. "You're a sweet boy, but not much of a conversationalist."

She stroked his chest absently. "Besides, I really need to talk with her about Michael." *Too many people are related to each other. It makes it hard to know who to trust because you don't know where their loyalties lie.* How would she tell her? *Lying and cheating have always been deal-breakers for me.* Whit's words added another figurative matzo ball to her unsettled stomach. Surely she'd understand when Mae explained everything. Wouldn't she?

Her thoughts settled on Whit. She definitely felt drawn to her. It was probably because they both were in situations where they had no one else to depend on. It made perfect sense for them to want to help each other.

Some people might think it was more than that. Whit *was* a lesbian. Maybe she was, too. But she'd never felt compelled to hang out with her lesbian sorority sisters. Well, no more than any of the other sisters. She'd never really felt drawn to any of the guys she'd dated either. Hmm.

Whit wasn't what most would call pretty, but not bad looking, either. Big Mae would have said she was a handsome woman. Her hazel eyes were like pale jewels against her thick, sable lashes and tanned skin. Mae even liked the small crow's feet starting to form at the corners. Whit had nice, full lips, too.

Her brain jumped to an image of Avery kissing Whit. She frowned. No, Avery was all wrong for Whit. She was a blond, plastic Barbie. She shook Avery from her head, only to have her replaced by the image of Whit's lips. Mae licked her own and noticed that she needed to apply some gloss because they were dry. In fact, her whole mouth had suddenly gone dry. She licked her lips again. What would it feel like to kiss a girl, to kiss Whit? Mae had kissed a lot of guys, mostly chaste kisses, but she'd had her share of heated ones, too. Most guys were rough, like they were trying to chew her face off. But some weren't so bad. She closed her eyes and let herself imagine moving closer and brushing her lips against Whit's. She jerked in surprise at the shiver that ran through her.

Then she laughed at herself, and Rhett wagged his short tail. The teapot began to whistle, so she placed him gently on the floor as she stood. "I think we need to fix something to eat. Even if I don't feel hungry, I'm apparently delirious from lack of nourishment." Why else would she be thinking such silly thoughts about Whit? She poured the water over her tea bag and cocked her head at Rhett. "If Jean Paul doesn't ask me out pretty quick, I just might break Big Mae's cardinal rule and call him."

CHAPTER TWELVE

"Add a jug of wine to a barrel of slop and it's still a barrel of slop."

Whit stared into her Crown and Diet Coke as she swirled the dark liquid, then gulped the last of it down. She held the empty glass to signal her waiter for another.

If nothing, Avery was consistent. She'd always felt her time was more important than anyone else's, so was persistently late to everything except court.

She was also predictable. When Whit checked in with the hostess, she was led promptly to a very private booth in the rear of the restaurant. She ignored Avery's usual pacifier, the chilled bottle of expensive wine sitting on the table, just to be cantankerous, and ordered a highball instead. The fresh drink the waiter placed on the table was her third.

"Didn't like my choice of wine?"

Avery was stunning in low-slung dark slacks and a champagne silk blouse with French cuffs and one too many buttons open at her breasts.

"You ordered it. I thought I'd let you have the first glass." Whit stood and waited for Avery to sit down. Her dress clothes were still in her condo, so she'd settled for a new pair of black jeans and a crisply starched white shirt. Accented with a gold necklace, bracelet, and earrings, she had felt fairly presentable until Avery arrived. Now she felt a bit like the wait staff.

They were quiet as the waiter opened the wine. Avery made a show of tasting it, then nodded her approval. Whit didn't protest when Avery indicated that he should also fill her glass, but that didn't mean she'd drink it.

"I hope you weren't waiting long."

"Twenty minutes."

"I had a hard time getting away from the campaign office. We have a million things to do and never enough people to handle them."

"I still can't believe you're working for your father's campaign. When did you become a Republican, for God's sake?"

"You never have understood politics, have you? We're not going to change things if we try to take the Republicans head-on. They have too much money. We need people like me on the inside to guide them to a more moderate platform." Avery held up her hand when Whit started to answer. "Please, I don't want to talk about Daddy or politics. I wanted this dinner to be about us." She reached across the table to capture Whit's hand. "I've missed you, baby."

Whit hated that her fingers reflexively tightened around Avery's. She also hated the burn flushing her neck as her traitorous body responded to the overtures. She was floundering. The part of her that had just downed three highballs wanted to drag Avery to the nearest hotel. It'd been a long time and she was horny, damn it. But another part of her was screaming, "Warning, warning, Whit Casey."

Avery seemed to sense this reaction and, like the skilled attorney she was, changed her line of questioning. "When did you cut your hair short again?"

"This morning. Long hair is too hot when you have to work outdoors most of the day." She fingered the hair cropped close to her neck and over her ears, then fluffed the longer curls that spilled forward onto her forehead. "You were the one who liked it long. I always preferred it short."

"My mistake. That haircut's a very attractive look for you." Avery scanned her menu. "Have you decided what you want? My treat."

"In that case, I'll have the lobster." She wasn't sure what to make of this new, nicer Avery, and she was still peeved that she was late.

Avery ignored Whit's sarcastic retort. "That sounds really good. I'll have it, too." She waved their waiter over and placed the order. "Now, tell me about this fantastic colt you have. Michael says he's the talk of the track."

This wasn't the old Avery that Whit knew. She'd never cared anything about the horses Pop ran. It was on the tip of her tongue to remind her of that, but she stopped herself. Maybe Avery *was* trying to mend fences, and she should quit being so defensive. She shoved aside her skepticism and began to explain her plans for Raising the Bar.

They also talked about Avery's last big case that she won and caught up on what their mutual friends had been doing in Baton Rouge. By the time dessert arrived, Whit felt like she was spending the evening with the woman she once loved. She excused herself to the ladies' room while Avery waited for their waiter to return with her credit card. She was drying her hands when the door opened and closed, and then its lock clicked into place. Avery stood with her back against it, her gaze hot enough to incinerate Whit's clothes.

"I've been dying all evening to do this."

Two steps and Whit was held fast between the vanity and Avery's soft, lithe body. It was just as she remembered, Avery's breasts fitting perfectly against hers, her slim hips melding to Whit's. She groaned as Avery's mouth found hers, hot and tasting of the cherries jubilee they'd just shared. They explored each other's mouths thoroughly before Avery finally pulled back, resting her forehead against Whit's.

"God, I missed that."

Whit was silent. Her brain was too scrambled, her feelings too conflicted. Her body was screaming "yes!" and her brain was reasoning "no." Why did Avery want her so badly now? She obviously hadn't given Whit much thought for the past two years.

Avery took her hand and closed Whit's fingers around a plastic card.

"What's this?"

"It's a room at the Hilton. I want you to spend the night with me."

"Avery. I need to go home. I have to be at the track at dawn."

"I don't care if it's only for a few hours."

Whit started to protest again, but Avery covered her mouth with her hand. "Don't say no yet. Just hold on to it for a bit and let's take a walk."

It was a beautiful, mild September night. Lafayette's downtown, the center of Louisiana Cajun culture, was alive with tourists and students hopping from restaurant to pub to club. Street musicians performed in front of shops and throughout a downtown park.

It should have been perfect. With the right person, it would have been. But while they walked through the park among the couples who strolled arm in arm, hand in hand, the flame of arousal that Avery had sparked in the restroom faltered. Whit was acutely aware that now they were in public, Avery kept a careful distance. God forbid somebody think they were together. The fantastic food they'd just eaten soured in her stomach.

When they came upon a park bench secluded from the flow of foot traffic, Avery sat and gestured for Whit to join her. Dusk had settled around them, sufficient to cloak their identities unless someone walked right past. Still, Avery crossed her legs and sat at an angle that prevented Whit from sitting too close. That irritated her even more, so she left more space than necessary between them and crossed her arms over her chest.

"I have a proposal to make."

"Well, if it's a marriage you're going to propose, you need practice. This sounds like a business deal."

"It's a job proposal."

"I have a job. In fact, two jobs. I'm not in the market for a third."

"Just hear me out."

"I'm listening."

"This proposal to develop the eighteen miles between Carencro and Opelousas is really important to Daddy's campaign. If he can make this happen, he'll run for the U.S. Senate next time."

"What's that got to do with me?"

"We're prepared to promise an in-depth exclusive for your magazine's next edition. After that, you'll get first notice of every new investor, every new business that signs on."

She stared at the complete stranger before her. "What would you want in exchange?" It didn't really matter since Whit would never bargain her self-respect or journalist ethics, but she was curious.

Avery held her gaze. "You know as well as I do the power of the media. We want you to write about the economic benefits of this project. We want you to write about the families that will get good jobs with benefits, health care for their children. Write about the millions of tax dollars it will generate, money that can be used to improve our schools, pave our roads, and help save our bayous."

Whit sprang from the bench and stood over Avery. "You are asking me to slant my report to pave your father's way to Congress?"

Avery stood, too, forcing Whit back a step. Her voice remained calm. "I'm not asking you to print anything that's not true. I'm only asking that you don't interview every bleeding-heart landowner who'd rather stand in the way of progress than sell his swampland for a development that could benefit thousands of people."

Whit struggled to keep from raising her voice. "I happen to *be* one of those bleeding-heart landowners."

"That's exactly why you shouldn't report it. You can't possibly be objective. I can even have the articles written for you, so you don't have to do it. All you have to do is publish them."

"You can't be the woman I've spent the past twelve years with, because you obviously don't know me at all. Thanks for dinner." She turned to leave, but Avery's hand closed around her forearm.

"There's more you need to consider."

"I seriously doubt it."

"When Daddy's elected, we'll need a point person to manage the flow of information about the project to the general media. I can guarantee the job is yours for a salary that would let you hire someone to manage *Quarter Track*. You can just sit back and collect the profits."

Whit stood perfectly still, her insides turning cold with fury. If she moved one muscle, she was afraid it would be to punch the woman standing beside her. What in the hell made Avery think she could be bought?

Since she didn't walk away, Avery forged ahead. "Daddy can make sure you get top dollar for your farm, so Clinton will have the best care money can buy. You can move back to Baton Rouge. Several great facilities there handle Alzheimer's patients." She stepped close enough that her distinctive perfume filled Whit's senses. "We can be together again. It won't be like before. We'll see each other all the time because we'll be working out of the same office. I'm going to be working for Daddy full-time, too."

Whit yanked her arm from Avery's grasp. "I'd rather be homeless than become one of the godless souls who sell themselves for political power. But it was a very pretty speech, Avery. You should run for office yourself."

"Actually, I do plan to run for Daddy's seat in the legislature when he runs for Congress. You need power to be able to change things, Whit."

"So…what? You're going to get elected as a Republican and then come out of the closet to get the conservatives to embrace same-sex couples? You can't even tell your parents you're a lesbian. How do you plan to tell the world? I don't want to live in the closet with you for any amount of money or power."

Turning again to leave, she jammed her hands into her pockets and her fingers closed around the hotel room key. She stopped, her back still to Avery, and stared at the card in her hand. "Mae was right to warn me about you. You thought I'd sell my soul for a fuck." She tossed the card key on the park bench and started walking. "You were wrong."

Avery followed, matching Whit's long strides. "Oh, I see. You're screwing *her*, aren't you? God, how old is she? Twenty? For God's sake, Whit, you're forty-two. If she's the problem, then don't let me stop you from getting what you can. You should still consider what I'm offering, for Clinton's sake if nothing else."

Whit glared at Avery. "I'm not sleeping with Mae. The problem, as you call it, is that you just aren't that good of a fuck."

❖

"I was surprised to hear from you," Jean Paul said as he clasped Mae's elbow to guide her to their table.

Actually, Mae was the one who had been surprised earlier. When she'd opened the door of his Jaguar for Rhett to hop in, the backseat was strewn with dog toys to keep him busy while they were in the restaurant. It had been unexpectedly thoughtful. "I hope you don't think me too forward, but Michael said you wanted to get in touch with me."

He held her chair for her and then took his seat on the other side of the small table. "I enjoy certain things in life, such as fine dining." He gestured to the rest of the room. The tuxedoed wait staff and white linen tablecloths suggested that this restaurant was probably the most expensive in town. "It's difficult enough in this god-forsaken bayou to find a woman with all her teeth, much less someone refined enough to appreciate the finer things society has to offer. The short time we spent together at the track told me you were a woman who knew which fork to use."

"That's not very complimentary of the native population," she said. "I've seen plenty of other women in Opelousas who don't eat with their hands." She kept her voice mild to temper the reproach.

"They're all old or unavailable or simple." He regarded her solemnly. "None are as beautiful and intelligent as you."

"Surely the landscape isn't that bleak."

"Perhaps my expectations are too high after experiencing what other parts of the world offer."

"I had the impression you grew up here."

"I am the first generation of Broussards to be born here, and my mother, a native to the state, insisted I stay with her until I was twelve. Then my father, who is French, enrolled me in a boarding academy for young men, where he went to school in that country."

"That must have been very lonely for you, a young boy that far away from your parents."

Jean Paul cocked his head, his expression amused as if he was enjoying a private joke. "Not at all. I found living in a dorm full of boys my age a wonderful, enlightening experience. We forged a brotherhood that followed us as we attended different colleges around the world and began our business careers. I still see some of them from time to time."

The waiter discreetly interrupted, and Jean Paul gave him a complete order for both of them. Mae hadn't even looked at the menu and started to object, but something about Jean Paul seemed a little off. He was charming one minute and an almost insufferable snob the next. She decided it was best to hold her tongue until she had a better read on the man sitting across from her.

"Did you go to college in France?"

"No. I attended Oxford, then returned stateside for law school at Yale. As payment for that expensive education, my father demanded that I return to Louisiana to handle his legal affairs." He frowned at the salad the waiter set before him. "Otherwise, I would have preferred to return to Europe or settle in New York, at the very least."

"I was wondering about your unique accent. It doesn't quite match the Cajun twang I've heard around here."

"Cajun is a bastard brother to French. My accent is a blend of my Southern-belle mother and my French father."

Mae lifted an eyebrow at his snub to the local culture but let it pass. "Do you go back to France often?"

His face darkened. "Not since I began practicing law. My father—" He stopped and nearly drained his wineglass. "My father's legal work leaves little time for me to travel."

"I'm sorry. I didn't mean to bring up a sore subject."

He refilled his glass and redirected the conversation. "Enough about me. Let's talk about you. All I know is that you're from Georgia."

"I almost made a career out of attending Emory University because I loved college so much. By the time I graduated, I had enough credits for three bachelor's degrees."

He sat back in dramatic, mock surprise. "Three degrees?"

"Nearly four. I'd have one in criminal justice, too, except I couldn't make myself take the forensics class."

"Forensics?"

"You know, gathering evidence at the crime scene. They actually required you to observe a real autopsy. Can you believe that? I would have had nightmares for years of them cutting the top off some poor person's head to take their brain out. If I could stand that sort of thing without fainting or throwing up, I'd have gone to medical school."

Jean Paul laughed. "So, indecision kept you at Emory so long?"

"That was my excuse." Mae looked down at her plate and smiled. "I actually stayed because I didn't want to leave my sisters," she said softly.

"I thought you didn't have any other immediate family."

She looked up at him. "My sorority sisters. Like your school chums, they were the large family I never had before I went to Emory."

His eyes searched her face, his expression suddenly unguarded, as if he was waiting for her to say something more. Then as quickly as the door had opened, his expression was closed again. "I doubt they were like my school chums." He sat back, the aloof, charming persona firmly in place. "And what persuaded you to leave your university nest?"

"Big Mae, my grandmother, basically told me to pee or get off the pot."

He chuckled and shook his head. "You have such perfect manners, it catches me off guard when you use expressions like that. I think you'll have to explain that one to me."

"Big Mae considered college as a sales lot for husbands. She was tired of me test-driving but never signing a contract to buy."

"You don't plan to marry?"

"I've never met a man who made me want to get married."

He studied her. "I wouldn't guess you to be like your boss."

"My boss?"

"The Casey woman. I don't know her personally, but I have met Senator Perrault's daughter." He tapped his finger on the table and pursed his lips. "She is rather aggressive for a woman, even though I wouldn't have picked her to be a les-bi-an." He drew the word out as though it was a nasty taste in his mouth. "Michael says Whitley Casey is just what you'd expect."

Mae didn't like where this conversation was going. "What exactly would you expect a lesbian to be like?"

"They walk and dress and talk like men. They know nothing about what it is to be a woman."

Her steel magnolia began rising. "No offense, Jean Paul, but, as a man, what do you know about being a woman? Your ideas are pretty stereotypical. I could be a lesbian."

He shook his head, smiling. "You're too beautiful and have a fabulous sense of style."

She narrowed her eyes. Did he just say fabulous?

"It's true," he said, holding up his hands to ward off the glare she directed at him. "Try to picture Whit Casey in the dress you're wearing." He laughed when she hesitated. "See. You can't do it." He turned his palms toward the ceiling. "I can't imagine it, either."

She pictured Whit's tall, graceful body. Just because she was strong didn't mean she was masculine. She thought of those viridian eyes and soft sable curls. "I don't think a woman has to wear a dress to be beautiful."

He looked surprised at her reproach. "I apologize. I meant to compliment, not offend you."

She sucked in a breath and straightened her shoulders. She had to rein it in or she'd never get the information she needed for her story. "No, I'm sorry. I didn't mean to snap. Where were we before our conversation got off track?"

"You were about to tell me what led you to Opelousas."

"My grandmother was my only immediate family. After she died, I decided I needed a fresh start."

"Why would you come to the bayou for that?"

"I've always loved New Orleans, and a letter my grandmother left with her will suggested that I ask Michael for help. He was a close friend of my mother before she killed herself."

He blinked at her, as if at a loss to comment.

"It was a long time ago." Mae waved dismissively. She was tired of this conversation and wondered what Whit was doing with Avery at that moment. God, she was so unfocused tonight. They had finished their main courses, and she still didn't know anything more about the deal Michael, the senator, and Jean Paul were brokering. It was time to wrap up the story of her pitiful life and get down to business. "Anyway, Michael helped me find a place to live and a job."

"Dessert, sir?" The waiter interrupted and flashed a tray of decadent samples in front of them while another waiter cleared their dishes.

Mae held up her hand when Jean Paul opened his mouth to speak. "Dinner was delicious, but I can order for myself," she said softly.

Jean Paul shrugged. "By all means."

"I think I've eaten all I can, but I'd like something sweet to sip. Can you please ask the bartender to make me a double-shot Buttery Nipple?"

The waiter hesitated a second. "Buttery Nipple?"

"Yes. It's equal parts black sambuca, Bailey's Irish Cream, and Buttershots. He may not have black sambuca on hand, but Kahlua will be fine if he doesn't."

"Yes, ma'am." He turned to Jean Paul. "You, sir?"

"Just coffee."

Their waiter conferred with the bartender, then disappeared into the kitchen.

"Since you brought up my boss, she and I met with Michael yesterday about the casino deal. He said several of the landowners between Carencro and Opelousas have already signed options on their properties. That would be your area, wouldn't it?" She offered her warmest smile. "I wanted to interview some of the landowners about why they've decided to sell. I don't suppose you could point me toward a few?"

"Real-estate transactions are confidential until the property transfer is recorded with the parish," he said.

"I wouldn't want you to betray any confidences, but it probably would help some others to make up their minds if I could write an article about why some feel it's in the best interest of the community for this project to go forward." She schooled her face into what she hoped was her most innocent, hopeful expression, the same one she'd used to ask for a kitten when she was eight.

Jean Paul chuckled and shook his head. "Did you just bat your eyes at me?"

"Did it work?"

He was about to answer when his gaze jerked from Mae's face to whoever was approaching behind her. His body went still and his eyes gave a clear warning, but the blond man wearing a huge grin and a chef's jacket didn't seem to notice when Mae turned to face their visitor. He set Mae's drink, the liquors neatly layered, on the table.

"You forgot to ask for a dot of grenadine for the nipple, darling."

He held out his arms, and Mae could barely refrain from squealing her excitement as she jumped up and wrapped her arms around her old friend.

"Robbie! How did you know I was here? Are you the chef? Dinner was delicious."

"Still asking fifty questions a minute." He returned her hug, then pushed her back down in her seat and pulled up a chair to join them. "Honey, when my bartender came in the kitchen to ask me for some sambuca from my private stash, I knew only one other person besides me would ask for a Buttery Nipple with those ingredients." He held out a swizzle stick. "But I know you'll want to sip it, so go ahead and stir it."

"I had no idea you were in Louisiana. I just moved here." Mae stirred her drink to mix the layers and glanced over at Jean Paul, who was scowling at the interloper. "Oh, where are my manners? Jean Paul, this is Robbie, one of my favorite escorts at Emory."

"We already know each other well," Robbie said, giving Jean Paul a friendly wink. "We're business partners."

"I'm an investor in this restaurant," Jean Paul said, nailing Robbie with a hard stare. "Aren't you needed in the kitchen?"

If it weren't so totally ill-mannered, Mae would have laughed. Men were so territorial. But Jean Paul had nothing to fear from Robbie. He'd had more boyfriends at Emory than she did.

Jean Paul's pointed dismissal didn't dampen Robbie's enthusiasm. "I do have to get back. My best sous-chef is out sick and the kitchen is bedlam." He scribbled a phone number on the back of a business card he took from his pocket. "Here's my cell number. Call me so we can catch up." They both stood for another hug, and then he winked at Jean Paul again. "The meal is on the house. Bringing this lovely belle to my doorstep is payment enough."

Mae almost laughed at the tense set of Jean Paul's jaw as Robbie retreated to the kitchen. "You know he's gay, right?" She felt safe revealing that because Robbie had never been one to hide.

Jean Paul seemed to relax a bit. "What I know is that he's a great chef and my investment in his business has already been profitable."

There seemed to be more to it, but Mae needed to get back on track. She took a sip of her drink and licked the sweet liquor from her lips. "We were talking about land options, I believe."

Jean Paul leaned forward. "If you want a real story, you should look into the horse cloning I told you about." He sat back. "But then I wouldn't expect your boss would want you poking into that."

"Whit says that it's all rumor and a waste of time."

"I'm not surprised she'd say that, considering that her colt is rumored to have come from a test tube."

"That's just ridiculous."

"That's why the old man is so deep in debt and about to lose that farm. He took out a loan to pay for the cloning procedure. It's very expensive."

Mae put her drink down and pushed it away, suddenly queasy. "Why would he do that?"

"An old lion looking for one last kill, one last big race to put his name in the track records." He studied her. "I mentioned it to Michael, but he told me to leave it alone. I heard he was responsible for finding the money to have it done."

Mae placed her napkin on the table and Jean Paul stood to pull her chair out.

Could that have been what Michael wanted to talk to Whit about privately? She hadn't known Whit very long, but she couldn't believe she would be mixed up in anything like this. "And exactly how would you go about proving a horse has been cloned?"

He shrugged as they made their exit. "That's a little outside the field of real-estate law."

The evening was a perfect seventy degrees as they walked along the sidewalk under the huge oaks to Jean Paul's car.

"We're only about eight blocks from my apartment. Would you mind if we walked instead of taking the car?" Mae's thoughts were a jumble of casino deals and cloned horses, and walking usually helped her sort things out.

"I can't think of a better way to share a beautiful night with a lovely lady." His words were pretty but seemed to lack feeling. Perhaps he was preoccupied, too.

Mae clipped Rhett's leash to his collar and they strolled the distance in silence, pausing several times for the dog to mark a tree or hydrant. When they reached the broad porch of the house that held her apartment, Mae hesitated at the door.

"Thank you for a lovely evening. Forgive me for not inviting you in, but it's been a long week and I'm deathly tired." She wasn't really fatigued, but she was tired of Jean Paul's company, and she had more than a few burning questions for Whit.

Jean Paul actually appeared relieved, so it startled her when he stepped forward and grasped her face in his hands. His mouth covered hers, and his tongue pushed inside for a brief, but thorough, exploration before he released her.

"If I wanted to interview someone who signed a land option, I would look for an old widower, a young man who has just inherited a farm he doesn't want, or a childless couple burdened with a lot of medical bills," he said softly.

Mae watched him stride down the sidewalk they had just strolled until he disappeared into the dark. Well, sir. She wasn't at all sure what to think about Jean Paul Broussard.

CHAPTER THIRTEEN

"Staying drunk ain't no cure for a hangover."

Mae's cell phone rang while she was waiting for her laptop to boot up for a night of research into cloning. Despite her apprehension over Jean Paul's implication that Raising the Bar was a clone, a rush of pleasure swelled her chest when the caller ID showed Whit Casey.

"Pillow talk usually means a conversation with the person next to you in bed, not on the phone with somebody else." Her joke was met with silence, and in those few rapid seconds her mind traveled light-years. Her heart lurched that her emotionally reserved friend might be reaching out to share, only to be scared off by her flippant tease. Then her brain registered the late hour, and the possibility that something might be terribly wrong with Clinton or the colt blossomed in her mind like a mushroom cloud. "Whit?"

"No, ma'am."

She was surprised to recognize Tyree's deep, soft tones. "Tyree?"

"I'm sorry to be calling so late, ma'am, but I didn't know who else could help."

"What's wrong? Is Clinton okay? Where's Whit?"

"She's right here with me at the training track."

"Did somebody hurt the colt? Is he sick?"

"No, ma'am."

"Where's Clinton?"

"He's at home asleep. My mama sat with him tonight."

"Why is Whit at the track? I thought she was meeting a friend in Lafayette."

"Well, ma'am. That's why I'm calling. She needs to go home so Mama can leave. She has to be at church early in the morning. Mama never misses church."

"Is her truck broken down?"

"No, ma'am. I don't think so."

Getting information from Tyree was like plucking deer ticks off a hound dog. For every one you pulled off, twenty more were still burrowed deep.

"Can I speak to Whit, please?"

"Uh, she's, um, not feeling well. I think she needs somebody to drive her home. I'd do it, but Mama borrowed my truck to go sit with Mr. Clinton."

So, Whit needed a ride. She could have been halfway there already if Tyree had just spit it out to begin with. "Tell her that I'll be right there."

❖

It was near midnight and the only movement was the night watchman patrolling up and down between the barns. The backstretch bedded down early even though it was Saturday night, because horses had to be fed and trained at daybreak Sunday, just like every other day of the week.

"Ms. St. John?" The watchman's voice was loud in the stillness.

"Yes."

"Tyree said you were coming. He's down by their stalls, waiting for you."

"Thank you."

During the twenty minutes it took to drive to Carencro, her concern had grown into worry, and the sight of Tyree pacing along the barn's overhang turned that worry into a cold ball of fear. Rhett at her heels, she broke into a trot until she reached Tyree and grabbed his shoulders.

"Where is she? Is she all right?"

He pointed to the colt's stall. "She ain't hurt or nothing, but I ain't never seen her like this."

"You wait out here." Mae stuck her head over the half door. The colt was relaxing against the far wall, head drooping and one hind foot cocked at rest. Whit was slouched on an upturned bucket in the corner to the right of the door, her long legs sprawled haphazardly with a brandy bottle clutched in her hand and resting against her crotch. Mae took in the starched white shirt and jet-black jeans. Whit Casey sure did clean up well. But something was different. She looked closer and realized Whit had cut her hair. Dark curls tumbled rakishly across her forehead while the close-cropped sides and back accentuated the strong line of her cheekbone and jaw. Mae had thought Whit attractive before, but she was gorgeous now. She appeared to be asleep, so Mae stepped into the stall. "Whit?"

Whit stirred and her head lolled in Mae's direction. "He-e-ey. It's the Jaw-juh peach." Her eyes were hazy, her speech loud and slurred. "I like peaches, an' you're jus' in time." She held up the empty bottle. "'Cause I'm fresh out." She squinted at it. "Didn't know peaches could taste so good." Her gaze swung back to Mae, eyes wide. "Maybe they're from Georgia," she whispered.

An unfamiliar tingling spread through Mae's groin, and she laughed nervously. "Tyree said you needed a ride, and I agree."

Whit frowned. "I hardly know you."

"I don't think you're in any condition to drive."

"Oh, that kind of ride." She grinned at her apparently private joke. "Okay."

Mae handed her keys to Tyree, who stood just outside the stall door. "I'll try to get her up while you go get my car. I don't think they'll mind if you pull up right here so we don't have to carry her all the way to the parking lot."

Tyree sprinted for the car, and Mae grabbed Whit's hands to haul her up. Once she got her long legs under her, she rose and teetered for a minute. Rhett sniffed the brandy bottle she dropped and sneezed. She settled Whit's left arm across her shoulders and wrapped her right arm around Whit's waist to steady her. "Ready?"

Whit nodded, but swayed toward the center of the stall and away from Mae when they took the first step, then overcorrected to fall against Mae, pinning her to the wall. Mae tightened her grip as Whit struggled against her like a newborn foal trying to find her balance. Mae was breathless when she finally stilled, a swirl of unfamiliar feelings swelling up every place Whit's body touched hers. Whit's head rested on her shoulder, her warm breath bathing Mae's neck with each exhale, igniting a trail of goose bumps that spread down her arms and across her chest.

"You smell really good," Whit mumbled against her neck.

Mae froze. Was that Whit's tongue on her skin?

"Mmm. Taste good, too."

The tingle started between her legs and spread outward. She felt Whit push off the wall so she grabbed the first handhold she could find, the waistband of Whit's jeans, and pulled to stop her from stumbling backward. Whit groaned and fell against her again. Her nipples were hard against Mae's breasts. Her forearms bracketed Mae's head and Whit nuzzled her ear. "Damn, you're beautiful."

Whit's words made her shiver. Her knees felt like jelly, and she had a fleeting vision of them both falling to the floor because neither was capable of standing. She tightened her grip on Whit's jeans and pulled her hips closer, eliciting a second low groan that flowed over her like a hot wave.

Whit's eyes, darkened to a shade of blue, blinked lazily at her. "Do people tell you that a lot?"

"Never. No one, really. No one that counts." She barely breathed the words, afraid to break the spell, afraid the sound of her voice would scare Whit away.

But Whit moved closer, so close Mae could almost feel her lips move when she spoke again. "I want—"

"Yes."

Whit's lips were so soft Mae wondered if she was imagining them. Just a teasing brush at first, and then Whit's mouth closed on hers. When Whit began to withdraw, she tugged her down again. And, when Whit's lips parted, she opened freely to suck her in. The brandy was sweet and thick on Whit's tongue. Her body felt both heavy and light as her insides clenched so tight she would have surely suffocated if not for Whit's breath filling her, feeding her. The slam of a car door nearby and Rhett jumping against their legs jerked Mae back to reality, and she gently disengaged.

"Tyree's back. We need to get you in the car so I can take you home." She slipped around and shouldered under Whit's right arm so that, this time, she was between Mae and the wall. Whit put her hand out to brace against the wood as they shuffled forward. Outside the stall, Tyree steadied her on the other side, and the three of them staggered to the open car door. Once they had her in the car, Mae closed the door and Whit slumped against the window.

"Tyree, you need to get that bottle and bucket out of the stall before the horse steps on them and hurts himself."

"Yes, ma'am." He hesitated. "Miss Mae, what about tomorrow morning? We've got track time at six thirty."

Mae looked back at the car. Whit's eyes were closed, her cheek pressed against the window. "I doubt she'll be sober in six hours. I'll drive Clinton out here."

Tyree nodded. "That'll be fine. Mr. Clinton forgets a lot of things, but if you get him to the track, he'll know what to do. Don't let him forget his stopwatch." He opened the door so Rhett could jump into the backseat.

"I won't. Thank you, Tyree, for calling me."

"Yes, ma'am."

She drove carefully, keeping a close eye on her passenger. She tensed when Whit stirred, and quickly scanned the road shoulder to evaluate whether there was enough room to pull over if she became sick.

Whit swiped her hand over her face but didn't open her eyes. "I'm so tired," she muttered.

"Why don't you lie down on the seat until we get home?"

Whit didn't answer, but slumped sideways. "Avery's a bitch."

"I know, sweetie." She gave Whit's arm a reassuring rub and was surprised when she scooted closer to lay her head on Mae's thigh, then tucked her hands under her chin like a child. Seconds later, the only sound in the car was Whit's soft, deep breathing.

❖

Tyree's mama was standing on the porch when Mae pulled up to the house. She was a small woman with sharp eyes and peered in the passenger window as Mae slipped out and around the car.

"You gonna need help getting her inside? Mr. Clinton went to bed hours ago, and he's like a baby. If you wake him up now, he'll never go back to sleep tonight."

"If I can't wake her up, I'll just let her sleep in the car." Mae offered her hand but spared the woman only a glance. She couldn't seem to take her eyes from Whit's prone body for more than a few seconds. "I'm Mae."

"I'm Bernice, Tyree's mama." She held onto Mae's hand while she gave her an approving once-over. "Uh-huh. Tyree was right. He said you were pretty. He also said you might be the one to get the Caseys back on course." She released Mae's hand and shook her head at Whit. "Lord knows getting drunk ain't gonna fix anything."

"Whit's carrying the weight of the world on her shoulders, Bernice."

"Child, don't I know it." She opened the car door so Mae could crawl in to wake Whit. "But it's gonna seem twice as heavy when she wakes up in the morning."

Mae shook her gently. "Whit, honey, we need to get you inside." No response. She stroked her cheek and pulled at her arm, but Whit remained limp.

"Lord, girl, you ain't gonna wake a drunk like that. Let me try. I'd like to get home before church services start in the morning." Mae backed out and Bernice took her place. She slapped Whit hard on the rump and raised her voice to drill-sergeant level. "Get up, Whitley. You can't sleep in the car like some old wino." Whit stirred and Bernice smacked her again. "The Almighty has no patience for fools and drunks."

Whit mumbled and sat up, blinking as she tried to orient herself. Bernice tugged on her arm until she was sitting with her feet on the ground. "Now stand up and go get in your bed."

Mae helped her stand and stagger to the front door. As soon as they stepped inside, Whit broke into a stumbling run for the bathroom. Mae started to follow, but Bernice stopped her. "Give her a few minutes. She wouldn't want you to see her at her worst."

Mae nodded. "Thank you for staying with Clinton. Tyree should have called me sooner so you wouldn't be out so late."

"It's no burden. Those two have been lost since Miss Celeste passed on. It was time for Whitley to come home so they could face things together." She patted Mae's arm. "Still, they may need some help to find their way. Without Miss Celeste, they're just two empty cans rattling around in this house."

Mae watched her leave, then locked the door and went in search of Whit. The door to the bathroom joining Whit's bedroom was closed, so Mae pulled back the bed covers and waited. Gagging noises intermittently filtered under the door for another ten minutes, and she was about to knock when she heard the toilet flush and then water running. She nearly jumped out of her skin when the door jerked open and Whit, eyes barely open, plowed past in nothing but black bikini briefs. She dove for the bed and hit it crossways, face-first, then didn't move.

She stared at the smooth lines of Whit's long back and the defined muscles of her legs. This wouldn't do. Her feet were hanging off the bed. She moved closer and reached hesitantly to touch Whit's back. She stopped and withdrew. She'd never touched a naked woman before. Certainly not one who'd kissed her like Whit had. Her body flushed with the memory of it. She'd been kissed plenty of times, but those kisses were nothing more than tongues and slobber compared to how Whit's kiss made her feel. It made her want to strip off her clothes and rub her burning flesh against the naked back stretched out before her. She wanted to entwine her legs with Whit's and hump that muscled rump. God, she felt like a pot about to boil over. She was actually fantasizing about taking advantage of a woman who was passed out cold.

She gently pulled Whit's feet around to tuck them under the covers, but that bent her body in a ninety-degree angle that looked terribly uncomfortable. So, she placed one hand on her hip to push and the other on Whit's shoulder to pull. A little firm pressure and Whit straightened in the bed. What she hadn't anticipated was what rolling Whit onto her back would reveal. Mae stared, fascinated by the smooth abdomen and small, firm breasts. She jerked back in horror when she realized her fingers were inches from touching a pebbled nipple.

She yanked the covers up to cover the temptation, then retrieved a bottle of water from the refrigerator and some aspirin and antacid from the bathroom. She grouped the offerings on the night table for when Whit woke and paused for one last, long look. She finally gave in to her need to touch her. The thick sable curls were impossibly soft. She loved Whit's new hairstyle. It exposed the clean lines of her long neck and wide shoulders.

Mae snagged one of the extra pillows from Whit's bed and found a blanket in the hall closet. The long sofa was comfortable enough, and Rhett and Ellie jumped up to curl against her chest and behind her knees. She set her cell-phone alarm and snuggled into her cocoon with a sigh. Then she closed her eyes and relaxed into a restful slumber and dreams of peach-brandy-laced kisses.

Chapter Fourteen

"Elvis is dead and I don't feel too good either."

Whit rolled over and groaned when her eyes finally focused on the two-inch-tall numbers of her digital clock. It was ten o'clock. Why didn't Pop wake her? Pop! Crap. Her head was pounding. She swung her feet to the floor and a sickening wave of nausea hit her. When her stomach stopped flopping about from the sudden motion, she examined the offerings on her night table. She popped the aspirin in her mouth and downed the entire bottle of water. That was a mistake.

She barely made it to the toilet to throw it right back up. When she was done, she brushed her teeth and got two more aspirin from a bottle that had been left on the bathroom vanity. This time, she chewed the two antacid tablets first and then went to the kitchen for another bottle of water. She downed the aspirin, drinking slowly as she read the note left next to the butter dish and three slices of bread.

Don't make coffee. The caffeine will only dehydrate you more and make your headache worse. Drink lots of water and eat some toast. The bread will help settle your stomach.

I've taken Clinton to the training track. I told him you had some bad seafood for dinner and were under the weather. We'll be back as soon as he and Tyree are done.

Mae

Whit toasted and buttered the bread, then took it and a third bottle of water into the living room, where she sank onto the sofa. The unusual quiet was welcome since the pounding in her head had yet to fully abate, but it was a bit cool for the T-shirt she'd pulled on. Pop had probably turned the air-conditioner up again.

A blanket was neatly folded on top of a pillow at the end of the sofa. When she drew it over her bare legs, a faint whiff of something made her lift it to her nose and sniff. The familiar scent danced at the edges of her brain, but she couldn't quite place it. The cream-colored case identified the pillow as the one missing from her bed. She didn't remember sleeping on the sofa. In fact, she didn't remember driving home. She burrowed her nose in the soft flannel. It smelled like the beach, like cocoa butter. It smelled like Mae. Did Mae sleep here last night?

Whit chewed her toast. What was the last thing she remembered?

She was in the park with Avery and they argued. She didn't feel like coming home to Pop's twenty questions, so she went to the track. The rest of the night was a big black hole in her memory. She frowned and rubbed her temples. The headache was getting better, but things were still really fuzzy. Why had Mae been here? She'd left Pop with Bernice. Maybe Bernice had to leave for some reason. Maybe she'd been too drunk to answer the phone, so Bernice called Mae. She sniffed the pillow again. Was Mae here when she stumbled home drunk? God, she hoped not.

She managed to finish the toast without dashing to the bathroom to throw up again, so she showered, dressed, and settled in to update quartertrack.com. Although she hated the extra expense, she was glad she'd upgraded to more bandwidth for the website. The short story they'd posted on the casino deal had doubled the number of hits they had for the entire year. She also had an email from the company that sold ads for *Quarter Track*. They had sold four full-page color ads already for the next quarterly installment of the magazine and needed to talk to her about new ads for the website. Holy crap. She'd have to drive to Baton Rouge next week to meet with them and her website designers.

She held her fourth bottle of water against her still-pounding temple. She'd think about all this web stuff tomorrow when she felt better.

She stared into the living room. That sofa and the cocoa-butter scented pillow were looking better and better. Thank God it was Sunday, no pun intended. A short nap would probably do worlds of good. She was a split second from giving in to her need for more rest when she heard the rumble of a diesel-truck engine outside and a door slam. Crap. She forgot she'd agreed to let the Quarter Horse Breeders Association guy come out this afternoon to tattoo the yearlings with their official registration number. She pulled on her jeans and pushed through the front door to stand on the porch.

"Morning."

"Morning. Brian Baird. This is the Casey farm, right?"

"You've got the right place."

The man pushed his Stetson back and mopped at his brow with a faded bandana. Summer apparently was making one last appearance before giving way to cooler weather. "Damn. I thought Texas was hot, but I believe Louisiana's got it beat. You can just about bathe in the humidity down here."

"You get used to it, I reckon. I expected Hubert Johnson today. Is he okay?"

"You probably know that his wife is doing poorly."

She nodded. "Breast cancer. His office scheduled him to do this on Tuesday, but he needed to take her for a treatment that day, so I told him we could do it today."

"Well, she's having a bad day, so he called me. Getting close to racing season and we're pretty booked up. I've got another appointment Tuesday, but I told him I could do this for him if we went ahead and did it today like y'all planned."

She'd been through a few of those "bad days" when her mother was ill. But she didn't want to remember, much less talk about it. "Let's get to it then so you can get back to your usual Sunday afternoon."

The yearling auction went hand in hand with the fall racing season, and theirs had to be tattooed and registered in case she could pay off the farm lien in time to clear them for the sale. It wasn't his fault her head still hurt and her gut burned.

They were preparing to tattoo the last of the three yearlings when she heard her truck pull up. Mae's soft, melodic tones were interspersed with Clinton's low, hoarse ones, but Mae was alone when she appeared in the barn a few minutes later. A blush rose to her cheeks when she glanced at Whit with a shy smile.

Whit blinked. Shit. She must have done something stupid last night that embarrassed Mae. But what? Damn it. No matter how tightly she scrunched her brow and searched her tender brain, she couldn't squeeze out what had happened after she found that bottle of brandy in the camper.

"Clinton is taking a nap," Mae said softly.

Whit cleared her throat. "Thanks for driving him to the track this morning." She kicked at the hard clay of the barn's wide corridor where the yearling was cross-tied. "I don't think I was up to it." She glanced purposefully at Brian, who was checking his paperwork and selecting the correct numbers for the tattoo, and gave Mae a look that she hoped would be interpreted as "I don't want to talk about it right now." Mae nodded her understanding and turned to Brian.

"Hi, I'm Mae."

Brian touched the brim of his hat and held out his hand. "Brian Baird." He stuck his chest out and held her hand a little too long. "Nice to meet you, Mae."

Whit narrowed her eyes. She wanted to slap that leer right off his face.

Mae extracted her hand and looked up. "What are y'all doing? Is something wrong with the horse?"

"The yearlings are getting their registration tattoos. They have to have them to race."

Mae perked up. "Rhett has his AKC number tattooed on the inside of his back leg. I thought they branded horses."

Brian answered helpfully. "Nope. Racehorses have to be tattooed on the inside of their lip."

"Oh, my. That must hurt. How do you get them to stand still for that? When I got a tattoo, it took the guy about thirty minutes to do it. I thought I'd scream."

"You have a tattoo?" Whit's hazy brain spun into sudden, sharp focus.

Brian chuckled. "It's not like tattooing a person." He showed her the rectangular instrument that resembled a large rubber stamp. The stamp part, however, was a tray that held individual numbers.

Each number he inserted into the tray protruded small, sharp, inked needles. "I'll show you."

He dipped a large swab into a bottle of liquid and wiped it liberally inside the colt's upper lip while Whit gripped the halter. The colt comically puckered his lip and raised his nose upward when she released him.

"That's the same stuff the dentist swabs on your gum before he shoots you full of Novocain," Brian explained. "It'll deaden the lip so that the horse will hardly feel a thing. We'll give it a minute to work."

He held up the papers Whit had supplied for Mae to see. "The owner has to get a DNA test and submit it to the Quarter Horse Registry to confirm it against the DNA records for the dam and sire. Once the parentage is confirmed, the papers are issued and the horse can be tattooed." He held the stamp he had prepared next to the papers. "The tattoo has to match the numbers on the registration."

"How do you know you're tattooing the right horse?"

"See this drawing of a horse? These marks are made on this paper by a veterinarian when blood is drawn for the DNA test." He gestured toward the colt. "According to the papers, he has one white hind foot, a star on his forehead, a scar on his knee, and a whorl under his mane, right behind his ear."

"A whorl?"

He lifted the colt's mane and showed her a spot where his coat swirled in a sort of cowlick.

Whit blew out a breath. "That lip should be good now." The gurgling in her stomach and Brian's self-important tutorial were irritating her. Or maybe it was the big blank spot in her memory and the way Mae glanced away every time their eyes met. She swiped at the trickle of sweat making its way past her ear to her neck and wrapped her arm around the colt's nose to hold him firmly.

"You got him?"

The question was unnecessary, but Whit nodded curtly. She was wishing for the tenth time in the past ten minutes that Hubert Johnson's wife wasn't having a bad day. This strutting little rooster of a man was making her day worse. She wanted to toss him in his truck and send him on his way.

Brian rolled the colt's lip up and pressed the tattoo stamp against it. When he took it away, the number was embedded neatly into the skin. He spread some petroleum jelly over the tattoo and stepped back.

Mae picked up the papers Brian had laid on a hay bale and studied them. "So, how would you tell if somebody was registering a cloned horse?"

Whit's patience was all but gone. "For God's sake, Mae. It would never happen. It would show up when the Association compared the colt's DNA to his parents' and they'd refuse to register the horse. Besides, who would have the money to pay for a cloning? There's no guarantee the horse would be a winner. Training and feed and a lot of other things figure into the making of a champion."

Brian, on the other hand, warmed to the question while he signed each of the three registrations and handed them to Whit. "There ain't nothing more important than bloodlines when it comes to racehorses. But you could get a clone on the track if you bribed the veterinarian who took the blood sample or somebody that was comparing the DNA at the lab. Hell, you could pay somebody to hack into the registry and put whatever they wanted on a horse's records."

Whit snapped. "We're not wasting time chasing a story on something that's not happening." She pulled cash from her back pocket and counted off two hundred and twenty dollars. "Three tattoos and an extra twenty-five for helping Hubert out and coming on a Sunday. Appreciate it." She unclipped the colt from the cross ties and led him away.

After she released the colt into the pasture, she stood propped in the barn's entrance a moment to watch the yearlings graze as though they'd already forgotten their sore lips. The faint breeze was hot and did nothing to dry the sweat sliding down her neck and soaking her shirt. She only relaxed a bit at the sound of Brian's diesel truck cranking and heading away.

Still, she felt oddly out of balance. She wasn't just physically ill; she seemed emotionally unsettled. She'd had hangovers before and wasn't this grumpy. Maybe it was her argument with Avery. She frowned. That couldn't be it. She'd hardly given it a second thought. They were done.

"Are you okay?" Mae's soft question startled Whit, and when she whirled, the barn spun at a sickening tilt. She put her hand out as she stumbled to brace against the nearest wall and closed her eyes to settle her churning stomach. When she opened them, Mae was pressed against the wall, looking up at her. It felt familiar. Mae's fingertips brushed her sweaty cheek, and the memory of another barn—Mae sandwiched between her and the wall—flashed across her brain.

"God, Whit. You're soaked with sweat. You need to go in the house and lie down before you pass out."

Whit stared at her. The image danced away, and the harder she tried to grasp it, the farther away it seemed. "You were at the track last night?"

Mae met her gaze. "Yes." It was almost a whisper.

Whit pushed away from the wall, away from Mae, and scrubbed her hands over her face. "I can't remember. Christ, I think I was nineteen last time I drank so much that I couldn't remember."

"You were very drunk, and Tyree called me. I brought you home and put you to bed."

Whit froze. "You put me to bed?" She'd been nearly naked when she woke up this morning. She always slept in just her underwear, but—

"Well, I waited until you stopped throwing up, then you sort of put yourself to bed. I slept on the sofa so I'd be here to take Clinton to the track this morning."

Whit let out a breath. Hopefully she'd waited until Mae was on the sofa before she stripped down. But Mae was probably used to her sorority sisters walking around in various stages of undress. Straight women did that, didn't they?

Another image flashed across her brain. Her nose pressed against Mae's neck. Whit blinked.

"Whit, you're shaking. You're still too dehydrated to be out in this heat. Please come in the house."

Mae shouldered under Whit's arm and firmly wrapped hers around Whit's waist. Another image flashed of Mae and Tyree helping her to the car.

"I can walk, Mae." Even as she said it, she wasn't sure she could.

"Shut up, Whit. I'm helping you inside and that's final."

Maybe she did need help. The press of Mae's body against her side, the silky feel of Mae's hair brushing her arm, and, God, the scent of cocoa-butter made her dizzy. "You have a tattoo?"

"My sorority's Greek letters, but I'm not telling you where."

Damn, she was in trouble.

Chapter Fifteen

"You gotta put the hay down where the goats can get it."

Mae turned her Lexus north onto Interstate 49. Alexandria was only an hour away, but she'd have to hurry to make it back in time to interview a few of the landowners that Jean Paul had discreetly pointed out to her. She had promised Whit an update on the casino-project story by the end of the day.

She set the cruise control, settled into the worn leather seat, and let her mind wander. It went straight to the same memory it had played over and over since Saturday night. The kiss. Mae brushed her fingertips across her lips as though she could recreate the sensation of Whit's mouth on hers. She could almost taste the brandy on Whit's tongue, and it made her shiver.

Was it Whit who made her tingle, or just the fact that she was a woman? Mae examined this idea. She'd lived in a house filled with attractive women for nearly ten years. Some were even lesbians, but she'd never wanted to kiss any of them. If one had kissed her, would she have experienced the same awakening that came with Whit's kiss? She didn't think so.

She'd felt drawn to Whit the first day they met. She'd told herself it was because she empathized with Whit's situation, that she simply felt a kinship because they both were trying to find their way. But that didn't explain why she wanted to constantly touch her. It sure didn't explain why she wanted to tear her clothes off and rub her skin against Whit's naked back. Whew. She needed to think about something else.

She fanned her face with the copy of *Quarter Track* that had been on the seat beside her. Okay, okay. Something else. Think about something else. What questions did she need to ask when she arrived at the Louisiana Quarter Horse Breeders Association headquarters? She began to form a list, but her mind drifted back to Whit. Why was Whit so opposed to an article on the cloning lawsuit? Was there something to the rumor that Raising the Bar was a clone? Big Mae always said every false rumor usually had a grain of truth. At least that's what people thought. She'd just have to prove this rumor wrong. She'd find out all about this cloning thing and stop people from spreading lies about the Casey colt.

That decided, she let her thoughts drift to the day before. Despite her protests, Whit had let Mae lead her to the sofa where she reclined and dutifully, but slowly, downed three more bottles of water. They talked as Mae updated the website and posted a few things through social media. Whit told her about the new ads and the trip she'd have to make to Baton Rouge on Tuesday. Mae smiled at the memory.

"Whit! That's great news."

Slumped against the sofa, Whit rolled her head to look at Mae. "I have you to thank for it, Mae. I need to be paying you, but I've got every penny tied up in Raising the Bar and expanding the website to meet the demand."

Mae closed her laptop and walked over to sit next to her. She took Whit's hand in hers. "I'm fine financially. We can talk about salary when you start seeing money from the new ads." Whit started to protest, but Mae held her hand up to silence her. "I practically forced myself on you, even though you told me you didn't have the resources to hire an employee right now. I was lost after Big Mae died, and you gave me purpose. You and Clinton mean more to me than just a job."

Whit's hand clasped hers, but she didn't speak. She closed her eyes and the silence stretched out so long, Mae thought she might have drifted off to sleep. When she opened them, Mae marveled again at how her hazel eyes seemed to change color with her moods. They were more grayish-green this time, the color of the ocean at a Georgia beach. Whit had the face of a mature woman, and Mae found that extremely attractive.

"Tell me I didn't do anything to embarrass myself last night."

"You really can't remember?"

"Mae." Whit's tone was pleading.

"No. You slept all the way from the track and bolted to the bathroom when I woke you up to come inside. I didn't even see you throwing up. You had the door closed."

Whit sighed. "Thank God."

"But you were in there so long, I was about to knock on the door when you came charging out nearly naked and dove for the bed, where you immediately passed out." She chuckled when Whit covered her face with her hands. "It was nothing to be embarrassed about. You're very, uh, fit. Not that I looked, mind you. I just covered you up and came out here where the pups and I spent the night."

When Whit lowered her hands, her face was red. "I'm sorry."

Mae patted her knee. "Don't be. We'll laugh about it next week when you're feeling better." She stood and tossed the pillow that was still there to the end of the sofa. "Now, why don't you stretch out here for a bit? I'm sure you need to take care of the horses later, and I promised Clinton I'd cook him a spaghetti dinner tonight, but I want to get some research done before I start cooking."

Whit must have felt pretty bad, because she didn't argue. Mae went back to the dining-room table to work, and Whit shucked off her boots and settled in for a nap. She was asleep almost immediately. When her hands began to twitch, Mae had wondered what Whit was dreaming about. Horses, websites, Avery? Avery was a bitch.

Still lost in her thoughts, Mae turned into the parking lot of the office building where the Quarter Horse Breeders Association was located.

What had happened on Whit's date with Avery? Did she want to know? Damn right, she did. It had to be Avery's fault that Whit drank herself into a stupor. But then, if she hadn't gotten drunk, the kiss probably wouldn't have happened. Huh. Guess she owed Avery a thank you.

The only problem now was how to get Whit to kiss her again. Hopefully sober, the next time. There would be a next time, wouldn't there? Come hell or high water, Big Mae would say. Even if *she* had to do the kissing. Sometimes you just had to put the hay down where the goats could get it.

❖

The woman who approached her from a cluster of empty work cubicles was tall, like Whit, and had flashing dark eyes. She had a long face that spoke of perhaps some Native American in her bloodline, and her long black hair was pulled back in a French braid. The way she carried herself screamed lesbian. Huh. Had the kiss switched on a gaydar that had been latent within her? Was she viewing women differently now?

"Can I help you with something?"

Mae smiled at her. "I sure hope so. I'm Mae St. John. I work for *Quarter Track* magazine, and I'm writing a story about the process of registering a quarter horse for racing. I was hoping to talk to someone about the steps required."

"The steps are listed on our website, but I have a flyer with the same information. Would you like me to get one for you?"

"Yes, thank you. I saw the information on the website, but I also have a few questions. Maybe you could answer them for me, Ms.—"

The woman pulled a paper from a desk drawer and handed it to Mae, then extended her hand. "Jodie Redmond."

Mae smiled warmly and slid her hand into Jodie's grasp. "I'm very pleased to meet you. That's a good Southern name. Are you related to the Virginia Redmonds?"

Jodie shook her head. "Not that I know of." She studied Mae. "You're not from around here, are you? St. John sounds like Louisiana, but your accent is different."

"Busted. I'm from Georgia. I just recently moved here. Well, not here, but to Opelousas. It was kind of scary moving here by myself and not knowing anyone but a friend of my mother."

Jodie brightened. "Georgia's loss and Louisiana's gain."

"That's sweet of you to say so, Ms. Redmond." Batting her eyes was simply a reflex. Did lesbians fall for that like men did?

Jodie flushed. "Please, it's just Jodie."

Apparently, eye-batting was effective. Good to know. The tactics for manipulating lesbians apparently weren't so different from the ones she used on men. A little flirting and they'd fall over themselves to please her. It would be easier than she thought to get the information she needed.

"Since it's lunchtime, I'm the only one in the office at the moment, but I'll be happy to try to answer any questions you have. Would you like to go to a conference room where we can be more comfortable?" She gently clasped Mae's elbow and guided her past the cubicles to a room with rich wood and thick Berber carpet that spoke of money. Mae was beginning to realize the organizations that supported horse racing were rich like casino owners, while trainers, jockeys, and the rest were like the gamblers. Some were successful but most lived barely above the poverty level, as they put every cent they made from this year's horse into their next promising colt. She settled into a plush leather chair and opened her notebook while Jodie sat next to her. When Jodie angled her chair toward Mae and brought one foot up to rest on her knee, Mae touched the snakeskin boot.

"I love your boots."

"Handmade, right here in Alexandria. I've got a business card from the guy in my desk, if you'd like it."

"Thank you. Perhaps on my way out." Mae scanned her notes. "Could you explain a bit more about how the whole DNA thing works?"

"A vet draws blood from the horse and sends it to one of the laboratories approved to do DNA testing for the Association. The horse owner then submits the DNA report to the Association. The DNA markers are compared to the DNA markers of the parents listed on the registration and either verified or rejected."

"Are very many rejected?"

"It's rare with racers. Those people are all about bloodlines and breeding, so they know a horse's heritage before they buy it. Most of the rejections are from inexperienced owners who buy from bad sources or take a seller's word on the pedigree. Then when they test the DNA and it doesn't match up, they realize they've been bamboozled."

"What about cloning? I'm working on an article to explain the lawsuits that have been filed against quarter-horse and Thoroughbred racing to allow clones like some other groups do."

Jodie chuckled. "It's a big fuss about nothing, the way I see it. The few cutting horses that have been clones prove there's too many variables to guarantee the clone will be as good as the original horse."

"That doesn't stop the rumors whispered around the track about certain colts being clones."

Jodie shifted nervously in her seat. "It would be nearly impossible to get a clone registered to race." She scratched at her cheek and drew a deep breath. "But I guess if somebody was determined, they could."

"How can you tell if a horse is a clone?"

"Their genetic markers would be identical to those of the parent."

"What if the horse was the offspring of a clone?"

Jodie shook her head. "Wouldn't work. Both parents have to be registered and their parentage verified. A clone wouldn't have been eligible to register, so any offspring from the clone wouldn't be eligible either."

"You said it would be nearly impossible. What would I have to do to get around the registration process?"

Jodie stood. "I'm gonna get a cup of coffee. You want some?"

A single-cup coffeemaker sat on the credenza, and Jodie picked through the coffee selection.

"Yes, if you're going to have some."

She turned back to Mae while the coffee dribbled into the first cup. "We do have a complaint pending that includes a colt expected to race in Opelousas. It's being investigated, but that information isn't for public consumption."

"Oh, I'm not interested in who, just how. Can't you tell me in general terms?"

"If I told you how someone managed to register a clone and you put it in your article, then other people might think they could try the same thing."

"I wouldn't dare print anything that would encourage criminal activity. I know people don't believe it, but responsible journalists often don't print everything they know if it's not in the best interest of the public—like the names of sexual-assault victims. If you tell me something is off the record, then I can't print it."

"How do you like your coffee? We have mild to dark roast, and both cream and sugar."

Extracting this last tidbit of information called for the big guns. She gave Jodie a slow smile. "I like it bold and sweet."

Jodie's face reddened again as she selected the appropriate coffee. "I hate to disappoint a woman as attractive as you, but truth is I don't have the information you want. I'm just a technology specialist here. The director would be the only person who could tell you about the complaint being investigated, but she's out of the office, and I can guarantee she won't tell you anything."

Okay. Maybe that was coming on a little too strong. "A technology specialist?"

"Yep. If you want to talk about the firewall that protects the registry from hackers, I can bore you all day with that."

Mae smiled. "You've been very helpful anyway and answered a lot of my questions."

She gathered her notes and they walked out to the lobby, where Jodie pulled a business card from her pocket and handed it to Mae. "If you have any more questions, feel free to give me a call. If I don't know the answer, I'll try to find out for you."

"That's very sweet of you."

Jodie shifted her feet and stuck her hands in her pockets. "Sweet enough for you to have dinner with me sometime? Alexandria has a lot of great restaurants. I'd be happy to show you around...since you're new to the area and all."

Mae turned to study her. She was asking for a date, wasn't she? Jody was attractive, but Mae wasn't drawn to her the way she was to Whit. Maybe she just needed to spend more time with Jodie, like she'd spent time with Whit. Perhaps her sudden attraction to a woman needed broader research. Big Mae did say you should look at the whole litter before you pick a pup.

❖

It was a very productive day. It was only two o'clock when Mae returned to Opelousas, so she still had time to interview two landowners who had already sold options on their farms, and she talked to the third on the phone. Clinton knew all his neighbors within five miles either way and easily had put names to two hints Jean Paul had dropped. She found the third by searching recent parish land transactions.

Despite her elation at success, the telltale twinges of menstrual cramps had shown up on her drive back. The aspirin she'd immediately downed had held them at bay, but she was tired now. If she hadn't wanted to see Whit so badly, she would have gone home and curled up in her bed.

She was typing her notes when Clinton and Whit came stomping in from feeding horses. Their presence lifted her flagging spirits. Clinton flopped into his recliner, the pups went straight to their water bowl, and Whit wandered into the kitchen.

"God, what smells so good?"

Mae paused her typing. "There's beef stew in the Crock-Pot."

'We have a Crock-Pot?"

"I found it in the bottom cabinet next to the refrigerator."

"You don't have to cook for us, Mae. You certainly don't have to buy groceries for us either."

"I took the stew meat out of your freezer this morning, and the potatoes and onions out of your pantry. I did buy the carrots, but since I'm planning to eat some of your stew, it's a fair trade."

"Ha. Guess she told you," Clinton said.

"Who asked you, old man?" Whit said, smiling at him.

Mae resumed typing, pleased with the happy banter. Whit obviously had survived yesterday's hangover.

"What'cha working on?"

"I interviewed three landowners who have already signed options to sell their land to the casino-project investors. I'm typing up my notes, but I need the other point of view to balance the story. I really need to talk with a couple of people—not you or Clinton—who don't want to sell."

"Pop probably can give you a few names." Whit lifted the lid of the cooker and the stew's rich aroma filled the house. "We also can talk to the parish management, public-school officials, and local law enforcement to get their perspective on the impact that much development will have on their resources. That should balance out the talk about jobs and money pumped into the economy."

"Oh, I hadn't thought about that. I guess I've got more work to do."

"I'd help you with some of those interviews, but I've got to spend all day in Baton Rouge tomorrow in meetings."

"Not a problem. Do you need me to take Clinton to the track?"

"Thanks. I'll drop him off on my way to Baton Rouge. He's going to hang out with Tyree until I get back."

Mae felt Whit's eyes on her and she glanced up from her laptop. Whit looked so relaxed and happy, she had to stifle the impulse to jump up and wrap her arms around those strong shoulders. Clinton let out a long snore, and they shared a smile.

"It's really nice to come in and smell dinner cooking," Whit said softly. "I feel like we're taking advantage of you."

"No," Mae said quietly so they didn't wake Clinton. "It's hard to cook for one, and I enjoy the dinner company as long as I'm not overstaying my welcome."

Whit's gaze was soft. "Not at all."

Was Whit aware of how much her emotions showed on her expressive face? Probably not.

"When's dinner ready? I'm starving," Clinton said, his impromptu doze abruptly ending. He struggled to climb out of the recliner. "Damn dogs snore so loud, they woke me up."

Whit laughed and shook her head as Mae closed her laptop.

"You just stay right there, Clinton. I'll bring you a bowl of stew and some iced tea," Mae said.

He settled back again. "You'd make a good daughter-in-law."

Whit blinked at him. "Yeah, if you had a son."

Mae ignored Whit's comment. "Why, thank you, Clinton. I happen to think you'd make an excellent father-in-law, too."

The rest of their dinner conversation concerned horses and race times. Raising the Bar's first race would be in less than two weeks. Clinton and Whit were pleased with the jockey they'd been able to hire and excited the racing season was getting close.

Shortly after dinner, Clinton retired for the night, and Mae sat with Whit in the rockers on the front porch while the dogs sniffed around the yard. The nights were cooler, with a hint of Indian summer, and the stars were bright diamonds against a midnight-black sky.

They rocked and enjoyed the night sounds of the crickets and peepers for a while, until Mae could no longer keep quiet.

"So, judging from your condition and what you said when I drove you home Saturday night, I'm guessing your date with Avery didn't go well."

"What exactly did I say?" Whit asked slowly.

"Verbatim? 'Avery's a bitch.'"

Whit chuckled. "I guess I'm more succinct when I'm drunk."

The memory of the kiss made Mae shiver for the millionth time. "You do have a tendency to get right to the point when your guard is down." She turned her gaze on Whit. "You really should consider doing that more often. Not getting drunk, but letting your guard down."

Whit picked at a splinter on the arm of her rocking chair. "I don't think she was intentionally being a bitch. She actually was trying to help, but we just see the world differently." That fact seemed so clear now that she could hardly understand why she hadn't realized it before. "She wanted me to sell the farm and go to work for the casino project so I'd have the money to put Pop in a nursing home."

Mae stopped rocking and sat forward in her chair. The nerve of that woman. "Put Clinton in a nursing home? He's a long way from needing twenty-four-hour care. And, what about *Quarter Track*?"

"She suggested that I hire somebody to run it for me."

"It would be a clear conflict of interest for you to own the magazine and work for the casino project."

Whit pointed at her. "Bingo. I'm the only loud opposing voice out there. If they can bring me into the fold, they'll have clear sailing."

She really didn't care about Avery's politics, but to suggest Whit put her father away so somebody else would take care of him made Mae fume. "I can't believe she thinks you'd just lock Clinton up in a nursing home. He's not some puppy you can dump at the pound, not that I'd ever do that. I hate people who dump their animals at a pound to be killed when they decide they want a baby or they don't want to train them."

Whit chuckled. "Not all dogs come with a trust fund."

Mae stared at her. "Is that what you think of me? That I take care of Rhett just because he has a trust fund?"

"Well, it doesn't hurt. At least it pays for those silly haircuts."

It was irrational, really, the anger that rose up in her. But menstrual cramps were twisting her insides, and it'd been a really long day, and she'd consented to go on a date with a woman she hardly knew, and, damn it, she didn't want to talk about dogs. She just wanted Whit to take her in her arms again and kiss her. But Whit didn't seem to have any inclination to do that. "I'm stung that you think so little of me," she said stiffly.

"You're really upset." Whit looked at her in surprise.

Mae stood and went into the house to get her laptop and notes.

"I was just teasing, really." Whit stood in the doorway, confusion etched on her handsome face.

But Mae's frustration had finally found an outlet, and there was no stopping it. "You just think I'm some little trust-fund rich, straight girl. Well, I'm not. Rhett's trust fund is a measly fifteen thousand a year. Right now, I'm living off ten thousand my grandmother stuffed between the pages of *Gone with the Wind* to hide it from the bankruptcy court. After that's gone, I'll be living off whatever you can pay me and Rhett's dog support." She was gaining momentum so fast, she couldn't have put on the brakes if she'd thought to. "And, who said I was straight?"

Whit sputtered. "You…you had a date with that Broussard guy just the other night."

"And you had a date with a bitch. Does that mean you only date bitches?"

"I, uh—"

"Just so you know, I have a date this Friday night with a woman."

Whit's eyebrows crawled up into the curls that spilled across her forehead. "A woman? What woman?"

"The woman I met today at the Louisiana Quarter Horse Breeders Association office."

"In Alexandria? What were you doing there?"

"I was doing research for an article on the cloning lawsuit."

Whit scowled. "I thought I told you not to waste time on that. That lawsuit isn't going anywhere. The racing people have too much money to allow it to get past the first court hurdle."

"Maybe so, but we can't just ignore it." She pushed past Whit but stopped on the porch. "You shouldn't ignore the rumors at the track."

"There are always rumors at the track. Nobody pays any attention to them."

"Even when they are saying that your colt is a clone?"

"What? That's ridiculous. Somebody's just messing with you."

"Because I'm just a stupid, silly sorority girl? A trust-fund baby who never had to think for herself?"

"No. Mae, no. That's not what I meant. You just don't know these people. Open your eyes. They're just having fun with you."

"No, Whitley. You need to open your eyes and realize what's right in front of you." To her dismay, tears threatened. Damn hormones. She turned away so Whit wouldn't see. Hell, she didn't really see Mae anyway. "Rhett, come. We're going home."

CHAPTER SIXTEEN

"Don't climb an oak tree expecting to find pecans."

Mae was pleasantly surprised when Jodie met her outside a pricey Indian restaurant. No boots and jeans this time. Her dark hair loose around her shoulders, Jodie wore dark-gray trousers and a smoke-gray blouse, with black loafers. The woman knew how to dress up. Mae was relieved that she'd decided against the linen shorts she'd considered wearing and opted for soft camel-colored slacks with a cream shell.

"This is wonderful," she said as she unfolded the cloth napkin and placed it across her lap. "I love Indian food."

Jodie smiled. "You thought I was going to take you to some steak house with big slabs of meat and loud-talking men. Or maybe a seafood restaurant with a noisy Cajun band, right?"

"No."

Jodie raised an eyebrow.

"Okay, maybe." Mae chuckled. "Yes. I do enjoy those restaurants sometimes—especially the seafood and Cajun bands—but this is a nice change from the usual places people take you when they find out you're new to Louisiana."

"Good. That's good." Jodie paused. "You look lovely tonight."

"Thank you. You clean up very well, yourself. Although I think I miss the snakeskin boots."

Jodie laughed and opened her menu to discuss their food choices. In the end, Jodie called the waiter over and asked for a sampler dinner for two. He seemed to know her and immediately nodded his understanding.

"I didn't see that on the menu," Mae said.

"I come here pretty often and recommended them once to cater an Association function, so they allow me some special treatment."

"So, you bring dates here a lot?" She hesitated. "This is a date, isn't it?"

Jodie grinned. "Yes. This is a date. Are you asking me if I date a lot of women?"

Heat rose to Mae's cheeks. "You're certainly attractive enough. I guess I'm curious in a broader sense. Are there a lot of lesbians in Alexandria?"

Jodie shrugged. "Probably not as many as some places, but I have a pretty big circle of friends."

"No steady lover?"

"I wouldn't be in this restaurant with you if I did." Jodie picked up her fork and turned it over. "I lived with a singer for three years. We split about two years ago. She got a great opportunity in New York, and I just couldn't make the move with her. It's hard to keep horses in a New York apartment."

"You have horses?"

"I might be a tech geek, but I work for the Association because I own a small farm and a couple of quarter horses. I ride them in reining competitions. It's sort of a Western version of dressage. Anyway, things just didn't work out for me and the singer."

"I'm sorry if I brought up bad memories."

"No problem. When we got together, I think we both knew it might end up like that. Our interests were too different. But enough about me. Tell me more about you."

They spent the next hour sampling Indian delicacies while Mae regaled Jodie with her experiences living with Big Mae and in a sorority house full of women. Jodie reciprocated by recounting a few horse misadventures, and, afterward, they strolled through downtown Alexandria to walk off their meal. When they arrived at the parking deck where Mae had left her car, she turned to Jodie. They were alone for the moment, and a few missing bulbs dimmed the lighting enough to create an illusion of privacy.

"You're a natural storyteller. I enjoyed tonight," Jodie said, stepping close and taking Mae's hand in hers.

Mae lifted her face to Jodie, inviting more. She had to know if what she'd experienced with Whit was unique. Jodie obliged and brushed her lips against Mae's. It wasn't enough, so she slid her arms around Jodie's neck and deepened the kiss. Then she pulled back and sighed. She dropped her arms and propped her hip against the side of her car.

"Somehow that didn't sound like a 'wow' kind of sigh," Jodie said.

"You're very attractive, and our dinner was wonderful. I had fun, too." She shook her head, groping for the right way to explain.

"But?"

"You're only the second woman I've kissed."

"Ah. And the first?"

"My boss. She was drunk. Otherwise, I'm sure it wouldn't have happened."

"And?"

Mae closed her eyes, reliving Whit's mouth, her tongue sliding against hers. She sighed again.

"Okay, that was a 'wow' sigh."

She opened her eyes. "I don't really know what I'm doing. I didn't know if it was her or if any woman could make me feel that way." She gave Jodie a weak smile. "I'm sorry. I really did have a very nice time tonight."

"So you thought you were straight, but you're rethinking things because your boss kissed you? I mean, you're certainly not butch, but I didn't read you as straight. I've had plenty of straight women flirt with me for fun, and it doesn't feel the same."

"I don't think I was anything until she kissed me." She pondered what Jodie said. "Exactly how is it not the same?"

Jodie shrugged. "I think scientists are just figuring that out. Human sexuality is complicated. I read that recent studies indicate the scent of pheromones has something to do with it. Maybe it's unconscious body language. Nobody knows for sure yet."

"This is all so confusing. I mean I've dated men and even had sex with men, but I've never met one that I wanted, needed to be around."

"But that's the way your boss makes you feel," Jodie stated.

She covered her eyes with her hand. "God, I hope you don't feel like I just used you. I meant it when I said I had a good time."

Jodie leaned against the car alongside Mae and took her hand again. "Dating is the same, no matter which team you play for. You date to have a good time and find out how you might feel about the other person you just met. That's what we did. Who knows what decides chemistry between two people? It doesn't matter if it's a man and a woman or two men or two women. Attraction is about a lot more than gender." She squeezed Mae's hand. "I hope we can be friends. Your sorority stories are really funny."

Mae squeezed back, relieved that Jodie wasn't hurt or angry. "I'd love that. Thank you for not being upset with me."

"I'm not upset. In fact, I'd like to give you a 'friendly' memento of our date."

"A memento?"

Jodie dug into her pocket and pulled out a snakeskin change purse about the size of a credit card. She held it out to Mae. "Since you liked my boots so much, I got you this. Inside is the business card of the guy who made the boots and this little wallet."

"That's so sweet." She stood on her tiptoes to peck Jodie on the cheek. "You're sweet."

Jodie smiled and began to back away. "Call me next time you're coming to Alexandria. We can have lunch or dinner…as friends."

She waved. "I'd like that very much."

❖

Whit propped her shoulder against a support post of the Evangeline backstretch barn's overhang and absently kicked at it. A hollow restlessness had been churning her gut over the past ten days. She kicked the post again. The solid wood meeting her booted foot drained off a tiny, very tiny bit of her frustration, so she kicked it again. She couldn't remember when she'd last slept soundly, and she could hardly stand still now. She blamed it on the fact that Raising the Bar would run his first race tonight. She began a rhythmic thump of boot versus post.

"Stop that racket," Pop growled behind her. He sat in a camp chair next to Bar's stall door, his head resting against the barn and his hands folded calmly in his lap. "You're getting on my last nerve." He pulled a pouch of Red Man from his pocket, extracted a generous plug, then stuffed it in his cheek. "I'm hungry. Haven't had a decent meal in more than a week."

"What are you talking about? I've been feeding you."

"Leftovers and sandwiches. That ain't eating."

"If we win tonight, we'll all go out for a big, juicy steak."

"Mae, too? I want Mae to come."

"Maybe she's got other things to do." Whit kicked the post again, hard this time. Mae went on a date with a woman. The battle between her curiosity and not wanting to know about this other woman Mae found attractive was confusing. Maybe they were out together tonight. "She's probably got a date or something. It's Friday night, you know."

"I don't think so."

"You don't, huh." Whit turned on him, her nerves snapping. "Why don't you just tell me what you *do* think?"

"I think you two had a spat or something."

"Why on earth would you think that?"

"'Cause you've been acting like a sore-assed duck swimming in salt water, and Mae ain't been around."

Damn. Whit was happy Pop had seemed less confused after the most recent adjustment to his medication, but she'd prefer that he stay out of her business. "She's been working from home. No need for her to come out to the farm when we're here at the track."

"She ain't even come out here to the track to see us."

"She's busy." Busy with that woman, probably. Or maybe with that Broussard guy.

"Shows what you know. She's been feeling poorly."

"What?" Mae hadn't told her that she was ill.

"If you'd taken a minute to talk to her, you'd know that."

"We've been talking—well, emailing. She's been doing interviews and writing her next article. She didn't say anything about being sick."

Pop snorted and spit tobacco juice into a paper cup that once held coffee. "Said she was in bed for two days last week. You didn't know because you probably didn't ask."

"How could I know I needed to ask?"

"God almighty, you're even dumber than I was, and I don't know how your mother put up with me." Pop glared at her. "That girl has been around every day, either at the farm or the track, ever since you asked her to come work for you."

"I didn't ask. She talked me into hiring her."

"Will you shut up and listen, for once?" He spit again.

Whit eyed him. "I'm listening."

"She's been around every day and then, all of a sudden, she ain't around at all. That should tell you something's wrong. Hell, I knew something was wrong the minute I talked to her on Monday. She sounded right pitiful when I called to see if she would come out and cook us some real food."

Her heart raced in sudden panic. Could Mae be hiding some serious illness? She looked perfectly healthy. Really healthy. Images of Mae's cheeks coloring with a rosy flush when she was excited, her eyes bright with amusement, her smooth, gliding stride flashed through Whit's thoughts. Mae couldn't be too sick. "Why didn't you tell me? What if she needed somebody to take her to the doctor?"

"She said not to worry. It was just the usual female problems." Pop eyed her. "She was well enough to keep her date in Alexandria last Friday night, so that ain't what's keeping her away this week."

"Figures." Whit frowned and kicked the post one more time. "Wait. She told you about that?"

"She said she had a real good time."

Whit snapped without thinking. "What? Are you two girlfriends now? Do you call each other every day to gossip?"

Pop rose from the chair, slow but steady on his feet, to grab her by the scruff of her neck and give her a firm shake. "I might be losing my faculties half the time, but I'm still your father, missy."

She hung her head. "Sorry, Pop. It must be the race tonight making me all jumpy."

"I don't think it's the race at all." He shook her again to stop her protest. "My mind's not completely gone. I know what's riding on this colt. But that's not what's eating at you today."

Whit took a deep breath and let her shoulders slump. "What is it then? You tell me, because I don't know. I just know I've felt lately like I'm gonna crawl out of my skin."

"I think you miss having Mae around even more than I do. I think you're sweet on her, but you won't admit it to yourself because you think you're still hung up on that blonde."

"Avery and I are done."

"Then there ain't nothing standing in your way. You need to wine and dine that pretty young Mae."

"I didn't say I was interested in Mae. I'm her boss, Pop. That would be sexual harassment."

"It ain't harassment if she wants you to ask her."

"This is ridiculous. I've got to be twelve or fourteen years older than she is. I'm not even sure she likes girls."

"She said her date was with a woman." His tone dared her to deny it. "And she didn't cook that peach cobbler two weeks ago for me. I told her I don't like peaches, but you do."

Whit shifted uneasily, then kicked the post again.

Pop exploded. "For God's sake, quit kicking that damned post and go get Mae before we have to start getting the colt ready for the race."

There was nothing to do but fess up. "I can't. She's mad at me. We had an argument. At least I think we did."

"You don't know?"

"Well, I said something teasing that she took wrong, and before I knew what was happening, she'd chewed my head off and stormed out the door." She thought about it a moment. "But now that you told me she, uh, wasn't feeling well, it was probably just hormones more than anything I said."

Pop nodded and spit for emphasis. "Then hitch up your wagon and go get her. I didn't raise you to be a coward."

She closed her eyes and sighed. She needed to put things right. Seeing Mae didn't scare her. It was why she was so desperate to see her that was frightening.

Chapter Seventeen

"You can't shoe a running horse."

Whit knocked on the door to Mae's apartment and waited. Pop might not have raised her to be a coward, but she sure felt as scared as a dog with her tail tucked between her legs. She'd had to drive all the way to the farm to get the address, and she'd sat in her truck outside Mae's residence for at least ten minutes, trying to figure out what to say. She still didn't know when the door swung open.

"Whit!" Mae was breath-stealing in simple worn jeans and a red V-neck sweater. Her dark hair lay like silk against the soft cashmere covering her shoulders.

"Hi." Whit swallowed and cleared her throat, hoping the words would come to her. She shuffled her feet.

"Oh, where are my manners? Come in." Mae stepped back and waved her inside. "Was the story I sent you that bad?"

"What? The story was fine. I mean, I made a few editing changes, but overall, it was fine. Why'd you ask that?"

"Well, I thought maybe it was so bad that you had to come by in person to sort it out."

"No. I, uh…Bar's first race is today and Pop sent me…I mean, I came to get you because you shouldn't miss it."

Mae stared and chewed her lip.

"Listen, if I said something…I'm not really sure what I said… but I obviously upset you before, and I'm sorry…for whatever I said wrong." It was a lame, totally lame apology. In fact, she had a sudden déjà vu moment, only she was the one listening to a half-hearted apology from Avery. She had really wanted Avery to understand how she'd hurt her feelings. Otherwise, the apology was frivolous. "Okay, you're right. We can't ignore writing something about the cloning lawsuit. And, if rumors are circulating that my colt is a clone, then not writing about the issue will only add fuel to the impression that we have something to hide."

"Okay." Mae's expression was still uncertain.

"I'm not saying you can't work from home if you want to, but, uh, Ellie misses Rhett and Pop hates my cooking, or lack of it, and he's been complaining since we finished off the leftover beef stew you put in the freezer."

"Poor Clinton." Mae appeared to seriously ponder this situation, but her eyes were alight with amusement. "I have to admit Rhett's been moping around, too."

"Will you come with me to the track? If Bar wins, we're going out to get a big juicy steak to celebrate."

"You mean *when* he wins."

Relief washed through Whit and she grinned. "Absolutely. When he wins."

❖

"You're second from the rail and he hates the rail, so if you're out front and there's room to drift out, let him." Whit walked alongside, giving instructions to the jockey, Tommy, as Pop led Raising the Bar to the track from the paddock where the horses were saddled. "He's got enough speed to make up the extra distance."

"Whatever you say, Boss." The tiny man perched on Bar was a hundred and twelve pounds of pure muscle. He adjusted his helmet and pulled the chinstrap tight under his jaw.

"This is his first race, so I don't want to see you go for the whip unless his attention drifts, which it won't. This guy is really competitive, but I want to find out what he can do more than I want to win."

The jockey looked doubtful. "He's pretty laid back."

"Don't let that fool you. When that gate opens, you better hold onto your seat."

Tommy nodded.

Whit knew he would do exactly as she asked because he'd be paid a flat fee for this minor race. Jockeys only got a percentage of the winnings in the major races. Tommy didn't ride in a lot of minor races because of that, but he got his start as a jock on Casey horses, so he owed Pop this favor.

"Just a couple of taps if you think it's necessary. I don't want to risk injury or strain this early in the season, so don't take any chances or push him too hard." Whit was more nervous than the horse. She wasn't afraid of losing. She was afraid of an injury that would end Raising the Bar's racing season and leave her with no chance to save Joie de Vivre.

Pop unclipped the lead clipped to Bar's bridle and stepped back to allow room for the track's mounted outrider who would accompany Bar and Tommy to the starting gate. He gave the jockey a nod. "Just let him run, Tommy."

"Yes, sir, Mr. Casey."

It took all of Whit's patience to walk at Pop's pace, rather than run, to the owners' area where Mae was holding seats for them. When they finally made it to their seats, Bar was the next to be loaded into the gate. Being the gentleman that he was, Pop motioned Whit down the row first, seating her next to Mae.

"I'm so nervous," Mae said. She held out her hand. "Feel how cold my hands are."

"I should have told you to bring a jacket," Whit said. Although the days were still warm, the evenings had turned cool since they were well into October. "I'm just the opposite. I'm about to burn up with nerves." She peeled off her quilted vest and held it up for Mae to slide into. When they sat, she took Mae's hand in hers without thinking and wrapped it in her warmer hands as they turned their attention to the track.

Bar went quietly into the starting gate, and Whit dropped Mae's hand to lift her small binoculars to her eyes. She watched Tommy arrange his goggles and check to his right to see when the last horse was loaded. Bar's ears twitched and he shifted in the narrow chute. Tommy crouched forward and his lips moved. Was he praying for a good race or talking to Bar? Pop moved restlessly in his seat, his only indication that he was nervous, too.

"Don't take your eyes off the track," Whit said to Mae. "It's only a short quarter-mile sprint, and it'll be over in about twenty seconds."

The last horse loaded and Whit tensed. Mae's hand had dropped to Whit's thigh and her fingernails dug into Whit's jeans. The claxon sounded and the track announcer needlessly shouted, "They're off!"

The horses burst from the gate, Bar and two others abreast in an early lead. Bar's ears flickered as if he was evaluating this new sensation of running in a pack of ten horses.

The announcer's chant began. "It's Raising the Bar, Sipping Corona, and Jet Blue Black out front early."

As he continued his litany of each horse's position, Whit watched Sipping Corona drift left, crowding Bar against the rail. Bar's ears laid back and Tommy crouched farther over his neck to urge him forward. Bar pumped his powerful hindquarters in a burst of speed that pushed him clear.

"It's Raising the Bar taking the lead, with Jet Blue Black keeping pace and Sipping Corona dropping to third."

Bar drifted outward, allowing Jet Blue Black to gain ground as they matched strides.

"It's Raising the Bar and Jet Blue Black all alone out front, with Dash Away moving up to third and Sipping Corona fading to fourth."

Several shoulders off the rail, Tommy straightened Bar out and pushed his hands forward along his neck, giving him free rein. Bar jumped ahead like Jet Blue Black was standing still. Whit and Mae sprang to their feet. "Go, go, go!"

Raising the Bar crossed the finish line a full body length ahead, and Mae jumped into Whit's arms. Whit lifted her up in a hug and swung her around to deposit her back on her feet next to Pop.

Mae hugged Pop and gave him a quick kiss on his stubbly cheek and then turned back to hug Whit again. Mae's body was warm against hers. Her eyes were shining pools drawing her in, drowning her. With absolutely no thought, only reflex, she lowered her head and pressed her lips against Mae's. Whit blinked when she drew back. Her lips tingled and her heart thudded.

"Go," Mae said, her gaze soft. "I'll walk down with Clinton. You go see about your horse."

She hesitated only a second before climbing over seats to get around them and sprint down to the track.

❖

"I know she's here. Her truck is parked out front." It was after noon on Sunday, and Mae hadn't seen Whit since Bar's race on Friday night. She'd checked in the barn before she came inside, but Whit was nowhere to be found.

Clinton grinned up from his recliner and turned the sound down on the movie he was watching. "Running like a scared rabbit."

"Clinton." She flopped onto the sofa in exasperation. Ellie and Rhett jumped up to bracket her in a canine show of sympathy. "Somehow I don't think you're helping."

"She kissed you right there in front of God and everybody. Don't think I've ever seen her actually kiss anybody before."

Mae ducked her head to hide her embarrassed smile. He obviously was happy about it, and she wanted to be happy, too. But Whit had done a one-eighty and avoided her like the plague since.

After the race, she'd pressed a hundred-dollar bill in Mae's hand and told her to take Tyree, Clinton, and herself out for a big steak. Mae protested, but Whit said she had to stay to take care of the colt, and Clinton needed to eat before it got too late. When they returned to the backstretch with Whit's dinner in a take-out box, Clinton was exhausted. So, Whit asked Tyree to drop Mae off and drive Clinton out to the farm and stay with him overnight. She had done everything possible to avoid looking at Mae, keeping her eyes on the take-out box and muttering a quick "thanks" when Mae thrust it at her.

"When did she come home?" After the kiss on Friday, Whit hadn't answered Mae's calls or her text messages all day Saturday.

"Sometime last night after I went to bed," Clinton said. "She was here when I got up and Tyree had gone to take his mama to church."

"That's sweet of him," Mae said absently. She turned to look down the hallway, wondering if Whit was still in her bedroom. Had she stayed out until early this morning?

She could feel Clinton watching her as he rapped his fingers lightly against the arm of his recliner. "She's not back there."

"She wasn't here when I called yesterday and she wasn't at the track either."

"I told her you'd been looking for her."

"What did she say?"

"Said she went to Baton Rouge for something." Clinton frowned and scratched at the stubble on his jaw. "I can't remember what." The tapping of his hand against the chair picked up speed. "Tyree's gone with Bernice. Their church is having dinner on the grounds." It seemed to be the only thing he could dredge up.

Mae covered his hand with hers. "That's okay. It's not important." He seemed relieved to be let off the hook. "Do you know where she is now?"

He rested his head against the back of the chair and closed his eyes. After a minute or two, Mae thought he'd drifted off to sleep. His deeply lined, weathered face was still handsome, and she resisted the impulse to smooth down a lock of white hair that stuck out at an odd angle. When he opened his eyes, his gaze was hazy, his mind somewhere else.

"I was training a colt once that she took quite a fancy to. He was midnight-black, followed her around like a dog. Then the fella that owned him decided to ship him out to California to race. Whit cried like a baby the day they came for him."

His fingers drummed a tense staccato beat against the chair's worn leather. "I warned her not to get attached because he wasn't our colt, but she didn't listen." His eyes grew watery. "She ran off, and when it got dark, Celeste started to worry. I looked for her everywhere, but no Whit." He returned his attention to the television where a crew of young boys was driving a herd of cows hundreds of miles. "John Wayne dies in this movie."

She realized he wasn't ignoring her question but was sifting through things he could remember for an answer.

"Where did you finally find her?"

Clinton smiled and slapped his hand against the chair. "At the south pond, huddled in the dark under the big oak. It's a pretty good walk through the yearling pasture and over the rise. That's her thinking place."

She grasped his restless hand and squeezed. "Thank you." She stood, but uncertainty filled her. Would she be intruding? Should she just wait and come to work in the morning like nothing happened? Like Whit hadn't kissed her?

"She's different since she moved back from Baton Rouge—spooks easier than a whitetail during hunting season," Clinton said, quirking an eyebrow at her.

Mae winked at Clinton. "Wish me luck. Big Mae used to say it's hard to shoe a running horse."

❖

When she topped the rise, a horse stood saddled next to a huge oak tree. The pond was on the other side of the tree, and she suspected Whit was, too.

The mare nickered as she approached, giving her away, but no one stirred behind the tree's thick trunk. She squared her shoulders and stepped around it.

Whit sat on a large gnarled root, long legs stretched toward the pond. She wore knee-high leather boots over well-worn, doe-colored riding breeches and a polo shirt that brought out the green in her ever-changing eyes. The worn newsboy cap she'd favored since she cut her hair was pulled low over her brow, her eyes avoiding Mae's.

She had been tracking Whit for two days with single-minded determination, and she'd spent hours in one-sided conversation with herself, rehearsing exactly what she would say. But now, her words stuck in her throat. The speech she'd planned flew out of her head like a covey of quail flushed from their thicket. "Hi."

Whit glanced up. "Hey."

"I went to the track yesterday, looking for you."

"I was in Baton Rouge all day."

"Visiting Avery?" She grimaced. She hadn't meant to say that. It sounded like whining, petty jealousy. Damn it, she was jealous even though she had no claim on Whit, no right to question her.

Whit shook her head. "I closed on my condo last week. The buyers wanted some of the furniture, but I had to meet the movers to show them what needed to go in storage."

"I see." Hope swelled in her. This was good. Whit hadn't run to Avery, as she'd feared. Still, what she wanted to say froze in her throat, so she began to ramble. "Well, since I didn't find you, I poked around and found another feature story for the magazine."

Whit picked up a small stone and threw it into the water. "You don't have to work seven days a week, Mae. Hell, I haven't even paid you for working five days a week yet. We need to talk about that, though. Bar won a thirty-thousand-dollar purse Friday night. We need to settle on a salary for you so I can figure your back pay."

"We agreed to do that when *Quarter Track*'s advertising revenue starts pouring in. That's not until the end of the month. Your winnings should go back into your horse business."

Whit finally looked at her, her gaze sharp. "You've got to eat, Mae, and pay your bills just like the rest of us. Don't forget that when you were pissed at me two weeks ago, you told me exactly how much money you have."

"Huh. I must have forgotten to tell you about the trifecta I won on Bar's race."

Whit raised an eyebrow and Mae grinned.

"Five thousand dollars. Can you believe it? I forgot about the ticket until Saturday. You should have seen the happy dance I did when the cashier counted it out in one-hundred-dollar bills and put it in my hand." She demonstrated a short Irish jig.

Whit shook her head and chuckled, the icy tension between them finally melting away. "How could you forget about a winning trifecta ticket?"

Mae stared at her feet and kicked at a rock sticking out of the dirt while she summoned her courage. "Well, I had something else on my mind." She gestured toward the tree. "Can I sit down? It was a long walk out here."

"Since you're apparently determined to disturb my peace and quiet, you might as well pull up a root and sit." Her tone was teasing, but it did little to soothe Mae's nerves as she sat next to her. Whit tossed another pebble into the water, so Mae picked one up and tossed it, too.

"Are we going to talk about it?"

Whit sighed. "Talk about what?" Her tone said she knew perfectly well what Mae meant.

Mae turned to face her. "The elephant in the room. The kiss that made me forget I had a winning trifecta ticket."

Whit's face reddened and she pulled her cap even lower. "I need to apologize for that. I was just excited about the race. It was a one-time, heat-of-the-moment thing. I promise it won't happen again."

"You mean a second-time thing." She wasn't going to let Whit off the hook that easily.

Whit stood to put space between them, shoved her hands in her pockets, and stared out at the pond. "What are you talking about?"

"It wasn't the first time you've kissed me."

Whit turned to her when Mae stood. "Yes, it was." She frowned. "Maybe you've confused me with your date last weekend."

"I did kiss Jodie, but it wasn't anything like kissing you." Mae stepped closer. "There's no way I'd confuse you with her."

She watched as realization dawned on Whit's face. "I kissed you when I was drunk."

"Yes."

Whit covered her face with her hands and groaned. "Oh, God. Tell me I didn't attack you."

"Well, you did pin me against the wall and kiss me very thoroughly."

"Oh, Christ."

"Yes. It seems to happen only when your defenses are down." She gently pried Whit's hands from her face and held them while she waited for Whit to meet her gaze. "So, I'm thinking that you either kiss any available person when you're drunk or win a big race *or*—and I like this scenario better—you find me irresistible, which means I've got a good chance at being kissed again."

Whit's mouth twitched. "You...you want me...to kiss you again?"

Mae blinked slowly, her eyes moving to Whit's mouth. "Bad enough to track you here and beg," she whispered.

Whit's long fingers were soft, her palm warm against her cheek, and Mae closed her eyes.

"Mae."

Whit breathed her name like a benediction, but the feeling that flared in Mae's belly was completely carnal. The tentative brush of Whit's lips against hers was a delicious appetizer, but Mae was hungry, starving to be thoroughly devoured the way Whit had kissed her the first time. She threaded her fingers into Whit's soft curls, refusing to release her until Whit let go and kissed her with the wild abandon that made Mae's heart race and her insides somersault.

"Wow." Mae blinked to clear her suddenly fuzzy vision. "That's the kiss I remember."

Whit grasped Mae's hands but stepped back, and the October chill replaced the warmth of her lean body against Mae's. Her eyes were bright with desire yet dark with doubt. "There are so many reasons why this is a bad idea."

Mae entwined her fingers with Whit's. She wasn't going to let her run away again. "I can think of a few reasons why this is an excellent idea."

Whit groaned but held just as tight to Mae's hands. "You're my employee."

"Technically, I'm not. You haven't paid me. Besides, nepotism is a Southern tradition."

"You're straight."

Mae wanted to roll her eyes. "Who said I was straight?"

"You date guys."

"Didn't you ever date boys?"

"Not after I kissed my first woman."

Mae closed the space between them, pressing against Whit's warmth and tilting her head back to stare into Whit's eyes. "I've never felt what I do when you kiss me. You absolutely melt my insides." She freed one hand to pull Whit down for another scorching kiss.

Whit's chest heaved when they finally broke apart. "Mae, you don't know the first thing about lesbians."

"I wasn't aware they came with instructions." She wrapped her arms around Whit's waist. She just couldn't stop touching her. "I figured I'd just follow my instincts." She rubbed her groin against

Whit's, enjoying the shudder she evoked. "When you charged out of that bathroom nearly naked and collapsed on your bed, my instincts screamed for me to tear off my clothes and jump you." She chuckled at Whit's groan. "But you were drunk as a sailor and passed out cold. It took a lot of restraint to cover you up and leave you to sleep it off."

"I need to sit down," Whit said, gently breaking Mae's hold and moving back to the tree.

Mae sat beside her and looped her arm in Whit's to press against her shoulder. "I'm a big girl, Whit. I'm perfectly capable of making intelligent decisions about who I date, who I sleep with."

Whit pulled off her cap and resettled it on her head. "A lot of lesbian relationships don't work out, Mae. They burn hot and bright, then two or three years later—boom, lesbian bed death hits or you just don't make time for each other. Then, by your fourth anniversary, you're selling the house and battling for custody of the pets."

"That sounds like a lot of relationships these days. I don't think lesbians have a patent on it."

Whit shook her head. "Maybe not. But we have the same pressures of heterosexual couples—money, in-laws, jobs—plus the stress of having to be guarded around those in society who disapprove of us. It can be dangerous to be gay and heartbreaking when you lose family and friends over it."

"I don't think Clinton will mind, and he's the only one who counts." Mae's face and other parts heated as she stroked her fingers along Whit's bare forearm. "I don't even know what lesbian bed death is. I can't imagine not wanting to touch you."

"You say that now, but will you feel that way six months from now? A year from now?" Whit captured Mae's hand and sighed. "I'm too old and too tired for a fling, Mae."

Mae withdrew her arm and stood. "Is that what you think I want? A casual fling?" She stared down at Whit. "I may not be a rich, beautiful, high-powered lawyer, but I've had a few opportunities recently for flings with people I wouldn't have to chase all over Louisiana and beg to kiss me."

Whit jumped to her feet and caught Mae's arm as she tried to turn away. "Wait. Geez, that didn't come out right." She blew out a breath and stared up at the sky. "For some reason, my relationships just don't work out. I'm doing something wrong, but I'm not sure what."

"Well, at least you have a track record. I've never even had what I'd call a relationship with anyone. How does it usually happen?" She folded her fingers around Whit's again.

Whit's laugh was a harsh bark. "Well, lesbians usually meet in a bar or at a party and end up in bed on the first or second date."

"Then we'll do things differently. Where I come from, a girl likes to be thoroughly courted."

"You mean like flowers and candy?" Whit smiled at the idea.

"Flowers are good, but no candy. My waistline doesn't need it."

Whit placed her hands on Mae's hips. "Your waistline and everything else are perfect."

Mae returned her smile. "Compliments are good, too." She cocked her head. "By my estimation, this is our third date."

"Third?" Whit's brow wrinkled.

"Yes. And, I've got to tell you, there's room for improvement."

"Improvement?"

"Well, our first date started out with a really hot kiss, but ended with you passed out cold. Our second date was better. It started out with an apology, and then we watched Bar win his first race and you kissed me. Again, the date went downhill after the kiss because you started avoiding me and I had to catch a ride home with Tyree."

"And you still want to date me?"

"Third time's a charm. The kissing today, as always, has been wonderful. We just need to work on what happens after."

"Any suggestions?"

"I think we should go back to the house and I'll cook my special five-alarm chili for you and Clinton. After dinner, we can sit in the front-porch swing and talk for a while before you walk me to my car and give me one more of those delicious kisses before I drive home."

Whit nodded. "I have a suggestion to add."

"Please, by all means."

"How about a short riding lesson on our way back to the house?"

Mae gasped. "Really? You'll teach me?" She hugged Whit, then jumped back. "Oh, my God. I'd love that."

Whit grinned and led Mae over to the patiently waiting mare. "Riding is sort of like dating. It feels awkward at first when you're trying to remember how to hold the reins, balance your weight, and guide the horse, but you have to stop thinking about it and just let it happen—" She stopped midsentence, her face clouding as quickly as a summer storm. "Crap."

"What? What's the matter?"

Whit shook her head and stared at her feet. "I don't know if I can do this, Mae. I'm tired of always coming up short. I don't know if I can, if I want to risk trying again."

Whit obviously wasn't talking about the riding lesson, and she wanted to slap Avery Perrault for hurting this gentle woman. Instead, she curled her hand around Whit's neck and brushed her thumb along her cheek. "Has every horse Clinton trained been a big winner?"

Whit frowned. "No. Pop's trained a lot who did well enough, but never one that's taken the Breeders Futurity."

"Has he quit training horses because he hasn't found that big winner yet?"

Whit slowly met her gaze. "No. Pop's not a quitter."

She kissed her softly. "I'm placing my bet on those strong Casey genes. I don't think his daughter's a quitter either."

CHAPTER EIGHTEEN

"Always dance with the one who brought you."

Mae held tight to Whit's hand as she led them through the crowd. The bar reminded her of the warehouse-sized lesbian hot spot her sorority sisters had taken her to in Atlanta. Here, however, clientele was mixed—young and mature, men and women, gay and straight—but it was predominately gay and lesbian, with a brace of beefy bouncers to make sure everyone played nice as the liquor flowed and sweaty bodies filled the dance floor.

"White wine?"

"Yes. Thank you."

Over the past three weeks, Whit had proven to be an attentive suitor, never failing to consider and remember Mae's preferences. Dating a mature woman was worlds better than her experiences with frat boys or even playing "beard" to one of her gay friends.

They passed their days at the track, watching Bar win every race he entered, or at the farm, working together on the website and magazine. Most of their evenings had been spent sharing dinner with Clinton, then enjoying some quality time in the front-porch swing, but Whit had taken Mae out to dinner or a movie several times. They even spent a wonderful evening at Robbie's restaurant. Robbie had claimed, of course, that he wasn't surprised when Mae showed up with a female date, and when they had said their good nights, he tugged her into a tight hug and whispered his approval of Whit.

If she had any complaint at all, it was that Whit was taking the "courting" ritual a little too literally. The excruciating pace of their physical relationship was driving Mae insane. One more unfulfilled make-out session and Mae was sure she'd spontaneously combust.

So, she had jumped at the invitation to go dancing in Baton Rouge while Clinton entertained his visiting cousin, Henry, over the weekend. She planned to lubricate Whit with liquor, tease her with lots of sexy dancing, and then whisk her off to a luxurious room she had secretly reserved at the Marriott a few blocks away.

"Hey, Casey! Over here."

Mae tugged on Whit's sleeve and pointed toward a table full of women waving wildly in their direction. "I think you have a fan club over in the corner," she said as Whit slipped a glass into her hand.

Whit grinned. "Some of my old softball buddies. Do you mind? We don't have to sit with them, but I'd like to say hello."

"I'd love to meet your friends." Mae felt oddly exuberant and a little nervous as Whit took her hand again. They were about to go public as a couple. God, what if Whit's friends didn't like her?

Broad grins greeted them, and several of the women who weren't trapped in seats against the wall stood to give Whit enthusiastic back-slapping hugs.

Whit drew her close and pointed to each one around the table in turn. "This is Dale, Amanda, Janet, Gail, Sue and Christie. Guys, this is Mae."

"Damn, Casey. You've traded up," Sue said as she offered the only empty chair to Mae. Christie snagged a chair from the table next to them for Whit, and they both sat.

"Thanks. I think so."

Mae's face warmed when Whit grinned and winked at her, but she smiled at Sue. "It's nice of you to say so. I've met Avery and she's very attractive."

The group looked surprised.

"Attractive in a stick-up-the-butt sort of way," Sue said, moving to dodge Gail's swat to the back of her head. "What? You know it's true."

"Yes, we all know that, but you didn't have to say it. Mae's probably thinking we were all raised in the barn with you."

Mae immediately liked Sue, but Gail was right. Public critique of the ex-girlfriend was very poor manners, so she demurred. "I don't really know Avery." She winked back at Whit. "Still, her loss is my gain."

"To Avery then," Sue said, holding her beer aloft. They clinked their glasses together and laughed.

"I like your haircut," Janet said. "You look like the old Whit we once knew and loved."

It was Whit's turn to redden. "Thanks." She stared down at her drink. "I'm sorry I've neglected you guys."

Gail patted her hand. "We're just glad you're back." She turned to Mae. "As we say in Louisiana, are your people from around here?"

Mae smiled. "No, but we ask the same thing where I'm from in Georgia. I moved to Opelousas a few months ago, and I've been writing stories for Whit's magazine."

"Are you a horsewoman, too?" Dale asked.

"No, but I'm learning. Whit's giving me riding lessons."

"I'll bet." Sue smirked.

"Will you shut up?" Gail scowled at Sue. "Since you can't seem to keep those feet out of your mouth, why don't you use them to go get us another drink before Whit pours hers over your head?"

"Yes, dear."

Mae chuckled at Sue's antics as she pretended to grumble when the others put in their drink orders, too. "Does she need some help bringing all that back?"

Whit shook her head. "She'll return with two or three young waitresses in tow, carrying it all for her."

"Well, I need to visit the ladies' room, so I'll check to see if she needs help on my way back." She stood, then bent to touch her lips to Whit's. "Visit with your friends. I think they've missed you. I'll be right back if the line isn't long."

❖

The restroom was large and the line to the toilets fairly short, but the row of sinks was crowded with women washing their hands or checking their hair and makeup. She felt someone watching her as she rinsed the soap from her fingers and was surprised when she looked up to meet Avery's gaze in the mirror before her.

"I saw you come in with Whit," Avery said when Mae turned to face her.

Mae's shoulders tightened. "I'm sorry. We didn't see *you*." Something like sadness passed briefly across Avery's fine features, and, God only knows why, she felt compelled to offer a gentle clarification. "I'm sure Whit would have wanted to say hello."

"I'm not so sure she would have. We didn't part on the best terms last time I saw her." Avery cleared her throat. "Can we talk for a minute?"

Mae's steel magnolia went on high alert—curious but ready to parry and strike if necessary. She'd lived her entire life with Big Mae, then spent years in a sorority house with a hundred other women. She had a full set of sharp verbal weapons in her arsenal and knew how to use them. She didn't trust Avery, but she wasn't afraid of her either. She held Avery's gaze in an unwavering challenge to let her know that. "Sure."

Avery inclined her head, a silent acknowledgement of Mae's worthiness on the feminine battlefield, and then led her to a less crowded, quieter spot in the dark hallway outside the restroom.

"I don't know how much you know about Whitley's situation."

Avery waited for Mae to respond to the apparent request for information, but instinct told Mae to hold her cards close. She simply raised a questioning eyebrow for Avery to continue.

"Well, I offered her a job—a really good financial opportunity—when I saw her last."

Mae nodded slightly, indicating she knew about it. "Whit already has a business and a training farm to run."

"That's just it. I know she manages well enough on the income from the website, but that was before she hired you. Now she has an…employee…to support, and she's not going to have the farm much longer."

She narrowed her eyes. She didn't miss the catty inference that she was a "kept" woman, under the guise of an employee at *Quarter Track*. "Whit will not sell Joie de Vivre as long as Clinton is alive."

"She's not going to have a choice," Avery said, her eyes darting to check who might be standing nearby and hear them. "Clinton took out a loan to stay afloat and put up the farm as collateral. I'm pretty sure the people holding the note on the farm are backing the casino project. If she doesn't give in and sell, they'll just take it from her."

Mae's stomach dropped. Jean Paul must have been telling the truth when he said Clinton was in debt. Was Whit really in danger of losing the farm? She struggled, but managed to keep her expression even. "I'm sure Whit can manage her own affairs without your help or selling her soul to work for your father's friends." She said it with more bravado than she felt and implied that she knew more than she really did. But it worked.

Avery slumped against the wall and her shoulders sagged. "Just because Whit and I didn't work out doesn't mean I don't care about her. Please talk to her. I don't want to see her and Clinton homeless. I don't want to see her hurt."

"That's between you and Whit. I don't think I should get involved." She wanted to believe Avery, but Big Mae was in her head, reminding her that the cruelest traps are baited with the sweetest honey. "I can tell her you're here and see if she'll talk to you."

Avery shook her head. "I've got a late meeting. I was about to leave when I saw you come in." She hesitated, then grasped Mae's forearm in a quick, gentle squeeze. "I don't want to spoil Whit's evening, but think about talking to her tomorrow."

Mae watched Avery disappear into the crowd and, for a moment, wished for a time when her biggest problem was what to wear to a sorority rush party. Then she thought about what Margaret Mitchell's heroine would have done. She gave a firm nod, her decision made. She would think about this tomorrow. Nothing was going to sidetrack her plans for this evening.

❖

The music changed to a thumping oldie disco tune, and Whit held out her hand when Mae returned to the table. "Dance?"

"I'd love to."

Whit was mesmerized by the sway of Mae's hips. She danced with a wild abandon she would have never suspected from a highbred debutante. In fact, she rarely thought of her in those terms any more. Mae was intelligent and sweet and treated everybody she met with the same respect, whether it was the guy mucking Bar's stall or that pompous Michael Dupree.

She closed her eyes and moved to the throb of the music. God, she loved to dance, and Mae was a fantastic partner. They were on their third song and Mae showed no sign of faltering. Avery never seemed to be able to let herself relax enough to enjoy dancing. She usually begged off after one dance, saying she might perspire and spoil her makeup. Mae's skin was so flawless, her eyelashes so thick and dark that Whit doubted she even wore makeup.

She faltered when the music turned to a hip-hop tune, not her usual beat, and opened her eyes as a body brushed against hers. Mae backed against Whit and pulled her arms around her. When she smoothly changed the timing of her movements, Whit realized she was showing her how to match the unfamiliar beat. It took every ounce of Whit's concentration to follow because the rub of Mae's ass against her groin was threatening to short-circuit her brain and overheat her body. When the song ended, Whit hugged Mae against her and put her mouth to Mae's ear. "If we don't sit down and cool off, I'm going to end up dragging you to a dark corner to ravish you, and that's not how I want our first time to happen."

Mae's lilting laugh floated out over the thump of the next song, but she allowed Whit to take her hand and lead her back to the table. A fresh beer and glass of wine had replaced their empty glasses, and Whit drained a third of hers as they settled into their chairs. Amanda and Janet also were just returning when Sue set a tray in the middle of the table. Sixteen shot glasses were filled to the rim.

"What's this?" Mae asked.

"Buttery Nipples, darlin'," Sue said. "Two rounds for everybody."

"I love Buttery Nipples," Mae said, smacking her lips together.

Whit shook her head with a smile. "Not for me, thanks. I'm driving, but you guys go ahead."

"No, you're not." Mae grabbed two, handing one to her. "I've reserved a room for us at the Marriott. We can walk from here."

Whit stared at her but took the drink.

"You might want to close your mouth before something flies in it," Sue said, lifting her shot along with the others. "To good company and sweet Georgia peaches."

They all laughed and tossed back their shots. Whit swallowed the sweet liquid, then downed the rest of her beer. When she set her empty glass on the table, Mae's amused gaze caught and held hers. Her eyes dropped to Mae's mouth, and she watched as her pink tongue took a slow, tantalizing swipe along her full, red lips.

Whit took another long draught from her glass that Sue had refilled from one of several pitchers on the table. She narrowed her eyes. Two could play at this game. She grabbed shots for each of them. They all lifted their glasses again, but when everybody else drank, Whit waited. She waited until Mae lowered her empty shot, and then she made her move.

Mae's lips, her tongue tasted of butterscotch schnapps and Irish-cream liqueur, and Whit drank from her until she was breathless, until Mae was breathless. When she released her, she held Mae's stunned gaze and slid her untouched shot toward her.

"You…you didn't drink yours," Mae stammered.

Her friends' delighted expressions, the pulsing music, and the writhing dancers faded away as though she and Mae were the only ones at the table. "It tastes better on your lips," she murmured.

Mae closed her hand around the shot glass. Her eyes gleaming, she tossed it back and rose from her seat to straddle Whit's lap. Then Mae's lips were on hers, her tongue stroking for entrance, and Whit opened to take her in. The demand of Mae's warm mouth ignited a hot blaze in her loins, and she wasn't sure if the pounding that reverberated through her body was coming from the music or her clit or her wildly beating heart. Just when she thought all the blood in her body had drained into her crotch, Mae broke their embrace and slid back into her own chair. Their surroundings slowly bled back into focus and Whit sucked in a deep breath.

"Damn." Sue fanned herself. "It's hot in here, isn't it?"

"You two need to get a room, before you burn the place up," Christie said.

Whit was still light-headed as she rose and offered her hand to Mae. "Somebody said we already have a room, and I think we're ready to call it an evening."

❖

The brisk November night did nothing to dampen the fire between them. Mae nearly swooned when the doors to the elevator closed and Whit gathered her in her arms. Her urgent, hungry mouth made Mae want, need to be consumed. She offered her lips, then her neck, and Whit feasted until she put her hands on Whit's chest and pressed her against the elevator's stainless-steel wall. Whit's nipples were hard against her palms, and she marveled at the searing jolt of pleasure that came from having her hands on another woman's—no, on Whit's breasts.

They stumbled from the elevator, mid-kiss and hands still groping, fumbled with the card key in their haste to get inside the room, and now finally stood next to the bed.

Whit hesitated, her brow creased with sudden uncertainty. But Mae was sure, very sure. She pulled her cashmere sweater over her head and dropped it to the floor.

"I'm not a virgin, Whit," she said softly. She decided to leave her red, lacy bra—the one Whit's eyes were glued to—for her to remove. "I've had sex before…when it felt like the thing to do. But this is different." Her hands were still chilled from their walk, and she unbuttoned Whit's shirt to warm them against her smooth belly, smiling as the muscles jumped and a soft hiss escaped Whit's lips. "I want you so badly that if you don't make love to me right now, I swear I'll torture you until you give in."

She almost cried for joy at the feel of Whit's long arms around her again, her hands drawing her close and her mouth laying her claim. The room was cool, but her skin burned under the heat of Whit's gaze when she stepped back and shed her jeans to reveal her addiction to Victoria's Secret. She smiled when Whit reciprocated by revealing a black pair of the store's cotton bikini briefs.

"Somehow, I can't picture you shopping there." She traced the outline of Whit's nipples puckering the matching seamless silk bra. "I had you figured for a Jockey boy-shorts kind of girl."

"I order online," Whit said, catching Mae's hand and lifting it to kiss the teasing fingers. "But I don't want to talk about my shopping habits right now." She held Mae's gaze as she stripped off her bra, revealing firm breasts and dusky, rose-colored nipples.

"God, Whit. You are so gorgeous." She tentatively trailed her fingertips along the sculpted collarbone. Whit watched her with hooded eyes as she took Mae's hands and pressed them against her bare breasts. Mae was transfixed as she cupped them and flicked her thumbs against the hard nipples. The tingle in her belly made her thighs clench when Whit dropped her head back and groaned. God. Oh, God. Parts of her body she'd never felt before were suddenly awake and screaming. She wanted to freeze the moment, but at the same time she was swallowed by an urgency to beg like a honky-tonk slut for Whit to do something before the wanting broke her into a million tiny pieces.

Whit's fingers traced the lace of her bra, finding and pinching her sensitive nipples. Then the bra was gone and she let Whit lower her to the bed and hover over her.

"Please."

They both groaned as skin met skin. They were belly to belly, breast to breast as the sweet pressure of Whit's thigh pushed against the damp silk of her panties. She raised her leg and found Whit just as wet and hot. Their kiss was deep, Whit's tongue still tasting of butterscotch and cream.

Whit moved away, but Mae's protest caught in her throat when Whit peeled off her briefs to reveal dark, glistening curls. Her breath caught and held as Whit curled her fingers into the red lace of her panties and lowered them slowly down her legs. She flushed with embarrassment at how wet she was—God, nearly halfway down her thighs. But Whit only smiled and licked her way from ankle to thigh.

She gasped and jerked when Whit parted her and ran her tongue along her aching clit, then sucked her into her mouth. It was too much, Whit was too much, and she came with a scream as the waves of pleasure washed over her. She hadn't caught her breath yet when Whit was over her again, her long fingers pushing inside and finding that spot that made her legs jerk as she wrapped them around Whit's hips, offering herself. She opened wider and pressed upward, urging

Whit's frantic thrusts. Her orgasm swelled again and burst with Whit's low growl.

"Mae, God, baby." Whit's lean body tensed, and she groaned through several stiff thrusts before rolling off to collapse on her back.

Mae's breasts heaved like the heroine in one of Big Mae's torrid romance novels as she fought to catch her breath and slow the thudding of her heart. "Oh. My. God." This was it. This was what all those books were about. She turned onto her side to rest her cheek in the well of Whit's shoulder. "You should be illegal."

Whit's arm curled around her. "I think what we just did *is* still illegal in some states."

She trailed her finger through the perspiration that dotted the shallow valley between Whit's breasts. She felt suddenly uncertain, unsure how to phrase the question looming in her mind. "You're probably used to this, having slept with other women," she said quietly, tracing a nervous pattern on Whit's chest. "More experienced women, you know, who are probably better—"

In one smooth roll, Mae was suddenly on her back with Whit hovering over her again. She trembled under Whit's gaze, caught helplessly in the swirling whirlpool of summer green and sky blue. She tasted the salty-sweet of her own arousal as Whit kissed her gently, then brushed her cheek against Mae's as she whispered in her ear. "You were perfect. But if you feel the need for more practice, I'll be happy to oblige."

CHAPTER NINETEEN

"A cold wind finds every crack in the house."

Whit woke slowly, the scent of coconut shampoo tickling her nose and a velvet blanket of naked woman warming her. She could tell by Mae's utterly limp body that she was still deeply asleep. She should be. They'd made love for hours, slept, then woke to make love again as dawn crept through the curtains. Mae had been like a woman emerging from an arid desert, with Whit her only source of water. Whew. That polite Southern belle sure hid a hellcat unleashed. For the first time in months, she felt happy—deliciously sore and a little raw in parts she didn't want to inventory, but happy. She felt like sunshine was finally peeking through, pushing aside the clouds. Hell, she felt so completely blissful, she imagined she could hear music. She frowned. On a morning like this, her subconscious should pick something less strident.

"Are you going to answer that?" Mae mumbled against Whit's breast without moving a twitch, which made her smile.

"I can't move. Somebody has me pinned to the bed." The phone stopped chirping. "Too late. It's gone to voice mail. It's probably Tyree. We need to take more of Bar's feed supplements to the track. There's only enough left for the morning feeding, and he probably wants to know what time we're coming out. I can call him back later."

"Good. I'm starving."

Teeth nipped at Whit's nipple and her groin tightened. "Jesus." She rolled them over and found Mae's mouth with hers. They shared tongues and breath and, when Whit pulled back, soft gazes. "How about we check with room service before I'm on the menu again? This old forty-something body needs nourishment."

"You order for us. Something sweet and fruity for me, please." Mae slid from under her. "I need to take care of my morning ablutions."

Whit sat up, enjoying her view of Mae's naked body as she crawled across the bed. "Ablutions? Do people still use that word?"

Mae hopped off the bed and raised an eyebrow at Whit's cheeky grin. "Big Mae did. She said it was elegant and efficient—one word rather than a handful." She picked up her red lace panties from the floor, then straightened and put her hands on her hips. "I can be more literal if you prefer."

"Just because I'm curious, give it a shot."

Mae disappeared into the bathroom, then stuck her head out. "I have to pee, wash my unmentionable areas, and brush my teeth."

Whit laughed as the door slammed shut. Ten minutes with Mae was more fun than two years with Avery. She climbed out of bed, wrapping the blanket around her to ward off the chill of the room, and began to search for a room-service menu. Clothes were flung everywhere. She finally located the menu under a jacket, but before she could open it, her cell phone began to ring again. She glanced at the caller ID. Pop. Whit mentally shook her head. He and Cousin Henry probably wanted to know where the coffee or pancake mix was. Men could be so helpless sometimes.

"What's up, Pop?"

"Whitley, this is Henry. I hate to bother you, but I think you need to come home and take Clinton to the emergency room."

Whit threw the blanket onto the bed and began gathering her clothes. "What's wrong?"

"I know you said he sometimes doesn't know where he is when he first wakes up, but that's not the only problem. He says his belly hurts, and when he urinates, it's pink with blood. I'm pretty sure he's running a high fever, too."

"I'm in Baton Rouge, but I can be there within the hour. Tell him to hold on."

❖

Mae shoved Whit's laptop and power cord into the messenger bag. What else? Oh, crap. She should have downloaded the photos from her camera into Whit's computer before she packed it. She frowned. No time now. She needed to run those feed supplements to the track, tell Tyree that Whit had taken Clinton to the hospital, then head that way herself.

Worry ate at her insides. Clinton was flushed with fever and bent over with pain when they arrived, and there was fear in Whit's eyes. Mae had wanted to go with them, to be at Whit's side and hold Clinton's hand. But Whit needed her to take care of other things so she could focus on her father.

The pictures. Right. The corrected galley proofs for the magazine were due back to the printer by noon tomorrow, and Whit wanted to sub out several of the photos and captions from a new shoot Mae had done at the track. She extracted the photo card from her camera and started to put it in her pocket. No. She might forget it was there. The snakeskin change purse Jodie had given her would be perfect. It was small enough to fit alongside Whit's laptop, but big enough that it wouldn't get overlooked if it fell out when the computer was pulled from the messenger bag.

She rummaged in her bag for the small purse and zipped it open. What was this? A thumb drive? It was probably Jodie's. Why would she put a thumb drive in a change purse she was giving as a gift? The purse was obviously new, the craftsman's tag still attached. Maybe it belonged to him, not Jodie. Mae chewed her lip. It would only take a minute to check, and her curious nature was itching to decipher the mystery. She switched on Whit's desktop computer to boot up while she gathered a change of clothes from Whit's bedroom. She didn't know if Clinton would have to stay at the hospital overnight, but Big Mae had taught her to always be prepared.

She paused in the doorway. It smelled of Whit's spicy scent, a mixture of leather and soap. Several pairs of boots were scattered around a chair that served as a hanging place for several caps, but the room was otherwise neat. She couldn't resist sitting on the bed and smoothing her hand over the down quilt. This was where Whit slept. A wave of arousal washed over her as flashes of Whit's body warm and soft under her hands the night before burned through her.

God, she'd never felt hungry for anyone before, but just the thought of Whit naked between these sheets made her want to tear her clothes off and roll around on them like a barn cat in a bed of catnip. She blew out a breath and tried to rein in her raging hormones. Focus.

She packed an overnight bag with clean socks, underwear—she had to force herself not to peruse that drawer—a long-sleeved polo shirt, jeans, and some basic toiletries. The computer was booted and waiting when she returned, so she popped the thumb drive in and opened it. What in the world?

The drive held two files, and she opened the text file. It was a report from a lab notifying the Quarter Horse Breeders Association that information from an anonymous source had cast doubt on the blood-test results used to confirm the parentage and, therefore, the registration of three race horses. The second horse on the list was Raising the Bar.

Mae clicked on the video. The camera work was shaky and seemed to have been covertly filmed, perhaps with a cell phone, at waist level from behind the left elbow of the man presenting the bribe. The lighting was dim and the voices had been run through a synthesizer to disguise them, but the lab-worker's face was in full view. He repeatedly licked his lips, his eyes nervously darting here and there.

"This is full payment," the briber said, holding out a thick envelope. "I don't want to risk meeting again."

"This could get me fired, maybe even arrested, if I get caught," the lab guy whined.

"Don't even think about backing out, cousin. Didn't I get you out of that accessory charge, then bring you here for a fresh start? You owe me."

The lab guy took the money and tucked it in his jacket. "This makes us even. That was twenty years ago, and I don't need you to remind me of it. For God sakes, when I look at my little daughter now, it makes me crazy thinking that something like that could happen to her."

The briber's laugh was harsh. "You should have thought about that while your buddies were raping that girl and you didn't do anything to stop them."

The video ended and Mae watched it again, listening carefully and trying to pick out something that would give away their location. That's the way they solved cases on television detective shows. But she couldn't find any clues to identify the briber other than a distinctive wide wedding band imbedded with a dark stone on his left hand.

Was the lab guy going to alter blood tests to make it appear the horses were clones? Or was he going to cover up that they truly were clones? She didn't have time to sort this issue out now. She closed the drive, then shut down the computer and her thoughts. Whit and Clinton were her priority right now. Horses be damned.

❖

Mae struggled to lift the five-gallon bucket of feed supplement. It didn't look that heavy when Whit had easily carried it to the car and set it in the trunk.

"Need some help with that?"

"Yes, please." She turned to smile at Jean Paul. "You look nice." He was a study in Southern yuppie, dressed in khakis and a deep-pink polo, a tennis sweater draped over his shoulders. The casual attire made him look younger.

"Thank you." He lifted the bucket. "Where were you headed with this?"

"I'm not sure. The Caseys' trailer, I guess. I think Tyree mixes the horses' feed there and then carries it to their stalls."

"I thought you were working for Casey as a writer. She's using you as an errand girl, now?"

"No. I offered to help." She followed him to the area behind the barns where horse trailers and RVs were parked together like a small village of temporary living quarters. "Clinton is very ill and she had to take him to the emergency room, but Tyree needed this stuff before he feeds tonight."

He opened the back of the trailer and set the bucket inside next to bales of hay stored there. The camper and compartment that held the feed and tack were locked. "Your delivery has been made," he said, closing the trailer. "I was about to head over to the casino for some blackjack. Care to join me? We could have an early dinner in the members-only restaurant on the upper level."

"Thank you, but I need to find Tyree to tell him about Clinton. Then I'm going to the hospital to see how he's doing."

"Tomorrow night then. I can get Robbie to cook something special for us." He put his hand on the trailer and canted his body so that he crowded her personal space, a clear message of his intent as a suitor.

Mae backed up. "Jean Paul. I'd love to have dinner with you as a friend, but I have to tell you that I'm seeing someone else."

"I know it's been weeks since we went out, but this casino deal has kept me very busy. I'm sorry you thought I wasn't interested in your company. I'm very interested."

"Thank you, but, as I said, I'm seeing someone else… exclusively."

"I refuse to believe Robbie's gossip." His eyes narrowed. "Tell me it's not true."

Mae shifted uneasily. "Exactly what did Robbie tell you?"

She and Whit hadn't talked about who should know they were dating. She'd seemed perfectly at ease letting Robbie know, and she certainly didn't mind letting everyone in the lesbian bar know. But she might feel differently about being outed to others like Jean Paul, who might try to use it against them. Mae didn't have a problem with it, but she'd like to tell Michael before it became common knowledge around town. He *was* her only blood relative, her father.

"He said you were hot for Casey." His eyes flashed. "He thinks everybody's queer. I told him there's no way you're a dyke like Casey."

Really? She felt like she was back in high school dealing with "mean girl" backbiting. Her steel magnolia seethed and begged to cut him down with a razor-sharp retort. But she wouldn't rise to his bait. Instead, she feigned surprise.

"I am personally offended and shocked that a man of your breeding would use such common slurs in my company." She stepped back, her hand at her throat as if she were a bit frightened of his callous behavior.

"I apologize for my crude language." His sarcastic tone didn't match his words, but Mae chose to ignore that fact.

"Apology accepted."

"You should be careful. Casey is tied up in some things that aren't going to end well."

Did he know more about the loan against the farm or the cloning investigation? She needed to learn what he knew, but she didn't have time to wheedle it out of him right now. "Like I said, I'd love to have dinner with you as a friend, but until I find out how much of the *Quarter Track* workload Whit needs me to handle while Clinton's sick, I can't commit to a time. I'll call you."

He regarded her, then nodded curtly. "As you wish."

❖

"Do you think Mr. Clinton will be all right? He ain't been sick hardly a day in his life. I just can't imagine how things would be without him around."

Mae had found Tyree lounging in front of Bar's stall with several other exercise jockeys. "Don't worry, hon. I'm sure the doctors will fix him up." She smoothed her hand down Bar's nose when he stuck his head over the half door and nickered to her. "You're such a good boy." She was becoming more at ease around horses since Whit had given her several riding lessons. She was anxious for another lesson, horseback or otherwise. The thought of "other" made her tingle low in her belly.

"Is there anything I can do?"

"I'm sure Whit will call you after the doctors have a look at Clinton."

"We've got the Breeders Futurity in less than two weeks. She's going to need to be here every morning for Bar's workouts, and she has two client horses running in other races."

"I know. I'll stay with Clinton when she needs to be here. We'll work it out." She made a quick decision. She could trust him. "Tyree, have you heard anyone talking about some horses being clones?"

Tyree dropped his gaze and kicked at the dirt. "That's just stupid rumors, Miss Mae. There has to be blood tests and paperwork and lots of stuff to get a horse registered. Mr. Clinton might have won Bar in a poker game, but Mr. Clinton's vet did the tests for registration."

"He won that horse in a poker game?"

"He sure did. But Mr. Clinton had him tested right away to make sure the loser turned over the right horse. People are just trying to stir the pot, but there ain't nothing to it."

Mae rubbed her temple. What else could possibly pop up to muddy the waters of Bar's heritage? "I'm sure. But those rumors could cause trouble at an inconvenient time. Big Mae said you should always have some hush puppies ready in case the dogs start barking."

Tyree smiled. "I think I would have liked your granny. Mama would have, too."

Mae clasped his shoulder. "You and your mama are good people, Tyree. Whit and Clinton are lucky to have you as friends."

The boy blushed and shuffled his feet. "So what do we need to do?"

"I know it's Sunday, but I'm going to arrange for the track veterinarian to draw some blood from Bar first thing tomorrow and send it to a lab the Quarter Horse Breeders Association doesn't use for DNA testing. That's going to be our insurance." She frowned. "The thing is, I don't want you to say anything to Whit. She's got enough to worry about."

He nodded. "I gotcha. It'll be our secret."

CHAPTER TWENTY

"A blind mule ain't afraid of the dark."

I'm sick of laying around in bed. I'm not tired. I want to go to the track."

Pop had been a difficult patient at best, and Whit was relieved to bring him home after three days. The problem had been a urinary-tract infection, aggravated by an enlarged prostate that kept him from fully emptying his bladder. That was really more than Whit wanted to know about Pop's plumbing, but she realized that as his Alzheimer's disease progressed, her role as his daughter would have to expand to include caretaker.

"Just sit here in your recliner and watch television for a while. Tyree and I already ran the horses this morning." She brought a bottle of water—flavored and reinforced with electrolytes—from the refrigerator and held it out with his noon medicines.

"I don't want water. I want a beer."

"The doctor says you can't have beer until you finish the antibiotic."

"I ain't drinking no more water."

"The doctor said you have to remember to drink lots of fluids."

"I don't care what the doctor said. He looked to be all of fifteen years old. He can't know much."

"Mae bought this especially for you. It's berry flavored. She said it's your favorite."

He eyed the bottle, then took it and downed the pills with a huge swallow. "Where's Mae? I'm hungry."

"She's out doing an interview. I'll fix you a sandwich."

"Cut it in half like Mae does."

Whit shook her head. "Okay, Pop." She put together ham sandwiches for Pop and herself, carefully cutting them diagonally like Mae always did. When she returned to the living room, Pop was snoring, his mouth open and his hands moving as he dreamed. The doctor said the Alzheimer's medicine made him dream a lot. She set his plate on the table beside him and replaced the now-empty water bottle with a full one. He would probably jump off a cliff if Mae said he should.

Actually, she might jump off a cliff in frustration if she and Mae didn't get some private time again soon. She'd passed the long hours in the hospital by reliving their night together over and over. By the time Mae would show up to sit with Pop while she went to the track for the morning exercising of the horses, she was ready to bribe a nurse into showing them an empty bed and guarding the door for thirty minutes. But that wasn't how she wanted to do things with Mae.

Instead, they stole kisses when Clinton slept and cuddled in the only comfortable chair in the hospital room. That got them some looks from a few self-righteous nurses, but Whit didn't care. Even better, Mae didn't seem to care. Their relationship was already so different from what she'd had with Avery.

She booted up her desktop computer to update the website and sorted through the stack of mail she'd brought in from the oversized mailbox at the end of the driveway. Junk mail went into the trash—household bills in one stack, farm business in a second stack, and *Quarter Track* mail in a third. She raised an eyebrow at a long white envelope addressed to Mae. Whit frowned. The return address was from a lab company she didn't recognize. Was Mae having tests for some reason? Nah. Probably some general information for the cloning lawsuit story Mae insisted on pursuing.

Her cell phone rang, and Whit's heart skipped a beat at the name on her caller ID. The day seemed suddenly brighter.

"Hey."

"Hey yourself. Did you get Clinton home okay?

"Yep. He's snoring in his chair."

"Did he eat lunch?"

"I made sandwiches, but he fell asleep without eating his."

"Whit, he needs to take his medicine."

"I gave him his medicine, which, by the way, he refused until I told him that you said he had to take it."

"Well, he needs to eat when he takes that antibiotic. Wake him up and get him to eat."

Whit held the phone away from her ear and raised her voice. "Pop. Pop, wake up."

He closed his mouth with a snap and blinked awake. "What? What's the yelling about?"

"You need to wake up and eat your sandwich before that medicine you took burns your stomach up."

He closed his eyes and muttered. "I'll eat in a bit."

"Mae says you need to eat now."

His eyes opened again and he sat up in the recliner. "Too many bossy women around here. A man can't get any rest." Despite his complaining, he picked up the sandwich and took a bite.

Whit returned the phone to her ear. "He's eating now."

Mae was laughing. "I didn't mean for you to holler at him. You could have walked over and gently shook him awake. You really were raised in a barn, weren't you?"

"As a matter of fact, I was." She loved Mae's lilting laughter and their teasing conversations. "Where are you?"

"Rhett, Ellie, and I are at my apartment, but we're headed your way in a few minutes."

Since Whit had been spending nights at the hospital, Ellie had been staying with Mae and Rhett. She missed her constant companion, but not as much as she missed Mae.

"Good. One of Pop's client horses, Dun Done It, is running at five o'clock. Do you mind staying with Pop while I take care of that? He'll probably feel like going to the track in the morning, but he's pretty worn out just getting home from the hospital today."

"Of course I don't mind."

"I know you haven't had much time to yourself lately, but I don't know what Pop and I would have done without you." She worried that she was asking too much, taking advantage of their fledgling relationship.

"Stop it. I love spending time with you and Clinton. I'll write up the interview I just finished, and then Clinton and I'll cook dinner while you're working at the track."

Whit closed her eyes and wondered, not for the first time, if some higher power had sent Mae to them. "Pack an overnight bag, okay? Stay with me tonight," she said softly.

Mae's voice was velvet in her ear. "I was hoping you'd ask."

❖

"It's Jack Junket first out of the gate, then Ide B Lyin' and Lotta Blue. Ain't Behaving is moving up on the outside, followed by Dun Done It, Sippin' Corona, Henry's Girl, Tweet Sensation, and Dash Away. Gray Shadow is bringing up the rear."

"Crap." Dun Done It had stumbled as he left the gate because the gray horse broke bad and bumped him. "Gonna file a complaint on that one," she muttered. "That gray never breaks clean." Whit followed the horses with her binoculars. "Come on, Dun."

"It's Ide B Lyin' in the lead, followed by Lotta Blue as Jack Junket fades to third. Sippin' Corona is fourth, then Tweet Sensation and Dash Away, with Dun Done It coming on fast." The announcer's deep drone raised an octave. "Sippin' Corona takes the lead, with Dun Done It sliding into second and Lotta Blue in third. It's Sippin' Corona and Dun Done It pulling away. Sippin' Corona and Dun Done It. It's Dun Done It by a nose with Sippin' Corona second, Lotta Blue third, and Tweet Sensation to show."

"Yes!" Whit pumped her fist in the air. She hurried down to where Tyree was waiting for Dun to come off the track, wishing again that Pop and Mae had been here to see him win.

It was turning out to be a good season. If Dun Done It's owner wanted to pay the entry fee, she'd have two horses running in the Breeders Futurity next week. The other client horse, Crawdaddy Red, wasn't winning like Bar and Dun, but he usually placed and was improving. Pop had said all along that Red, foaled late in the year, was on the young side and would probably race better as a three-year-old.

Tyree was practically dancing as he helped the jockey dismount. "Woo-wee. Dun ran like a fox with his tail on fire, didn't he?"

Whit matched his grin. “He sure did. I thought that gray had bumped him out of the running, but he came back like a bullet.”

“You gonna file a complaint on the bump?”

“Nah. I was thinking about it until we won. Not worth bothering with. I’m thinking Gray Shadow’s going to be packed up and hauled to the next auction. He hasn’t done much of anything here at Evangeline.” She gave her jockey a clap on the shoulder. “Good race, Rick.”

“Good horse, Ms. Casey. Are you going to run him in the Futurity?”

“I reckon we will if his owner wants to pay the fee. You open for a ride if we do?”

“I haven’t signed on with anybody else yet. I know Tommy is going to ride Mr. Casey’s horse, but if you get the owner to commit before I get another offer, I wouldn’t mind riding this one for you.”

Whit nodded. “I’ll talk to him tomorrow.”

“Hey, Casey.” One of the track officials waved her over. “They want you upstairs.”

She frowned. “What for?”

“Don’t know. I was just sent down to get you.”

“You go ahead,” Tyree said, taking Dun’s lead from her. “I’ll take care of Dun.”

❖

Mae burrowed against Whit’s warm body to stave off the night’s chill as they rocked lazily in the front-porch swing. Although Whit had arrived home well after Clinton had to eat and take his medicine, she’d waited so they could dine together, then swing and talk about their day. It was a comfortable habit she’d missed while Clinton was hospitalized.

“So, the interview with the Canadian trainer went well?” Whit asked.

“Yes, it did. You know, some of the older men just give you one-word answers, but this was a young guy, and he talked his head off about Louisiana tracks.”

“Was he handsome?”

"Are you worried?" Did Whit think she was the slightest bit interested in anybody else?

Whit shrugged. "Well, you were dating guys until about a month ago."

Mae tugged Whit to her and kissed her softly, then deeply, dancing their tongues together until a flush rose up Whit's cheeks. "I'm not interested in anyone but you. Not a man or a woman. Just you."

"You sound very sure," Whit murmured.

"I am." Mae hesitated. "But I do need to tell you about something." She closed her fingers around Whit's hand, hoping she wouldn't be upset. "Jean Paul knows about us."

Whit's eyebrows rose. "He does?"

Mae sighed. "Apparently, Robbie told him. You know they're business partners in the restaurant."

Whit nodded. "That's cool."

"You don't mind?"

Whit shrugged. "Not unless it bothers you. I've been out for a long time. It's not like people don't know about me."

"It doesn't bother me, but I ran into him at the track and he asked me out."

"He asked you for a date?"

"Yes, but I told him I was seeing someone else exclusively. I didn't name you, because we hadn't really talked about being public." She stared down at their hands. "Or being exclusive."

"Mae, look at me."

She raised her eyes and was warmed by Whit's gaze.

"I don't date more than one woman at a time."

"Okay." She smiled. "So, what made you late for dinner?"

Whit grinned. "I told you and Pop that Dun won his race, which qualifies him for the Breeders Futurity, but then we got into a discussion about whether his owner would pony up the entry fee, and I didn't get to tell you the rest."

"The rest?"

"I got called to the skybox where the track announcer and officials watch the races."

Mae's heart had nearly stopped. "What for?" Today was Wednesday and the report on the blood drawn Monday morning by the track veterinarian hadn't come in the mail yet, even though she'd paid extra to have it expedited within two days. Her first thought was that the test had come back suspicious and the vet had turned it over to the officials instead of mailing it to the farm. God, what if her meddling had gotten Whit's colt disqualified? She shook off the frightening thought. She wanted to wrap herself around Whit and shield her from anything, everything that could hurt her.

"They wanted to interview me for the Evangeline Downs website."

"Their website?" God, she sounded like a parrot.

"Yep. I went up there all bowed up, expecting that the guy training that gray was trying to claim Dun bumped his horse. Instead, it was this woman wanting to interview me. It's been a while since they've had a trainer with two horses qualified for the Breeders Futurity."

She was summoned by a woman? Maybe one that didn't stick her nose in places it didn't belong. "Was she pretty?"

"The woman who interviewed me?"

Whit's arm tightened around Mae's shoulders and she kissed her. Mae closed her eyes and relaxed, letting the taste of Whit's mouth, the silk of Whit's tongue against hers wash away her fears. They both sighed when Whit drew back.

"She was pretty ugly, I'd say, compared to you."

"Good answer." She wondered if she sounded as breathless as she felt.

Whit chuckled. "It always worked for Pop when Mama asked the same question."

"When are they going to post the story?"

"She said next week before the race."

"I hope you made sure they link it to your website."

"I might be a novice when it comes to social media, but I know the ropes when it comes to websites. I made her agree to mention our story about the casino project and link to it, and include our Facebook, Linkedin, and Twitter links."

Whit didn't seem to be offended by her prompt, but Mae was chagrinned at her faux pas. "I didn't mean to imply otherwise." She stared up at Whit, her eyes pale pools in the dim light. "I think you're one of the smartest women I've ever met. You started and run your own business, and you know all about horses and—"

"If you're trying to get in my pants, it's working."

Mae smiled, then rested her head against Whit's shoulder. "No. If I was trying to get in your pants, I'd tell you how incredibly sexy I find your confidence, your strength, and that tall, delicious body I'm dying to get my hands on again."

Whit stood and tugged Mae up. "Enough talk. Bed. Now."

❖

The house was silent as Whit led Mae to stand by her bed. This time, there was no alcohol in their veins to lubricate their desire, no lust fueled by dancing, writhing to a beat that reverberated through them. There was only the want in Mae's whiskey eyes and the unexpected intimacy of bringing her into the room, the bed that was hers. She touched Mae's cheek and traced the flush rising along her neck. She needed Mae to know this was special.

"I've never made love to a woman here before, in this room."

Mae trembled under her touch. "Oh, Whit. The things you say steal my breath."

She drew Mae into a soft, lingering kiss as her fingers found the buttons of her blouse. She undressed them—Mae's shirt, then hers, Mae's jeans, then hers—between kisses and caresses until they were both panting and naked.

Mae's skin was hot as she lowered her to the cool sheets and followed to gently pin her with her hips. Mae's dark hair fanned across the pillow like silk, her lips a red and plump contrast to her beautiful, sculpted features. She was slick and hot against Whit's thigh, and Whit wanted to touch and taste every inch of her, slowly and thoroughly. The thought of it made her belly tighten, and she groaned as she painted her desire along Mae's thigh, marking her with her scent and stoking the throbbing need building in her groin. Mae stirred things in her and drew them to the surface like a hot poultice applied to her damaged soul.

She held Mae's gaze as she bucked her hips again and gasped. "I don't know if I can wait." She moaned as Mae's lips closed around her nipple, and she grasped Whit's hips, urging her on.

Mae lifted her head, her gaze fevered. "God, don't stop, Whit. Please, inside me. I need you inside me."

Whit found her open and ready when she parted her to plunge inside and pump with each thrust of her hips. Mae took a sharp breath and held it, her eyes wide, her nails digging into Whit's ass. Hot muscles clamped around Whit's fingers. Mae whimpered, then bit off a scream. "Oh, God. Oh, Whit." Her surrender was a vortex, sucking Whit with her into the well of pleasure. She was drowning in it, drowning in Mae.

When her orgasm at last released her, Mae's lingering climax still pulsed around her. She withdrew to taste the evidence of it on her fingers.

Mae's eyes were bright as she pushed Whit onto her back and moved down her body to crawl between Whit's legs. Her tongue flicked across Whit's sex in a tentative taste, and Whit held her breath. She was still hard. Mae looked up and smiled, her fingers parting Whit, exposing her. "May I?"

God, she had to ask? Yes. Please. Please. She wanted to beg but had no breath in her lungs, no words she could speak, only the tremor that ran through her legs in answer. Mae lowered her head and took Whit's flesh into her mouth and feasted with a talent that made Whit want to weep with ecstasy.

She was boneless when her hips finally stopped jerking and her heart stopped pounding. Mae cuddled against her side and Whit reached deep into her resources, determined to have her again. And she *would* have her again, then maybe a third time, just because she could. Lovers never denied her this early in a relationship. It was only later that they tired of her, of her desire for them. Forever was rare, and she'd given up hope of finding it. So, she would take *now*.

And, at this moment, *now* was good. Mae was delicious, Pop was home again, her profit from selling her condo was holding off the loan collectors, and Raising the Bar was favored to win the Breeders Futurity. It was a heavenly oasis, and Whit intended to savor it.

CHAPTER TWENTY-ONE

"Shouldn't have trusted the dog to watch your food."

"I don't understand." Whit stared at the race director. "My paperwork is in order on Raising the Bar. He's been racing for the past six weeks. Why is there a problem now?"

Preston Wells sat back in his chair and tongued a toothpick from one side of his mouth to the other. "Did your father foal the colt, Ms. Casey?"

Whit's lunch suddenly soured in her stomach and lapped at the back of her throat. "No. He won him in a poker game as a yearling, but the bill of sale is valid, and the DNA test to register him was done at *our* farm. My veterinarian can vouch that we followed the proper procedure."

"Nobody is accusing you or Clinton. But the Association is investigating the lab that confirmed your colt's DNA. They have evidence that a worker there was taking bribes to alter certain records. Your colt is among the ones listed as suspect." He held up the folder that contained Bar's paperwork. "The bottom line is we have a protest filed against your colt, claiming he's an illegal clone."

"That's a load of crap." Whit wanted to jerk that toothpick out of his mouth and stab him in the eye with it. "You know it's crap."

Preston shook his head. "Maybe so, but Evangeline can't ignore a properly filed protest."

"Exactly what son of a bitch filed it? I've got a right to know."

"I don't know."

"What the hell do you mean, you don't know?"

"The complaint was filed by an anonymous client through an attorney. We, of course, checked with the Quarter Horse Breeders Association to make sure your colt is a suspect in an investigation, and they confirmed it. We're obligated to honor the protest and disqualify your colt until the Association clears him."

"And when will that be?"

"I have no idea. That's up to the Association."

"God damn it." She gave in to her anger and kicked the front of Preston's desk. He raised an eyebrow at her but said nothing. "My colt is favored in the Futurity this weekend, and this is nothing but an underhanded trick to keep him out of the race."

"That's probably the case, but my hands are tied unless you can get the Association to clear him."

She laid her hands on the desk and thrust her face inches from his. He didn't even blink. "And how am I supposed to do that? The race is in two days."

"I'm not the enemy, Whitley," he said softly. "Clinton knows a lot of people. I'd suggest that you two get busy calling in some favors to see what can be done. Standard procedure would be for me to scratch him from the race today, but Clinton Casey is one of the most honest trainers to race at this track. I'll give you until two o'clock Saturday before I take Raising the Bar off the entry list."

❖

Whit sagged against the bricks of the administration building, fighting to breathe against the failure that was squeezing her chest. They were so close, one race away from ending their financial worries. But if Bar didn't run in the Futurity, she was sunk and Joie de Vivre was lost. She'd still have *Quarter Track*, but she'd be dead broke and surviving on the monthly income from the magazine. She'd done that before, but she'd been young and single and didn't have Pop's health issues draining her finances.

She'd have to sell Bar. He was the jackpot, the winning lottery ticket, the colt of every owner-trainer's dream. A few more years of racing and his stud fees alone would have rejuvenated Joie de Vivre as a top training farm and ensured the best care money could buy for Pop. Was it nothing more than a pipe dream?

Her stomach churned with a new possibility. What if Pop had been set up? What if the guy who lost Bar in the card game had bribed somebody at the lab to alter the DNA tests and Bar really was a clone? She shook herself. God, she'd been watching too much television with Pop.

She straightened. This was only one thing. A big thing, but everything else was still good. *Quarter Track* was flourishing with Mae's added touches, Pop's medication had slowed his disease, and the three of them were starting to feel like a family. Despite her best efforts to remain guarded, Mae had burrowed into her life, into her heart. She squared her shoulders. Pop hadn't raised a quitter. She had two days, damn it. If they were going down, she'd do it fighting. First, she had to talk to Pop.

Head down, she strode toward the backstretch with single-minded purpose, checking off names. The bitter truth, however, was that the only people she knew with the influence to help were the same people who stood to benefit if Joie de Vivre went under. The obvious person would be Avery's father, but she'd rather make a deal with the devil than sell her soul to Senator Perrault. Not to mention that he had a vested interest in the new casino project, and Joie de Vivre Farms stood in the way. That left Michael. He was involved in the project, too, but he owed Pop. There was no telling where Michael would be today if Pop hadn't befriended him as a youngster.

"Whoa." Jean Paul caught Whit by the shoulders to keep her from running him down. "Casey, isn't it?"

"Sorry," she muttered, moving to push past him.

"What's the rush?" He stepped in front of her. "Oh, I guess you've been to see Preston Wells."

Whit froze. "Do I know you?"

Jean Paul removed his sunglasses and perched them on his head so they were eye to eye. "Jean Paul Broussard. I believe we have a mutual friend."

She stared. So this was the guy Mae had dated, the one who was buying up land for the casino project? She stood straighter, pleased to be several inches taller than him. "What do you know about my meeting with Wells?"

"I saw Michael on his way up to file the protest. Guess I'll be putting my money on somebody else's horse."

Whit felt, for the second time in an hour, the color drain from her face before a ball of fury crawled up her neck and blurred her vision. "Michael filed the protest?"

"Didn't Preston tell you?"

"He said it was filed by an attorney. Who's Michael representing?" She wished the cold edge in her voice were a real knife she could hold to his throat. "Who's his client?"

Jean Paul shook his head and clicked his tongue. "What makes you think he's not representing himself?"

Whit grabbed his polo shirt with both hands and jerked him to his toes. "Because Michael doesn't have the balls. I think he's representing some bastard like you who's trying to buy my land to build a casino on it."

He broke her hold and stepped back, brushing his shirt with his hands as if her touch had soiled him and puffing his chest like a scrawny bantam rooster. "I wish I could take the credit, but I'm just the paperwork guy. Michael's the one you should worry about."

"I won't pretend that I understand what Pop sees in him, but he's been Michael's only friend since they were kids. Michael wouldn't risk that."

Jean Paul smirked. "Michael doesn't have friends. He'd tear out his own mother's throat if she got in his way. He couldn't care less about some absent-minded old man and his dyke daughter."

She stared at him. Dyke. Why hadn't this occurred to her before? "This isn't really about the casino project, is it?" She should have guessed this was simply a pissing match over who had the biggest dick. "You had Michael file that complaint because Mae dumped you to be with me. Getting my land would just be extra gravy."

"You really are clueless, aren't you?" He laughed. "No wonder you played right into Michael's hands, like taking candy from a baby."

"What the hell are you talking about?"

He feigned surprise. "You really fell for that sweet-as-molasses act." He glanced around but no one was close enough to overhear. "You've been sleeping with the enemy all along, darlin'. That little Georgia peach is Michael's illegitimate spawn."

Before she could think, her fist connected with his jaw, and then Jean Paul was looking up at her from where he was sprawled on the ground. He got up slowly, working his jaw back and forth to test it. "You have me at a disadvantage, Casey. I'd never hit a woman—even though the label is questionable in your case."

"You fucking, lying son of a bitch."

"Ask her if you don't believe me." He began to back away toward the parking lot. "While you're at it, you might want to ask her who actually holds the note on your father's farm."

❖

Mae paced the length of the backstretch again. She knew Whit hadn't left because her truck was still in the parking lot. She wasn't at the trailer with Clinton and Tyree, and she wasn't in the track restaurant. The track and viewing bleachers were empty since the morning exercising period was over and the afternoon races hadn't started. So, where was she?

Bar stuck his head over the stall's half door and nickered to her as she started her third patrol around the barns. This was pointless. Whit was probably somewhere talking horses and handicapping, or interviewing someone for quartertrack.com or other such stuff. She should just wait for her to find her when she was done.

She went to the horse and stroked his long nose while he searched her hands for treats. "No treats. Whit says you're on a strict racing diet." His low, rumbling response let her know he didn't agree. She reached over the door to stroke her hand along his silky neck, and a faint movement in the corner of the dark stall caught her eye.

"Whit? Why are you sitting in the dark?"

Seated on an upturned bucket in the far corner, Whit didn't answer or move.

"Are you okay?" Bar stepped back as Mae slipped into the stall to go to her. Whit's elbows were propped on her knees, her hands covering her face. "Baby, are you sick? Has something happened?"

Whit mumbled something into her hands, but it was unintelligible.

"What'd you say?" She knelt before Whit and grasped her wrists to gently pull her hands away. Whit's eyes were bloodshot, even in the dim light, and she wouldn't meet Mae's gaze. "Please, you're scaring me."

Whit's jaw flexed and she lifted her eyes. "Who's your father, Mae?"

"Wh-what?" The question hit her like a sledgehammer. She knew Whit had trust issues. She should have told her. But it wasn't like she'd lied to her. She just hadn't found the right time to tell her. "Is it that important?"

Whit's eyes bored into hers. Her face was stone. "Is Michael Dupree your father?"

Oddly, Mae wasn't shocked. She instinctively knew Whit wouldn't have asked the question if she didn't already know. But why would Michael tell Whit? They didn't even like each other. Who else knew? She hadn't told anyone.

Whit clamped her hands on Mae's wrists like a vise and shook her. She growled through clenched teeth. "Is he?"

"Ye-yes, he is. At least, according to Big Mae's will."

Whit released her and stood so quickly that Mae toppled to sprawl in the thick wood-chip bedding. Whit stared down at her but didn't offer to help her up. "Just when were you going to tell me?"

She scrambled to her feet, and Bar shifted restlessly in the large stall, pinning his ears at Whit's harsh tones. "It just hasn't come up. I mean, he asked me not to tell anyone because his wife doesn't know."

"I didn't think I was just anyone." Whit slapped her own forehead. "God, I am so gullible."

"No. No, you're not. You *aren't* just anyone." Mae reached for her, but Whit stepped back. "It's not like Michael and I are close. I'd never met him until a few months ago when I first moved here. I don't understand why you're so upset. I know you don't really like him, but he is a friend of Clinton's."

"That fucking bastard isn't anybody's friend."

Mae wrung her hands. God, this was bad. Very bad. She had to fix this, whatever was wrong, whatever was making Whit stare like she didn't know her. "What's he done? I can't help if I don't know why you're so upset."

Whit's laugh was harsh. "Didn't daddy dearest tell you he'd filed a protest to disqualify Bar from the Breeders Futurity?"

Mae shook her head. "This has to be a mistake."

"It's no mistake. Preston Wells informed me this morning."

"On what grounds?" As soon as the words were out of her mouth, she knew. Had the rumors been true?

"You should know. It's your favorite subject. He's claiming our colt was cloned."

Was Bar a clone? Had Whit known it all along? No. She refused to even consider that Whit or Clinton would do anything illegal or immoral, no matter how desperate their situation. Damn it. She needed those blood-test results. "That's ridiculous. What proof does he have?"

"He doesn't need proof. All he had to do was to inform the track that the Quarter Horse Breeders Association is investigating Bar."

"Wouldn't they already know about that?"

"Apparently, they don't normally share notes, but you obviously knew." Whit stalked toward her. "I've been sitting here wondering how Michael could have found out about that investigation." She backed Mae against the wall. "Who else outside the Association would know? Oh, yeah. You have a girlfriend who works there. Did you fuck her to get that information, then hand it over to daddy dearest?"

The accusation was like a slap and she recoiled in horror. "I did not! How could you even say that?" Tears welled in her eyes and an icy panic seized her. Whit was acting like a cornered dog, biting everyone close to her.

"Because the first thing I did after leaving Preston's office was find the track veterinarian, just in case we could draw a blood sample and find a way to have Bar's DNA confirmed in time for him to race Saturday."

Mae's heart stopped. She knew what was coming.

"Funny thing, he said he'd just drawn blood on my horse Monday. Duh." Whit slapped her own forehead again for emphasis. "I saw the envelope from the lab, addressed to you, when it came yesterday." Hurt flashed in her eyes. "Do you know what I thought when I saw it in the mail? I was afraid you might be sick and were having some tests you hadn't told me about. It never occurred to me that I was sleeping with Michael's henchwoman."

"No. No, Whit." She shook her head adamantly. "I know what it looks like, but you've got it all wrong."

Whit moved away, her face hard again. "I don't think I do."

"Why would Michael even do this? I don't understand."

Whit slammed her hand against the side of the stall, and Bar pinned his ears again as he moved away to the far wall. "Why do you think? To get his filthy hands on Pop's farm," she roared. "You probably know something about that, too, don't you? Who actually holds the note on Pop's farm, Mae?"

Mae blinked. "How would I know?"

"Maybe because it's Michael, and not some consortium he represents. Did he promise you a cut, something to replace your lost inheritance so you can go back to Atlanta and resume your life of privilege?" Whit paced to the other side of the stall. When she turned back to Mae, she spread her arms as if offering herself. "Am I just the sow's ear you're selling for your next silk purse?"

"You've got to listen to me." She went to Whit, grabbing her hands when she put them out to push her away. She wouldn't let this happen. She wouldn't let her go. "I don't know anything about that loan. I'm not getting anything from Michael. I know how it looks, but when I found out Bar was part of a cloning investigation, you were on your way to the emergency room with Clinton. I did ask the veterinarian to do that test so you'd have proof. We just have to go get the lab report from the farm and everything will be okay."

Whit jerked her hands free and glared. "WE don't have to do anything. I've already contacted the Association and they say their investigation is more about fraud than cloning, so a blood test isn't enough to close the investigation." Whit pointed to the door of the stall. "I can't even look at you any longer. Go. I don't want you near me or Pop or our horse."

"No." Mae couldn't stop her sobs. "This is wrong. You're wrong. I would never hurt you. Whit, please. I love you."

Whit didn't answer. She turned away and went to Bar, smoothing her hands along his withers to calm him. Her angry words and, now, her silence stabbed into Mae like a cold, sharp shard. The pain was so excruciating, she could barely coax her legs to move as she walked away, exiled from the woman who had awakened her heart.

Chapter Twenty-two

"There's rats in the feed room and the cat's gone missing."

Mae stared at the farmhouse and sniffed. How could Whit speak to her like that? She didn't even acknowledge when Mae confessed that she loved her.

Her first impulse had been to curl up on her sofa with Rhett and sob. She did drive to her apartment from the track, but never went in. She sat in the car, with Rhett looking up at her. For a brief second, she thought she saw something of Big Mae in his eyes.

You are a strong, Southern woman bred from a long line of strong women. We all have survived by our own wits and resources. You will do the same.

She didn't really have a plan, but something told her the first thing she had to do was find the blood-test results. She drove quickly to Joie de Vivre. If she hurried, she could find the envelope and leave before Whit and Clinton came home from the track. She didn't want to face Whit again until some of this was straightened out.

"As long as there's breath in my body, I won't let them lose this farm."

Rhett whined and wagged his tail in agreement.

She let herself into the house and, after only a moment of shuffling papers around, found the report. She opened it and read quickly. She knew it! The results again confirmed Raising the Bar was foaled by Bar None and sired by Beduino's Dash.

But Whit said they needed more. The investigation was about fraud. The bribe must be the key, but why didn't the Association investigator just interrogate the lab guy? He was easy enough to identify on the video Jodie had copied for her.

She pulled out her cell phone and found Jodie's number. She answered right away.

"Hey, I was beginning to think you were never going to call me again." Jodie's voice was warm. "Are you here in Alexandria?"

"No, and I'm sorry I haven't called. I've been really busy."

"Ah. Work busy, or working-out-with-the-boss busy?"

Mae's laugh felt hollow, but the overwhelming loneliness she'd felt as she walked away from Whit eased just a little as she realized she had people she could turn to for help. "Some of both."

"I'm happy for you."

"Thank you, but I wasn't calling to catch you up on what's going on with me. I need your help, Jodie."

"What's up?"

"One of the horses listed in that cloning case is Whit's colt. He's favored to win the Breeders Futurity on Saturday, but a protest has been filed at the last minute to have him pulled from the race because of the Association's investigation. I have proof from another lab confirming he's not a clone, but they won't let him run unless the Association clears him."

"So, what's the problem? Just bring the new test results here and give them to our investigator."

"Apparently that's not good enough. They told Whit the case will remain open until they confirm exactly what the lab guy altered after he accepted the bribe. It's easy enough to identify him on the video. Why haven't they just asked him?"

"Hold on."

She could hear footsteps, then a door closing. When Jodie spoke again, her voice was hushed.

"They haven't asked him because he's disappeared."

"Disappeared?"

"Gone. His wife and daughter are gone, too. He told his neighbor he'd been promoted and relocated by his company. When our investigator talked to the lab, they said the guy quit. Didn't even work out a notice. Just called in and said he wouldn't be coming back to work."

Mae's heart sank. "Hell's bells."

"Sorry I couldn't be of more help."

"I guess I'll have to figure this out on my own."

Jodie's voice was hesitant. "You haven't told anyone where you got that video, have you? I could lose *my* job."

"No, absolutely not. I haven't even told anyone I have it. I wouldn't do anything to get you in trouble."

"Okay." A pause. "I really wish I could help." Mae could hear the sound of computer keys clicking. "I'll hack into the case file one more time and see if there's anything that might give you a lead. But, honestly, if there was a lead, we would have already followed it."

"I appreciate you trying. I'll think of something." Mae sighed. "You have my number?"

"Yeah, I do." The clicking stopped. "It's not the end of the world, you know. They'll eventually get this cleared up and there'll be other races for that colt."

"No, I'm afraid there won't be. But that's another story I don't have time to get into."

"Good luck, then."

"Thanks. I'm going to need it."

Mae drove slowly back into town. Who could she turn to now?

Whit said Michael had filed the protest. How would he have known about the investigation? She frowned. She couldn't believe Whit's accusations were correct. Michael had been nothing but wonderful since she'd arrived in Louisiana. Well, there was his temper-fit when she'd tweeted news about the casino deal. That was a side of him that scared her a little. But he'd set her up in an apartment and got her a job with Whit. Had she been an unwitting dupe? No, she'd never discussed the cloning issue with him. Not after that first lunch. She'd only talked about it with Jean Paul. He was the one who told her of the rumors about Whit's colt. That was it. Jean Paul had to be behind this. He was the one responsible for securing land for the casino project. Michael was probably just representing him when he filed the protest against Bar.

Maybe she was going about this all wrong. Maybe Michael *was* the key. She could show him the lab report proving Bar wasn't a clone. She'd even show him the video if it would help convince him the probe had nothing to do with Bar. Surely he wouldn't want to be a part of anything underhanded. If he could withdraw the protest, then maybe the track would let the colt run. It was worth a try.

❖

Michael's secretary wasn't there, but he was pacing behind his desk with his cell phone to his ear. She stood in the doorway and he waved for her to come in and have a seat.

"No, Helen, it's on the seventeenth. Let somebody else chair the hospital fund-raiser. This is important. Guys from the national GOP are going to be there to support Senator Perrault." He threw his hand up in an exasperated gesture. "You need to quit listening to that MSNBC propaganda. There is no war on women. It's all made up." He frowned as he listened to the person on the other end of the line. "Listen. I'm paying five thousand a plate for us, and you're going. Period. It's formal, so I need you to get my tux cleaned. I'm sorry. This is more important." He listened again. "Look, make a big donation to the children's hospital in my name and go buy yourself something new to wear to the senator's fund-raiser." He threw his hand up again. "Jesus, not that big. I'm not made of money. Give them a check for fifteen thousand. That's plenty. Look, I've gotta go. I've got someone waiting to talk to me. Yes. Okay. Good-bye."

He looked at Mae. "I still wonder sometimes why I married that woman. In her world, everything is all about her."

Mae smiled at him, a polite reflex rather than an agreement. "Well, I hope I'm not about to add to your list of needy women."

He smiled kindly at her. "What can I do for you?"

She handed him the envelope. "This is a DNA test done by an independent laboratory, proving that Raising the Bar is not a cloned colt."

His smile faded and he slowly slid the report out to read it.

"Whit said you filed the protest with the racing board to have him scratched from the race because the Quarter Horse Breeders

Association has listed him in their investigation. They won't dismiss the complaint as long as that case remains open, and the Association won't close it because they say it's about lab records being altered more than it's about cloning. But I was thinking that, since the Association didn't file the protest, maybe Bar would be allowed to race anyway if the complaint is withdrawn."

"This is unfortunate." He handed the report back to her. "I filed the protest on behalf of a client. He'd have to agree to withdraw it."

"You filed it on behalf of a client, not yourself?"

"Yes. I'm not at liberty to reveal who—attorney-client privilege, you understand."

She frowned. It had to be Jean Paul. He had the most to gain if Bar didn't race. "What if you showed the test results to your client? Surely, he wouldn't want to wrongly exclude the Casey colt."

"I don't think this report will change his mind. He has other concerns that this report won't address. It's not just about the Caseys and their colt. It's about corruption in our local racing industry that could sabotage the casino expansion endeavor."

"You must know somebody who can help. How did you find out about the investigation?"

"Through my client, of course." He turned toward the window and rubbed his fingers against the beginnings of the thin beard he was growing. When he turned back to her, the ring glinted in the sunlight and she froze.

She'd seen that ring before. It was large and distinctive. The video. It was the ring in the video. He was speaking again, and she forced herself to focus, praying he hadn't noticed her reaction. "I'm sorry, you were saying?"

"I was saying that I'm sorry, but I can't help you with this. I wish I could, if only for Clinton's sake. But my hands are tied."

She dropped her gaze, feigning resignation. "I guess that's it, then. I'd better go talk to Whit. I don't know how she's going to explain it to Clinton."

"I'm so sorry," he said, gently squeezing her fingers.

"I understand. Thank you." It took every ounce of her self-control to refrain from wiping her hand on her jeans. She might have inherited some of his physical features, but thank the Lord she hadn't inherited his lack of conscience.

❖

Whit's phone chirped and she checked the caller ID. Mae had called several times that afternoon and she'd let it go to voice mail. She didn't want to talk to anyone—anyone but the person calling from the number displayed on the screen now.

"Whit Casey." She hoped the woman on the other end couldn't hear the desperation in her voice.

"Ms. Casey, this is Lorraine Morris. My secretary said you needed to talk with me on an urgent issue."

"Thank you for returning my call. This *is* urgent or I wouldn't have bothered you."

"What can I do for you?"

"The Association is investigating records fraud at one of the labs that does DNA testing for registration. My horse has been incorrectly included in that investigation, and I have independent lab results that show he is not a cloned colt. I need for you to drop him from your case." It was a bluff. She hadn't opened the lab tests and they were gone when she got home, so she didn't actually know what the results showed. But she'd worry about that later.

"I'm aware of the investigation and your appeal to have Raising the Bar dropped from the case. I also know my investigator told you we can't drop your colt from the case until we figure out exactly what was altered in the records."

"My colt is favored to win the Breeders Futurity on Saturday. If you don't drop him from the case, the racing board is going to scratch him from the race."

"I'm sorry, Ms. Casey. The Futurity isn't the only million-dollar race this season. I'm sure this will be cleared up soon, but I don't think it would be appropriate for me to interfere with the case."

Whit took a deep breath to keep her voice even. "Would it be appropriate for you to take measures to prevent a lawsuit against the Association? Because if my horse misses that race on Saturday, even though I have proof he is correctly registered, I will sue to recoup the purse my horse would have won." It was a useless threat, she knew, because the farm would be lost long before a lawsuit wound its way through the courts, but it was the last card she had left to play.

"I don't respond well to threats, Ms. Casey."

"I'm sorry, but I'm desperate. I can't wait for the later race. I need to run my colt on Saturday." She closed her eyes. At this point, she wasn't above begging. "Please, Ms. Morris. This is nothing but an underhanded move by Michael Dupree to get his hands on my father's farm."

"Michael Dupree is mixed up in this?" She practically growled his name.

"Yes. He filed the protest with the racing board." Obviously there was some bad blood between Michael and Lorraine Morris, and Whit wasn't above using it. "He holds a lien against my father's farm that is due next week. That's why he wants my colt out of the race."

The silence seemed to extend forever.

"I've got another meeting in about ten minutes and then a dinner engagement immediately after, but I'll talk to the investigator first thing in the morning and see where the case stands."

"Thank you. I'd appreciate anything you can do."

"Don't thank me yet. I meant it when I said I won't interfere, but I promise to check the progress."

"I'll take what I can get."

Well, nothing to do but wait. Whit closed the phone as Pop approached with Ellie at his heels.

"Where the hell have you been? Mae's looking for you, and I'm so hungry I'm gonna eat one of these horses if they don't run fast enough."

Whit tried to smile. It was an old joke that had made her giggle when she was a kid tagging along after Pop while he readied his racers. "Sorry, Pop. I was taking care of the paperwork to get Dun Done It entered in the Futurity."

"You got a jock lined up?"

"Yep. Rick. Same as the last race."

"Good. He's good." Pop eyed her. "So, who pissed in your cornflakes?"

Even with his faulty memory, Pop knew her better than anybody. She'd never been able to hide her feelings from him, but she wasn't ready to tell him yet that Bar might be scratched from the race. Not while they still had a sliver of hope.

"I'm just a little under the weather." She rubbed her lower belly and offered the only excuse that would stop his questions. "Female cramps." It was a lie that would deflect any man, even Pop.

"Why don't you go lay down in the camper and I'll bring you something from the cafeteria," he said gruffly, pulling her into a one-armed hug.

"I've got a better idea. Why don't I call ahead and order some takeout from your favorite Cajun place, and let's go home. I want to lie down in my own bed."

"Sounds good. We've got ice cream in the freezer there."

It was a small gesture, but it nearly breached the dammed-up tears her anger had been holding back all morning. The disease shredded his short-term memory, but he could still recall her craving for ice cream when she had menstrual cramps. She wrapped an arm around his waist and leaned into his strong, steady shoulder. "Thanks, Pop."

"Let's find Mae and see what she wants us to order for her."

"Uh, she found me a while ago. She's got stuff to do this afternoon. We're on our own."

He frowned. "Okay. I reckon she'll be out later. We'll save some ice cream for her."

Whit didn't answer. Telling him Bar might be scratched from the race filled her with dread, but explaining that Mae had betrayed them left her completely, desolately hollow.

What would she tell him? The hard truth. Parents, memories, relationships, happiness. None of it lasted forever.

Chapter Twenty-three

"A fox always knows a way into the henhouse."

Mae sipped her chardonnay sparingly, although she really wanted one of those stiff toddies Big Mae said would curl your nether hairs. She needed to stay sharp, her mind focused. Besides, it wouldn't take much alcohol before she'd dissolve into sobs. Whit's angry rejection only hours earlier tortured the edge of her thoughts and made her chest ache. She was barely holding it together and nearly burst into tears when she saw her old friend Robbie behind the bar. He'd instantly read the despair on her face and wrapped her in a tight hug. She promised she'd explain later. Right now, her last hope was approaching.

"It'd be an understatement to say I was shocked and intrigued when I got the message to meet you here."

"Please, sit down, Avery." Mae indicated the chair next to hers at the bar. "Thank you for coming."

"The message said it was urgent."

"Yes. It is." She fortified herself with another sip of wine and a deep breath. "Whit needs your help."

"She's not in jail, is she?" It was a weak jest. Avery's eyes were sharp with concern. "God, it's not Clinton, is it? He and I never got along, but I know what he means to her."

Robbie returned from serving a customer at the other end of the bar and gave Avery a questioning look. "What can I get you?"

"Whiskey sour," Avery said, without taking her eyes from Mae.

"She's going to lose the farm."

Avery held her hands open in a no-shit gesture. "This is what you call urgent. I told you that a couple of weeks ago. I told her that more than a month ago."

Robbie placed Avery's drink in front of her and she threw a twenty on the bar. He ignored it and stood with his arms crossed over his chest. Avery gave him an impatient glance. "Do you mind? We're having a private conversation here."

Robbie didn't move. "I know who you are," he said. "And I'm not about to leave Mae at the mercy of Whit's ex, who has a reputation of taking no prisoners in the courtroom."

"He's a friend," Mae said, defusing the confrontation before Avery could answer. "And he owns this restaurant." She let out another huge sigh. "I might as well explain to both of you at the same time." She pulled a dollar bill from her wallet and laid it in front of Avery. "I want to hire you to represent Joie de Vivre Quarter Horses."

Avery stared cautiously at the bill. "I'm not sure I can take the case. I could have a conflict of interests."

"Let me explain first. If you can't, then you can return my dollar."

She began with her first visit to the Quarter Horse Breeders Association offices, leaving nothing out except Jodie's name. "I think the chance of someone else having that same ring is pretty slim, but Michael says he's representing someone. I think that person is Jean Paul. He has the most to gain from the Casey farm going into foreclosure."

"No way," Robbie said. "There's no way Jean Paul has the balls to put a scheme like that together."

"I know he's your business partner, Robbie, but this has nothing to do with the restaurant."

"That's not it, Mae." He glanced around and lowered his voice. "Jean Paul is a victim in this, too."

Avery looked doubtful. "How do you figure that?"

"Because he's under Michael's thumb. Jean Paul is totally on the down-low and craps in his shorts at the thought that Michael knows about his secret gay side and might tell Daddy Broussard."

Mae sat back and gave him a skeptical look. "You can't possibly mean the man who's been stalking me for the past two months. He doesn't have a gay bone in his body."

"Your little-baby gaydar just can't pick up the ones on the down-low yet. He totally overcompensates to hide it." He tapped her on the arm. "You'll get better at it. Don't worry."

Avery frowned. "That still doesn't mean he's not behind this. I have to agree with Mae. He has the most to gain."

Robbie shook his head. "Nope. You're wrong."

"How can you be sure, Robbie?" Mae trusted him, but she was having a hard time seeing the Jean Paul that Robbie was describing.

"Because it was my dick in JP's mouth when Michael caught him."

"Yuck. I did not need that image in my head," Avery said.

"I told him to go ahead and tell his father. Then Michael wouldn't have the ammunition to blackmail him. The man makes a good living. He doesn't need Daddy's money."

Avery drummed her fingernails on the bar and pursed her lips. "Okay. Obviously, we need to talk to Jean Paul, but it looks like unless we can find the lab guy, we can't get that complaint dismissed in time for Whit's colt to race on Saturday."

"Can't you—I don't know—file an injunction or get a search warrant or something?" Mae had hoped that Avery could use her legal skills to fix this.

"You've been watching too much television." Avery gave her a rueful smile.

"I can probably get JP over here now, if that will help," Robbie offered.

"So, are you two boyfriends or something?" Mae was a little hurt that Robbie hadn't told her if they were. He was the first friend she'd told about her and Whit.

Robbie grasped his own chin and mugged for her. "This face is too pretty to waste on just one guy. I have to spread myself around. We're just business partners with benefits."

Avery shook her head. "Could I get a refill, pretty boy?"

"Make that two," Mae added.

"Phone call, then drinks." Robbie pulled out his cell phone and punched a speed-dial number, then held the phone to his ear with his shoulder while he poured another glass of wine and mixed a second whiskey sour.

Avery turned back to Mae. "Before we interrogate Jean Paul, I've got another question for you."

Robbie ended his call and delivered their drinks, propping his elbows on the bar. "No fair exchanging information while I'm on the phone. Where were we?"

"She was about to ask me a question." They both looked at Avery with expectation.

"You deftly avoided my first question. Why isn't Whitley here?"

Mae's embarrassment burned along her neck and cheeks. There was nothing worse than having to admit to your lover's ex that you've had a quarrel. "Because she thinks I've been working with Michael to sabotage her efforts to keep their farm out of foreclosure."

Avery's eyes narrowed and Robbie's widened.

"What would make her think that?"

Avery's eyes bored into hers, but Mae met her gaze. "Because she found out I'm Michael's illegitimate daughter."

Robbie gasped. "No! I thought your father died when you were a baby."

"I did, too, until Big Mae died and her will included a confession that my father was alive and well in Louisiana."

Avery studied her. "I'm thinking you're here alone because Whit didn't learn about it from you."

Mae ducked her head. "No. I was going to tell her, but everything has been happening so fast, and it didn't seem that important until he filed the protest with the racing board."

"So, you've been convicted on circumstantial evidence."

In spite of everything, Mae didn't hesitate to defend Whit. "She's scared, Avery. She's poured everything into that farm during the past six months. She's going to lose her home, Clinton's home."

"Does she even know you're talking to me?"

Mae shook her head. "She's angry and feels betrayed. She told me to leave." She lifted her eyes to hold Avery's gaze again. "But I love her. Even if she never speaks to me again, I need to fix this for her."

Avery chewed her lip, a gesture Mae found oddly uncharacteristic for her usually self-assured demeanor. "I'll do what I can. I guess I owe Whitley that much."

Chapter Twenty-four

"Liquor talks mighty loud once you let it out of the jug."

They watched from across the street as the man got out of a small, non-descript car and let himself in the front door.

"Is that him?"

Mae squinted. It was early, but already the sunlight seemed too bright. "It's impossible to tell with that ball cap. I couldn't see his face clearly, but it's got to be." At least, everything in her wanted it to be him.

Once they had lured Jean Paul into the restaurant office, only Avery's skillful questioning and Robbie's threat to out Jean Paul himself had made him give them the information they needed.

He had confessed to using his phone to video the bribe and sending it to the Quarter Horse Breeders Association shortly after Michael sent an anonymous tip of tampering in the DNA records of three racehorses. It was all part of Michael's plan. He didn't care if the horses were eventually cleared; he just wanted to keep Raising the Bar from racing in time to pay off the loan. The other two horses implicated were simply a ruse. The last thing he confessed was the most important—Michael had relocated his cousin, the lab guy, to Alexandria.

They'd driven there the previous evening, but the man was apparently working a night shift at a new lab. So they'd returned at daybreak to wait.

Mae almost groaned when she got out of the car and stretched in the early morning chill. Bone tired, she'd never felt so adrift. Not even at Big Mae's funeral. She'd always known she would lose her grandmother one day. That was part of life. But she'd never imagined this wound that Whit's withdrawal had created. It was a great aching emptiness that threatened to consume her.

After sitting in Avery's car for hours the night before, they'd gotten rooms at a hotel. But lying in the dark had been torturous, her mind playing Whit's words over and over. She longed for Whit's soft skin, her strong body anchoring her. She'd finally cried herself into a fitful doze that left her even more exhausted.

She was relieved that Avery seemed fresh and focused when they returned to their stakeout. She was happy to let her take the lead because, even if they found the answers they needed, it would be a long day of interrogations and negotiation.

Avery rang the doorbell but got no response. She rang it again and the curtain in the front window moved slightly. She knocked loudly on the door. "Mr. Sheldon. We know you're in there. We are not the police, but I can call them if I need to."

After a moment, the lock on the dead bolt clicked and Danny Sheldon opened the door. His face was haggard and his shoulders slumped. He took a moment to size them up, then stepped back and gestured for them to follow.

He led them through a house nearly empty of furniture. The kitchen counters were barren except for a lone coffeemaker, and he silently scooped grounds into the filter and switched it on before he turned back to them. "I don't guess you're selling subscriptions to the local newspaper." It was a rhetorical question.

"I'm Avery Perrault and this is Mae St. John. I'm an attorney, representing Clinton and Whitley Casey."

"I don't know anybody named Casey."

"They are the owners of Raising the Bar. Does that name ring a bell?"

Mae could see the recognition in his eyes, then resignation on his face.

"I have evidence that you are mixed up in a conspiracy to defraud my clients." Avery was stern and to the point.

"I always knew Michael would throw me to the dogs when he didn't need me anymore. It's almost a relief. At least I'll be rid of him. Go ahead and call the cops. I'm tired of running."

She shook her head. "At this point, I'm not interested in turning you over to the police, Mr. Sheldon. I'm just here to get some answers."

He sighed. "It's Danny. Do you two want coffee? I've been at work all night, and I'm going to need some caffeine if this is going to take very long."

"Thank you, Danny. That would be wonderful," Mae said, keeping her voice kind. "We'd be grateful for anything you can tell us that would help."

She wasn't consciously trying to play good cop-bad cop. She truly felt sorry for the man. He looked so defeated as he poured coffee into three cups. They stood in the empty dining area, separated from him by a counter. Mae opened her laptop and booted it up.

Avery glanced around. "Where are your wife and daughter, Mr. Sheldon?"

"I've sent them to stay with some of my wife's relatives. I'd rather not say where because they're family that my cousin, Michael, doesn't know. I hope to join them if I don't end up in prison over this."

He set the coffee cups, creamer, and sugar on the counter between them and stared at the small digital recorder Avery laid next to the cups.

"I need your permission to record our interview."

He nodded his consent and Avery pushed the button on the side of the slim recorder.

"This is Avery Perrault interviewing Daniel Sheldon on Friday, November 15, 2012, seven thirty a.m. Mr. Sheldon, do you give your permission for this interview to be recorded?"

"I do."

Avery indicated for Mae to turn the laptop's screen toward him. "I'm going to show you a video that was recorded by Mr. Jean Paul Broussard. Then I'm going to ask you some questions about it."

He nodded.

"I need a verbal consent so that it records."

"Okay. I'll watch it."

Mae clicked to play it and they watched Danny take the money. He flushed red as he watched.

"I didn't know he recorded that."

"Is that you in the video, Mr. Sheldon?"

"Yes."

"Because it was recorded without your knowledge, I need to ask your permission to include it as evidence in this deposition."

"That's fine. I'm tired of hiding."

"Who is the third person in that room with you and Mr. Broussard? The man handing you the money and speaking to you?"

"That's my cousin, Michael Dupree."

"The same Michael Dupree who is an attorney in Opelousas?"

"Yes. That's him."

"How can I be sure you've correctly identified him?"

"Are you kidding? You can clearly see that gaudy ring he always wears."

"For the record, he is referring to a distinctive gold ring on Michael Dupree's left hand."

"Where did you work at the time this video was recorded?"

"I worked at Lesley Laboratories. We handled a lot of medical and forensic cases. I worked in the section that identified DNA markers. We processed a lot of DNA tests for the Louisiana branch of the American Quarter Horse Breeders Association."

"Why would you test the DNA of horses?"

"Mostly to confirm their pedigree for owners. Some of these horses are very expensive, and people want to know what they're buying. Also, quarter horse and Thoroughbred racers must have their parentage confirmed before they can be registered to race."

"Why is that?"

"About ten years ago, researchers at Texas A&M successfully cloned a horse. It's expensive and there's no guarantee a clone would perform as well as the original, but some performance horses—cutting horses, dressage horses, jumpers—were cloned. You can only imagine the interest it would generate if one of the past great racing horses were cloned. Would Secretariat's clone be as fast? The racing industry, however, has forbidden it. When we tested potential racers, we not only confirmed parentage, but also compared the DNA results with a worldwide database to make sure there wasn't an identical match on record."

"Back to the video. Why was Mr. Dupree giving you money?"

"He wanted me to alter the records of three horses to implicate them as clones."

"Why would he do that?"

"I'm not sure. I'd have understood if he'd wanted to race a horse that was cloned and needed to cover it up. I mean, all someone would need to prove his horse wasn't a clone is another DNA test."

"And did you alter those records like he paid you to do?"

"No. I didn't."

"Why didn't you?"

He stood and went to the sink to pour his cold coffee down the drain. When he turned back to them, he looked angry. "Because my cousin has been pulling my strings, having me do his dirty work for years, and I'm tired of it. He's laundered money through accounts with my name on them. He calls me in the middle of the night to pick up or drop off things—money or bags I'm too afraid to even open—and he's used me as a front man for shady property deals. He went too far when he had me go out to that farm and wrap barbed wire around a horse's legs, then throw nails in that stall at the track." Anguish filled his eyes. "I've never hurt a living thing in my life. My daughter has a puppy, and when I think about someone hurting him—" Whatever image was in his head choked off the rest of his words.

"Why would you let him do that?"

"Because he's blackmailing me."

"You are saying that Michael Dupree has been forcing you to participate in illegal activities."

"Yes."

"What is he using to threaten you?"

The muscle in his jaw jumped as he stared down at the table. When a strangled sound escaped from him, Mae realized he was trying to maintain his composure and she laid her hand on his. "It's okay, Danny. You can tell us."

He sniffed and cleared his throat before his tear-filled gaze found hers. He seemed to find strength from it.

"When I was only fifteen, I went to a party with a bunch of older boys who were football players. They were popular and I wanted to be part of their crowd. There was a girl there about my age, but she was trying to act older and flirt with some of the guys. Then all of a sudden, she seemed really drunk. I found out later that one of the guys had put a drug in her drink. I took her upstairs to lie on a bed. I was going to call her parents, but the older boys followed me. She was completely unconscious and I was scared. I thought that maybe I should call the paramedics. But the older boys said she'd be fine and they started taking her clothes off." He began to cry. "I told them to stop, but they pushed me out of the room and locked the door. I should have called the police or somebody, but I was scared. I was only fifteen. I could hear them talking about her and laughing. I knew from what they were saying that they were raping her." He wiped his nose on his sleeve like he was that fifteen-year-old boy again.

"Was Michael Dupree one of the boys?" Avery asked.

He shook his head, then realized he must answer. "No. Michael's a lot older than me."

"How did he use this to blackmail you?"

"The boys were stupid and bragged about it at school. A teacher overheard, and two of them were charged with rape. Several more were charged with second-degree rape because they watched. Some other kids had seen me take her upstairs, so I was charged, too. Michael talked to the prosecutor and got the charges dropped in exchange for my testimony."

"Legal deals like that are made every day. How could he use that to blackmail you, Mr. Sheldon?"

He pulled a handkerchief from his pocket this time, and they waited as he dried his tears and wiped his nose. "My wife and daughter are the only good things in my life. They don't know, but Michael kept the newspaper clippings from the court trial. He said he'd give them to my wife."

Mae's heart ached at the deep sadness in his eyes.

"That girl lived down the street from me. I'd known her all her life. I came home one day after the trial had been over a few weeks and a moving van was at her house. She was in the yard and saw me drive up to my house, so she walked down there." His voice was choked. "I'll never forget the way she looked at me. She said, 'Why, Danny? Why didn't you stop them?' All I could do was cry, and her father came to walk her back to their house." He took a few seconds to compose himself, then found Mae's eyes again. "I'd kill myself if my daughter found out and looked at me like that girl did."

By the time he finished, Mae was searching her laptop bag for a tissue to dry her own tears. Even Avery appeared moved, clearing her throat and staring down at her notes.

"But Michael doesn't know where my wife and daughter are now, and I'm ready to face whatever I deserve. I want to wake up and be able to look in the mirror without being ashamed of the man I see there."

Avery looked up from her notes. "What did you do with the money he gave you?"

"I didn't want Michael's dirty money. I donated it to a shelter for battered women. I have the receipt if you want it."

"That, Mr. Sheldon, might have been the first smart thing you've done." She stopped the recording.

"What do we do now?" Mae was terrified their time was running out.

Avery's smile was predatory, and Mae was glad she was on their side. "We're heading straight into Dodge City with guns blazing."

CHAPTER TWENTY-FIVE

"When the chickens pack the jury box, the fox is always guilty."

Whit idly pushed off with her foot again, trying to organize her thoughts with the slow, repetitious arc of the porch swing. She'd been sitting there for hours, hoping to work up the courage to explain to Pop that their colt would be scratched from tomorrow's race and they wouldn't have the money to pay the note on the farm.

Finding the words wouldn't be the hardest part. She wasn't even sure losing the farm would be the worst of it. The biggest loss would be the empty seat where Mae usually sat, snuggled against her side.

It'd only been about two months since Mae had walked into their lives, and in that time she'd become their bright light, the sun that shone each day and warmed the cold, lonely places in their souls, in Whit's heart. She had unconsciously gravitated to the swing where they'd spent many hours, sharing kisses and the details of their days. But being there cast her deeper into her well of desolation. Mae's absence was sharper, more consuming than the pain of losing her mother.

Maybe it would be easier if she saddled one of the mares and rode out to her pond, her thinking place, before she sat Pop down to tell him she'd been unable to stop life from crashing down around them. But riding across the lush acres where she'd spent her childhood at Pop's heels, absorbing everything he knew about horses, seemed little comfort.

She'd tried to call Lorraine Morris repeatedly all day, but her secretary kept saying she was still in an emergency meeting, and, when she phoned a final time, Lorraine had left the office. She'd also hit the ignore button when Mae tried to call several times Thursday, but the attempts had become more frequent this morning, and Whit just couldn't bear to see her name come up on the caller ID again. That's when she'd turned her cell phone off.

Now, sitting in the swing and about to go inside to talk to Pop, she realized that she needed to let her jockey know Raising the Bar wouldn't race. He might still be able to sign on to ride in a different race on Saturday.

She powered up her phone and it buzzed with a list of missed calls. She'd expected the ones from Mae, but was surprised to see Avery also had been trying to get in touch with her. Fat chance. Avery was part of that pack of rats stealing Joie de Vivre, so Whit was certain she knew about the protest Michael had filed. The last thing she wanted was to hear Avery gloat and offer her that pity job again. She and Pop would live in the small camper compartment of the horse trailer before she'd go to work for the casino group.

She started to dial Tommy to tell him to find another ride, but hesitated. The text icon indicated a message was waiting. She touched it and sucked in a breath when Mae's name came up on the screen. She closed her eyes to summon the courage to hit the delete command without reading it, but the small traitorous part of her that still wanted Mae wouldn't let her. She opened it.

"We have proof. One o'clock tomorrow. Evangeline racing offices."

Proof of what? That records were altered and Bar actually is a clone? When she'd tried to find the lab results yesterday she'd decided Mae was the only person who could have taken them. Her head was screaming "traitor," but her heart still refused to believe Mae could betray her.

It was getting late and she needed to make sure Pop took his medication before he went to bed. She sighed and stood to go inside. Tomorrow she'd do the only thing she could do. She'd go to the racing office and look every one of them in the eye. She was a Casey and she refused to cower for anyone, even if her head was right and her heart was wrong.

❖

"What the hell is this?" Whit scowled. Surprised to see Raising the Bar still on the list of Breeders Futurity racers, she'd left Pop with Tyree and waited, pacing outside the racing office's conference room until Avery appeared at exactly one o'clock. Whit had been ready to face Mae and Michael, not her ex-girlfriend and two people she didn't know. She glared at Avery. "I should have known you were tied up in this, too."

"Shut up, Whitley, and give me a dollar." Avery's stare was cool.

"Give you a dollar? Are you nuts?"

"I can't be your attorney unless you officially hire me. I didn't tell Mae this, but the dollar she gave me to represent you may not hold up to questioning. It's better if you actually do the hiring."

"Why would I do that?" She glared at the darkly attractive woman who stood at Avery's elbow. A new girlfriend already?

"You always were hardheaded." Avery sighed. "You will hire me to represent you because Mae and I drove all over this state yesterday and were up most of the night pulling your defense together. I don't have time for your attitude right now, but we'll be happy to accept your apology when we're done. Now, give me a dollar."

She didn't want Avery's help, but this wasn't the time to let her pride get in the way. And, though Avery's priorities might be in the wrong place, Whit trusted that she wouldn't be cruel. She dug a bill out of her pocket and handed it over.

"Are we ready to start?" Preston Wells was sitting at the head of the table when they entered the conference room.

"We're waiting on one more," Avery said.

At that moment, a tall man with thick white hair and Avery's blue eyes walked into the room. "I apologize for being late, but I have the warrants."

Senator Perrault? Warrants? Were they going to arrest her? Arrest Pop? For what?

Preston stood again and gestured to an empty chair beside him. "Please, have a seat, Senator. We haven't started yet." He turned to Avery. "Ms. Perrault, could you introduce the people you brought with you?"

Avery placed her briefcase on the table and pointed around the table. "This is Kevin Mackey and Jodie Redmond, from the Louisiana chapter of the American Quarter Horse Breeders Association. Kevin is the lead investigator on the case in question here, and Jodie is one of their information-technology people. You, of course, know my father and Ms. Casey."

Preston nodded. "Okay, let's hear it."

Over the next two hours, the investigator and Avery laid out the tangled conspiracy directed by Michael. They listened to the deposition Avery had recorded with Michael's cousin, Danny Sheldon, and a second deposition in which Jean Paul described the bribe he had videotaped for Michael. Both identified Michael as the man giving Danny a bribe to alter the DNA records of three horses. Then Jodie testified that she and a Lesley Laboratories computer tech had spent most of the night examining the DNA files in question and could confirm that, despite the bribe, they were never altered after the test results were initially recorded.

Whit listened, speechless. She couldn't believe Mae and Avery had done a month's worth of investigating in less than two days. They did it for her and Pop.

"So, am I to understand that the Association's investigation is closed and Ms. Casey's colt is legally registered to race?" Preston looked as relieved as Whit felt.

"That is correct, Mr. Wells," Kevin said. "The Quarter Horse Breeders Association is satisfied that the DNA analysis that confirms the parentage of Raising the Bar is authentic."

Preston smiled at Whit. "At least I won't have to explain to the gambling commission why that colt wasn't scratched right after the protest was filed."

Avery looked at her father. "Dad?"

"The district attorney is on vacation in Florida, so I walked these warrants through myself, charging Michael Dupree with conspiring to affect the outcome of a professional sporting event and conspiring to subvert legal gambling to his own purposes." The senator shoved some papers at Preston. "I understand he's here at Evangeline today, so I have a sheriff's deputy waiting outside to arrest him."

Preston pursed his lips. "I've got a big crowd out there. Do you have any reason to think he's dangerous?"

"No, but the best way to handle this might be to call him to this office under the pretense of discussing the complaint he filed. We can arrest him here, out of the public eye."

Preston nodded. "We can call him from my office."

Whit stood. "As much as I'd like to see that bastard in handcuffs, I've got two horses to ready for the Futurity." She shifted on her feet and shoved her hands in the pockets of her jeans. "I don't know what to say. Thank you doesn't seem sufficient."

Senator Perrault studied her. "I know we don't see eye to eye on a lot of things, Whitley, but I won't be dishonest about my involvement. I believe in this casino project and the jobs it will bring to our state, and I don't want what Michael has done to taint its chances." He stood and followed Preston out of the room.

Kevin stood, too. "Well, my only regret is that it probably wouldn't look right if I bet on your colt, so I guess I'll go put some money on my second choice. I hear a horse called Dun Done It has a good chance."

Whit smiled. "I won't say he can beat Bar, but you won't go wrong if you bet on him to place." She turned to Jodie. "Thank you for coming and testifying today."

"I did it for Mae. She's more than worth going out of my way for."

They stared at each other. Jodie's message was clear, and Whit nodded her understanding. She didn't deserve Mae, but perhaps Jodie did.

"Avery—"

"Go, Whit. Get your horses ready. But you at least owe me a seat for the race, so I'll see you in the owners' box. We'll talk then."

Whit turned to leave but jumped when the phone in her pocket rang. She glanced at the caller ID. "Hey, Tyree." Her eyes darted to Avery as she listened. "Shit. I'm on my way." She ended the call. "Avery, get that deputy and tell him to haul ass to the backstretch."

❖

Whit's heart nearly stopped when she saw Clinton on the ground in front of Bar's stall. Mae was kneeling next to him, clutching his hand as she talked to him. Ellie sat next to Pop, licking his ear while Tyree stood over them, nervously wringing his hands.

"What happened? Pop, are you hurt?" Whit sank to her knees and ran her hands over him.

His face was pale and twisted in a grimace as he struggled to speak through clenched teeth. "God damn…Michael. Tried to…tell me…Bar wasn't…racing today."

"Mr. Clinton slugged him a good one. Hit him right in the jaw." Tyree bent over them, vibrating with excitement. "Made Mr. Dupree mad. He started saying all kinds of stuff about he was getting Mr. Clinton's farm and he was gonna build a big hotel and casino on it. Next thing, they're slugging it out like a couple of farmhands."

"Tell me what hurts, Pop."

"I wrenched…my back," he said, but he rubbed at his hip. "Michael still fights…like a girl. Never did learn…how to use his fists. Pushed me down against…that post over there."

Mae smiled down at him, even though her eyes looked worried. "Hey, you're talking to a couple of girls here."

Whit glanced around. "Where's Michael now?"

"Ms. Mae ran him off," Tyree said.

Whit looked at her for the first time, but Mae wouldn't meet her gaze.

"I was afraid he was going to hurt Clinton even worse, so I told him that we knew about the bribe and that the police were looking for him because Senator Perrault had warrants for his arrest."

"He slapped Ms. Mae," Tyree said. "I was about to kick the shit out of him, but he lit outta here like his tail was on fire."

Whit realized Mae had been keeping her face angled away so she couldn't see the left side. She gently grasped her chin and turned it toward her. Mae's cheek was red and swelling a bit around the cheekbone.

"I'm okay," Mae said, her eyes never leaving Clinton.

"Got to get…my colt ready," Pop muttered. He moved his legs and grimaced.

"Do you think you can get up?" Whit asked.

Although they stood a respectful distance away, a crowd was beginning to gather to watch.

"Maybe I better…go home," he said. He gripped Mae's hand tighter and stared at her, his eyes cloudy now with pain. "Celeste knows what to do, don't you, honey?"

Mae looked at Whit for the first time and spoke quietly. "You need to call an ambulance. It might not be his back. His hip could be broken. I don't think he lost consciousness, but he hit the back of his head, too."

Whit was about to dig her phone out of her pocket when Avery arrived with a deputy and a track security officer in tow.

"What happened?"

"Pop got into a fight with Michael. To break it up, Mae told him the police were looking to arrest him and he took off."

"How long ago and which way?" The deputy scanned the crowd.

"About five, maybe ten minutes ago. I think he was headed for the parking lot." Mae looked at Avery. "We need an ambulance."

"I'm going with them to find Michael," Avery said, punching nine-one-one on her phone as she turned away. "I'll tell the paramedics where to find you."

Whit untied the bandana around her neck and wiped at the sweat beading on Pop's brow. He was quiet now. She wondered if he was going into shock and considered whether they should elevate his feet. But what if his hip was broken? Damn, she felt helpless.

But she didn't have much time to worry over it. The EMTs on duty at the Evangeline race complex were there in minutes. They quickly evaluated Pop and gently loaded him onto a stretcher. Whit, Mae, and Tyree followed, but when Whit started to climb into the ambulance, Mae grasped her arm.

"You can't go, Whit. You have to stay here and win that race. I'll go with Clinton. I'll call to let you know what's happening."

Too much was happening at once. Pop wasn't having a heart attack. His injury could be serious, but it apparently wasn't life threatening. He'd do anything, sign whatever paperwork Mae told him to. So why shouldn't she let her go with him?

"Wait." She looked around but saw only Ellie. "Where's your dog? Where's Rhett?"

"He's fine. He's spending the day with my neighbor across the hall."

"Celeste? Where's Celeste? Where are we going?" Pop raised his hand, searching, and the EMT securing the stretcher in the ambulance gave them a questioning look.

"I'll be right there, Clinton," Mae answered, before turning back to Whit. "Go. I can't get his horse ready to race, but I can go to the hospital with him. I promise I won't let anything happen to him."

Whit nodded. "Thanks." The rest stuck in her throat. She'd needed to tell Mae so much, too much that she was ashamed to say. But the doors slammed shut, and the ambulance pulled away.

Chapter Twenty-six

"You'll never ride that horse if you stay sittin' on the fence."

Okay, Tommy. We lucked up and drew midfield. Bar prefers that. I want you to break out fast before the others have a chance to crowd in on him. He's got the juice to get out front and stay there. But that means you need to make sure he stays focused. He has a tendency to be distracted by them loading the last horses in the gate. Give him a jiggle of the bit or something to pull his attention back to the track when they're loading the last one."

"I got it covered, Boss."

Whit grinned up at him, despite the knot of tension in her belly, as the line of horses walked toward the track. "I know. I'm really glad to have a jock riding who knows him. But I've got to give you some instructions for the people watching, right?"

He grinned back. "Sure."

"See you in the winner's circle." She slapped Bar on the neck and dropped back for a last-minute talk with Dun Done It's jockey.

Dun was dancing nervously and his groom—standing in for Pop—clung to his lead rope while Rick worked to calm him from his perch on Dun's back.

"He's really hyped up today," Rick said. "More than usual."

"It's good, then, that he drew the number-ten spot. You'll only be in the gate for a few seconds," Whit said. "Watch out for the horse next to you. He tends to break out toward the right, and we don't want him bumping Dun out of the gate. Also, Dun's never run on the outside, so you may have trouble keeping him straight. Don't let him drift in. Bar's gonna break out fast, but Dun runs better if he has somebody to chase, so don't worry about it."

"No problem," Rick said, still working the reins as he listened.

"Rick." Whit waited for him to meet her gaze. "You should already know this, but I want to be very clear. I know Bar is my colt, but I expect you to run this race to win, not place. That's what Greg Vickers pays Pop for—winning."

He nodded. "If I thought anything else, you'd be talking to a different jock right now."

"Good luck, then."

❖

Every nerve in Whit's body sang as she climbed the stadium seating to the owners' box. The months of getting up at daybreak seven days a week, training horses, poring over feeding charts, calculating racing stats, arranging veterinary checkups, and filling out hours of paperwork all boiled down to this—a million-dollar sprint of only 400 yards that would be over in fewer than twenty seconds.

It'd been nearly impossible to concentrate on the race preparations, but Mae had called twice to relay every bit of information as promised. An MRI indicated Pop only had a small bump on his head and extremely strained muscles in his back. No concussion, no broken bones, no slipped disc. Still, because of his confused condition, they were keeping him overnight for observation.

Their conversations, however, were brief. On top of everything else that needed her attention, Dun Done It's owner, Greg, was there to watch his horse run, and he was nervous that Clinton wasn't present. Whit wasted valuable time reassuring him that she knew Clinton's race plan.

She was surprised to find only Avery in their seats. "Where's Greg? The horses are coming out on the track already. He's going to miss it."

Avery pointed to a box ten rows below them. "He said his wife wanted to sit with some friends down there."

Whit stood and scanned the entry points among the stadium seating.

"Looking for someone else?"

Whit sat down again, but kept scanning the people hurrying to their seats after placing last-minute bets. "I called Bernice, Tyree's mother, and asked her to go sit with Pop at the hospital and send Mae to watch the race with us. I need to apologize to her, but I don't want to do it over the phone." She sighed and stared down at her hands. "I'm not sure she'll come, though. I said some pretty nasty things to her when I found out that Michael was her father."

"You can be sort of a hothead at times."

"I'm not denying it." She sighed. "I know I'm a shit and a coward. I don't deserve her. I should just leave her alone."

"That's not what I was thinking."

"No?" Whit had such a low opinion of herself at the moment she couldn't believe Avery wasn't judging her, too. As desperate as she was to apologize to Mae, she wasn't sure she could face her. Shame overwhelmed her every time she relived Mae's tears and the hurt on her face when they argued—no, when Whit verbally attacked her in Bar's stall. She speed-dialed Mae's phone again, and it went immediately to voice mail.

The number-one horse approached the gate, but an official waved the rider off. It was malfunctioning, and a tractor was already pulling a new one onto the track. There would be a delay. She turned back to Avery. "What are you thinking, then?"

Avery studied her. "As much as I hate to admit it, I'm thinking that Mae just might be the real deal for you, and you're about to blow it."

"Avery."

"No, you listen to me, Whitley Casey. We were never destined to work out, and I'll probably regret that until the day I die. But we want different things. You want a home and a wife. I want a seat in Congress."

"The U.S. Congress?"

"Yes. Working to get Dad elected is my first step. I'm tired of the courtroom. Things are about to change in the political landscape. I know you don't believe it, but the Republican Party is going to move back to a more moderate platform. I believe in their financial platform, and I'm willing to work from the inside to change the rest."

"I'd rather wade through a pit of vipers than be involved in politics."

Avery chuckled. "That's my point. But for me, winning a seat in Congress will be my shining moment." She closed her hand over Whit's and squeezed. "I'm sorry we had to hurt each other to figure this out, but I'm not willing to give up my dream for yours," she said softly. "And, you deserve someone who will share your dream." Her eyes were sad but not repentant.

Whit squeezed Avery's hand. "I'm sorry, too." Avery's honesty should sting, but it didn't. She was no longer willing to compromise her dream either.

She dialed the number for Pop's hospital room.

"Mr. Casey's room, this is Bernice."

"Bernice, is Mae still there?"

"No, she left maybe two hours ago. She's not there?"

"No." Mae should have had enough time to drive from the hospital to the track. "She'll probably be here soon. Pop still okay?"

"Sleeping. The pain medicine they gave him pretty much knocked him out."

"Okay. I really appreciate this. I'll be there as soon as I can get clear from here."

"You just worry about that race. I've got me a good book and a comfortable chair. I'm fine here. I can even stay the night if needed."

"Thanks, it may be late when I get there."

She ended the call and watched the ten horses closely as they were led in a wide circle to keep them moving. It was no problem for Bar, but she worried that Dun would get too worked up during the delay. The new gate was in place and the old gate was being dragged off the track. "They're starting to load." She stated the obvious to refocus on the race. But it didn't work. She scanned the crowd for Mae once more.

"I don't think she's coming," Avery said.

"Shit." She raised her binoculars. Bar walked calmly into the tight starting stall. Her heart should be pounding with anticipation, but all she wanted was to fling those glasses down and go find Mae. She didn't deserve her, but she still wanted her…desperately.

Dun loaded into the gate with unexpected ease, and Whit tensed.

"They're off!" The announcer's voice boomed over the crowd's cheering. "It's Raising the Bar out of the gate with Corona Gold inside and Dashin' Snow close. It's all Raising the Bar. Dun Done It and T Boy C are moving up to challenge for second. Raising the Bar now all alone. Here comes Lucky Crown. Raising the Bar takes the wire, but hold on to your tickets. We'll need a photo finish for the rest."

They did it! Bar won. But the huge weight that should have lifted still rested heavy on her shoulders. The victory was hollow. They had the money to pay off the loan and more, but she dreaded that house, knowing Mae wouldn't be there.

Whit turned to Avery. "Do you still represent me?"

"What?"

"The dollar I gave you. You're still my lawyer, right?"

"I guess so." Avery frowned. "Just so you know, I can't continue being your lawyer. I'm still committed to the casino project, and representing you would be a conflict of interest."

The announcer's voice interrupted them. "The results are in. Winner of the Louisiana Quarter Horse Breeders Association Futurity is Raising the Bar. T Boy C is second, Dun Done It third, and Corona Gold fourth."

"Just be my lawyer for the next few minutes and go represent me in the Winner's Circle," Whit said, her words tumbling together in her haste. "Tyree will take care of getting the horses off the track. You'll just have to wave at the crowd, get your picture taken with Bar, and sign paperwork in my place."

"What? No, Whit. Where are you going? This is *your* shining moment."

Whit gently shook off Avery's restraining hand. "You know what? I want more than a moment. I want a lifetime. I want forever. I just hope I'm not too late."

Chapter Twenty-seven

"Bruised peaches make the best cobbler."

Whit knocked again. The sound reverberated in the hallway outside Mae's apartment, like the sick feeling gnawing at her gut as two minutes stretched into more without an answer.

"She's not there."

Whit turned at the voice behind her. An attractive, thirty-something blonde stood in the open door of the apartment across the hall. This was evidently the neighbor who was keeping Rhett earlier. Whit looked past her, but Rhett apparently wasn't still there. "Do you know when she'll be back?" She was relieved that Mae wasn't home, rather than just refusing to answer the door.

The woman held up a set of keys. "Not coming back. When she picked up Rhett, she said she was leaving town and asked me to drop her keys at Michael's office on Monday."

"Gone? She left town?"

"Yeah. The apartment was furnished, so she only had her clothes and a few boxes of personal stuff. She said most of her things are still in a storage room in Georgia. Maybe she's headed there."

Whit glanced at the time on her cell phone. "What time did she leave?"

The woman shrugged. "Maybe thirty minutes ago?"

Whit's heart sank. She was probably thirty miles east on Interstate 40 by now. "I guess I missed her. Thanks, anyway." She was halfway down the hall when the woman called after her.

"She was on the phone with Robbie as she was leaving. You know, her friend who's a chef? If you know where he works, she might have gone by there."

"Great. Thanks." Whit jogged back to her truck. Maybe she wasn't too late.

She sped to the restaurant, parked illegally on the crowded street, then dodged the hostess and two waiters to burst into the kitchen. Robbie was standing at the stove, sautéing someone's dinner. He looked up and frowned.

"Is she here?" Whit didn't have time for pleasantries.

He cocked an eyebrow. "No, but I'm not sure I'd tell you if she was."

"I don't have time to explain or make excuses. I need to find her. I'll follow her back to Georgia if I have to." As she said the words, she realized they were truer than any she'd ever spoken.

❖

Mae stood in the dark farmhouse and closed her eyes. She didn't want to turn the lights on. If she did, she would see the sofa where she and Whit had cuddled, the dining-room table where they'd worked together, and the kitchen where they'd cooked together—well, where she'd cooked and Whit had chopped or peeled whatever Mae gave her. But even the darkness couldn't hide the scent of soap and fresh hay and horses that she'd come to associate with Whit. Warm tears trickled down her cheeks. In such a short time, this modest ranch-style house had become as much a home as the expansive brick two-story where she'd spent most of her lifetime with Big Mae.

She opened her eyes, finding the light switch in the moonlight that shone in through the windows. There wasn't much to take—just her favorite jacket, a pair of muddy boots, and Big Mae's teapot that had migrated here from her apartment. Her clothes and Rhett were waiting in the car. She didn't know where she was going—maybe back to Atlanta—but she couldn't stay here. Since her furnished apartment belonged to Michael, she'd gone to empty it first after Bernice relieved her at the hospital. Clinton had been sleeping as she kissed him gently on the cheek before she left. He, not Michael, was the father she'd never had. She'd be leaving him behind, too.

She knew she shouldn't, but she walked tentatively down the hallway to Whit's bedroom. It had been *their* bedroom for only one night. One unforgettable night.

She sat on the bed, smoothing her hands over the down blanket. She picked up Whit's pillow and hugged it to her. The flannel cover was soft, like Whit's shoulder, and images of Whit naked, the feel of Whit's long body wrapped around hers, and visions of the swirling shades of blue and green in Whit's eyes swamped her. She buried her face in the pillow as the torrent of her emotions gushed through the ragged tear in her heart. She cried wrenching sobs like the child she'd never be again, like a woman who would never love again.

You are a strong, Southern woman bred from a long line of strong women. We all have survived by our own wits and resources. You will do the same.

Big Mae was wrong. She wasn't strong. And she wasn't sure she could survive losing the best thing in her life, the woman whose life, whose soul fit so perfectly with hers.

❖

Whit was relieved to see Mae's Lexus still parked in the circular drive. She stopped her big dually truck next to it and stared at the front door. She'd been so rushed, so intent on finding Mae, she hadn't had time to think about what she'd say.

She got out of the truck and helped Ellie to the ground. Rhett stood on his hind legs, peering through the car window, his tail wagging furiously. She let him out of the car and the two dogs raced around the yard together. "Let's hope Mae is that glad to see me," she said to them.

The only illumination was a table lamp in the dining-room/office. Mae wasn't there, but her jacket and Big Mae's teapot were clustered on the table with a few other things. She listened in the darkness and then followed the muffled sobs.

Cradled in soft moonlight, Mae was curled on Whit's bed, her face buried in Whit's pillow. The sobs tore at her, but at the same time, hope bloomed. Mae was here, crying on her pillow. That meant something didn't it? "Mae?"

Mae jerked up. Tears glistened in the faint light as she turned to Whit. She tried to speak but only cried harder.

"Honey, don't cry."

"I'm sorry. I'm sorry." Her breath hitched between her words. "I just came to get a few things. I…I didn't mean for you to find me sobbing like an idiot."

"Mae—"

Mae shook her head. "I understand, Whit. I do, really. It's just… it's just, I lost Big Mae, but she leaves me a letter telling me that I'm flat broke and my father isn't really dead, but lives in Louisiana. Then I get thrown out of the house I grew up in, and all I've got is a dog with a trust fund and Scarlett's mad money. So, I come out here to find the only person I have left in the world, and I want to believe he's a good person because he *is* the only family I have left, but he asks me not tell anybody that he's my father, so I don't, then I meet you and—"

"Mae—" Whit turned on a lamp and sat on the bed to take the pillow Mae was clutching to her chest. She laid it aside and closed her hands around Mae's.

Mae refused to meet her gaze. "And, and, and I find out that it's not that boys are really that stupid, but it's just that I'm a lesbian and didn't know it, and I fall in love with you and I'm so happy, but then everything falls apart."

"Mae, I'm sorry—"

"I know you can't forgive me. I know lying is a deal-breaker with you. You told me that."

It was clear Whit wouldn't be able to interrupt Mae's tearful, rambling confession, so she pulled some tissues from the box on the bedside table and pressed them into Mae's hands. She barely paused as she wiped at her nose.

"I didn't mean to lie to you, Whit. I really didn't. I was going to tell you, but everything was happening so fast, you and me, then Clinton in the hospital, and, God, I had no idea Michael was doing all that." She wiped at her cheeks, finally winding down. "But now you don't trust me, and how can you love somebody you don't trust? I understand that. I do." She hiccupped and plucked at the pillow. "Now I've made a fool of myself...crying (hic) always gives me the hiccups...and I got mascara all over your pillow and—" She finally looked up at Whit. "I'll never feel the (hic) same about anybody else."

She crawled around Whit and stood. Whit stood, too.

"I love you, Whit, but I know I screwed it up (hic), and I know I don't deserve this, but could (hic)...could you just hold me one last time?"

Whit shook her head slowly. "I don't think I can do that."

Mae nodded and hiccupped, tears again welling in her eyes. She turned slowly toward the door, but Whit stopped her. She wrapped Mae in a strong hug and rested her cheek against Mae's silky hair. She closed her eyes as Mae's arms tightened around her, her shoulders shaking with renewed sobs.

Whit spoke quietly. "I'm not going to make excuses for not trusting you before, because I don't deserve your forgiveness. I knew in my heart that you weren't that kind of person, and I am so ashamed of the things I said." Whit drew back to gently cup Mae's damp cheek and lift her face so she could drown in those tearful whiskey-brown eyes. She brushed her lips against Mae's and then kissed her deeply, reveling in the taste, the warmth of her mouth.

"I love you," she murmured against Mae's lips. She hugged her again, clinging to Mae like she was the last life vest on the *Titanic*. She kissed her smooth cheek and whispered in her ear. "But if I'm going to hold you, it has to be forever."

About the Author

Jackson Leigh grew up barefoot and happy, swimming in farm ponds and riding rude ponies in rural south Georgia.

Her passion for writing led her quite accidentally to a career in journalism and North Carolina where she now feeds nightly off the adrenaline rush of breaking crime news and close deadlines.

She is a hopeless romantic with a deep-seated love for anything equine.

Friend her at facebook.com/d.jackson.leigh, follow her on twitter @djacksonleigh, or visit her website at www.djacksonleigh.com.

Books Available from Bold Strokes Books

At Her Feet by Rebekah Weatherspoon. Digital marketing producer Suzanne Kim knows she has found the perfect love in her new mistress Pilar, but before they can make the ultimate commitment, Suzanne's professional life threatens to disrupt their perfectly balanced bliss. (978-1-60282-948-0)

Show of Force by AJ Quinn. A chance meeting between navy pilot Evan Kane and correspondent Tate McKenna takes them on a roller-coaster ride where the stakes are high, but the reward is higher: a chance at love. (978-1-60282-942-8)

Clean Slate by Andrea Bramhall. Can Erin and Morgan work through their individual demons to rediscover their love for each other, or are the unexplainable wounds too deep to heal? (978-1-60282-943-5)

Hold Me Forever by D. Jackson Leigh. An investigation into illegal cloning in the quarter horse racing industry threatens to destroy the growing attraction between Georgia debutante Mae St. John and Louisiana horse trainer Whit Casey. (978-1-60282-944-2)

Trusting Tomorrow by PJ Trebelhorn. Funeral director Logan Swift thinks she's perfectly happy with her solitary life devoted to helping others cope with loss until Brooke Collier moves in next door to care for her elderly grandparents. (978-1-60282-891-9)

Forsaking All Others by Kathleen Knowles. What if what you think you want is the opposite of what makes you happy? (978-1-60282-892-6)

Exit Wounds by VK Powell. When Officer Loane Landry falls in love with ATF informant Abigail Mancuso, she realizes that nothing is as it seems—not the case, not her lover, not even the dead. (978-1-60282-893-3)

Dirty Power by Ashley Bartlett. Cooper's been through hell and back, and she's still broke and on the run. But at least she found the twins. They'll keep her alive. Right? (978-1-60282-896-4)

The Rarest Rose by I. Beacham. After a decade of living in her beloved house, Ele disturbs its past and finds her life being haunted by the presence of a ghost who will show her that true love never dies. (978-1-60282-884-1)

Code of Honor by Radclyffe. The face of terror is hard to recognize—especially when it's homegrown. The next book in the Honor series. (978-1-60282-885-8)

Does She Love You? by Rachel Spangler. When Annabelle and Davis find out they are both in a relationship with the same woman, it leaves them facing life-altering questions about trust, redemption, and the possibility of finding love in the wake of betrayal. (978-1-60282-886-5)

The Road to Her by KE Payne. Sparks fly when actress Holly Croft, star of UK soap Portobello Road, meets her new on-screen love interest, the enigmatic and sexy Elise Manford. (978-1-60282-887-2)

Shadows of Something Real by Sophia Kell Hagin. Trying to escape flashbacks and nightmares, ex-POW Jamie Gwynmorgan stumbles into the heart of former Red Cross worker Adele Sabellius and uncovers a deadly conspiracy against everything and everyone she loves. (978-1-60282-889-6)

Date with Destiny by Mason Dixon. When sophisticated bank executive Rashida Ivey meets unemployed blue collar worker Destiny Jackson, will her life ever be the same? (978-1-60282-878-0)

The Devil's Orchard by Ali Vali. Cain and Emma plan a wedding before the birth of their third child while Juan Luis is still lurking, and as Cain plans for his death, an unexpected visitor arrives and challenges her belief in her father, Dalton Casey. (978-1-60282-879-7)

Secrets and Shadows by L.T. Marie. A bodyguard and the woman she protects run from a madman and into each other's arms. (978-1-60282-880-3)

Change Horizons: Three Novellas by Gun Brooke. Three stories of courageous women who dare to love as they fight to claim a future in a hostile universe. (978-1-60282-881-0)

Scarlet Thirst by Crin Claxton. When hot, feisty Rani meets cool, vampire Rob, one lifetime isn't enough, and the road from human to vampire is shorter than you think… (978-1-60282-856-8)

Battle Axe by Carsen Taite. How close is too close? Bounty hunter Luca Bennett will soon find out. (978-1-60282-871-1)

Improvisation by Karis Walsh. High school geometry teacher Jan Carroll thinks she's figured out the shape of her life and her future, until graphic artist and fiddle player Tina Nelson comes along and teaches her to improvise. (978-1-60282-872-8)

For Want of a Fiend by Barbara Ann Wright. Without her Fiendish power, can Princess Katya and her consort Starbride stop a magic-wielding madman from sparking an uprising in the kingdom of Farraday? (978-1-60282-873-5)

Broken in Soft Places by Fiona Zedde. The instant Sara Chambers meets the seductive and sinful Merille Thompson, she falls hard, but knowing the difference between love and a dangerous, all-consuming desire is just one of the lessons Sara must learn before it's too late. (978-1-60282-876-6)

Healing Hearts by Donna K. Ford. Running from tragedy, the women of Willow Springs find that with friendship, there is hope, and with love, there is everything. (978-1-60282-877-3)

Desolation Point by Cari Hunter. When a storm strands Sarah Kent in the North Cascades, Alex Pascal is determined to find her. Neither imagines the dangers they will face when a ruthless criminal begins to hunt them down. (978-1-60282-865-0)

I Remember by Julie Cannon. What happens when you can never forget the first kiss, the first touch, the first taste of lips on skin? What happens when you know you will remember every single detail of a mysterious woman? (978-1-60282-866-7)

The Gemini Deception by Kim Baldwin and Xenia Alexiou. The truth, the whole truth, and nothing but lies. Book six in the Elite Operatives series. (978-1-60282-867-4)

Scarlet Revenge by Sheri Lewis Wohl. When faith alone isn't enough, will the love of one woman be strong enough to save a vampire from damnation? (978-1-60282-868-1)

Ghost Trio by Lillian Q. Irwin. When Lee Howe hears the voice of her dead lover singing to her, is it a hallucination, a ghost, or something more sinister? (978-1-60282-869-8)

The Princess Affair by Nell Stark. Rhodes Scholar Kerry Donovan arrives at Oxford ready to focus on her studies, but her life and her priorities are thrown into chaos when she catches the eye of Her Royal Highness Princess Sasha. (978-1-60282-858-2)

The Chase by Jesse J. Thoma. When Isabelle Rochat's life is threatened, she receives the unwelcome protection and attention of bounty hunter Holt Lasher who vows to keep Isabelle safe at all costs. (978-1-60282-859-9)

The Lone Hunt by L.L. Raand. In a world where humans and praeterns conspire for the ultimate power, violence is a way of life… and death. A Midnight Hunters novel. (978-1-60282-860-5)

The Supernatural Detective by Crin Claxton. Tony Carson sees dead people. With a drag queen for a spirit guide and a devastatingly attractive herbalist for a client, she's about to discover the spirit world can be a very dangerous world indeed. (978-1-60282-861-2)

Beloved Gomorrah by Justine Saracen. Undersea artists creating their own City on the Plain uncover the truth about Sodom and Gomorrah, whose "one righteous man" is a murderer, rapist, and conspirator in genocide. (978-1-60282-862-9)

Cut to the Chase by Lisa Girolami. Careful and methodical author Paige Cornish falls for brash and wild Hollywood actress Avalon Randolph, but can these opposites find a happy middle ground in a town that never lives in the middle? (978-1-60282-783-7)